Dear Re

They sa
Whether it's a small village on the coast, a
town nestled in the mountains, or a whistle-stop
along the Western plains, we all share the same
hopes and dreams. We work, we play, we laugh,
we cry—and, of course, we fall in love . . .

It is this universal experience that we at Jove
Books have tried to capture in a heartwarming
series of novels. We've asked our most gifted
authors to write their own story of American romance, set in a town as distinct and vivid as the
people who live there. Each writer chose a special time and place close to their hearts. They
filled the towns with charming, unforgettable
characters—then added that spark of romance.
We think you'll find the combination absolutely
delightful.

You might even recognize *your* town. Because
true love lives in *every* town . . .

Welcome to *Our Town*.

Sincerely,

Leslie Gelb

Leslie Gelbman
Editor-in-Chief

∽ OUR · TOWN ∽

STILL SWEET

DEBRA MARSHALL

JOVE BOOKS, NEW YORK

STILL SWEET

A Jove Book / published by arrangement with
the author

PRINTING HISTORY
Jove edition / August 1997

The Putnam Berkley World Wide Web site address is
http://www.berkley.com

ISBN: 0-515-12130-4

A JOVE BOOK®
Jove Books are published by The Berkley Publishing Group,
200 Madison Avenue, New York, New York 10016.
JOVE and the "J" design are trademarks
belonging to Jove Publications, Inc.

PRINTED IN THE UNITED STATES OF AMERICA

10 9 8 7 6 5 4 3 2 1

To the Warren Sisters Four
The spirit of McCurtain County

STILL SWEET

❖ 1 ❖

Old Oklahoma
March 1890

TARGETED BY SEVERAL unblinking gazes, Chaney White stood in the middle of the mayor's office, feeling as if he were about to lose a vital piece of his anatomy. The town council of Scrub in Old Oklahoma of Indian Territory stared holes in his hide.

The town council consisted of Royce Henry, owner and proprietor of Henry's Mercantile; Sada Pickins, editor for the daily *Scrub Herald*; Bonnie Bixler, owner of The Golden Goose restaurant; and Mayor Jeremiah Bushman, who also served as the banker.

They'd heard of his pa. He could tell by the way they were tiptoeing around instead of asking him direct questions. Cold sweat tickled Chaney's neck and slicked his armpits, but he showed no outward signs of his nervousness. He'd learned that from Axel.

Mayor Bushman squinted at him. "You're awfully young."

"And comely, too," Sada Pickins added kindly, her hands twisting nervously at a lace kerchief.

Bonnie Bixler simply stared, her round florid face scrunched in perturbed lines.

"Don't be a-flatterin' him, Sada," Royce Henry said

with disgust. "He's gonna be the new sheriff, not one of your People of the Week."

"He will if I say so," the tall, stately woman asserted.

Unease curled through Chaney and he shifted slightly. He needed this job as sheriff of the small town of Scrub. He *wanted* it, but the town council would take some convincing.

This wasn't the first or last time Chaney had run smack into his pa's reputation. Even in this little settlement tucked into the northeast corner of the recently opened Unassigned Lands the people had heard of Clarence White.

Chaney's pa had been the most notorious horse thief in Indian Territory, not to mention Arkansas and Kansas. But the people of Scrub would just have to learn, as had all the others, that he wasn't anything like his father.

"I say bad blood begets bad blood." Royce Henry eyed Chaney with suspicion.

"Nonsense, Royce!" Sada Pickins exclaimed. "If that were true, all yer young'uns would be scrawny and miserly, like you." She turned to Chaney, her gaze appraising. "I think the young man deserves a chance."

"Thank you, ma'am."

"We've all heard of your daddy, young man," Mayor Bushman said firmly. "Clarence White ran with a wild bunch."

"Yessir. But he's been dead for almost five years now." Chaney's Sunday shirt had been crisp and starched when he'd left Fort Smith, but it was now limp and grimy. Still it choked him and he fought the urge to run his finger inside the collar.

"Don't see how no outlaw's seed can be a lawman. Leastways, not one a body can trust," Royce Henry grumbled.

"I understand I'll need to earn your trust, just as I did the people of Fort Smith. I believe you've seen my references?" They could find nothing wrong with those. Axel had given him a glowing recommendation and Axel Dumont was legendary in these parts.

"Your references are fine." Mayor Bushman adjusted his spectacles and glanced down at Chaney's papers again. "What are your feelings about liquor? Do you imbibe?"

"Not much, but I believe my job is to uphold the law, regardless of personal preference."

The mayor and Mrs. Pickins exchanged a pleased look. Mrs. Bixler continued to stare at him.

"You shore like them fancy words," Royce Henry grumbled. "Can you get rid of moonshiners? That's what I wanna know."

"We do need them cleared out," Mayor Bushman drawled.

Sada Pickins spun in a flurry of skirts. "Hah, Jeremiah! That's your opinion, which not everybody shares."

"Well, I for one want to see it cleaned up," Mayor Bushman continued. "We need to be declared a territory, but until Congress decides to do that, we should establish our own government, just like the Five Civilized Tribes. That's the only way we'll ever make it into the Union."

"The *United States*," Sada emphasized with arched brows. "The war's been over for twenty-five years."

"And another thing," Bonnie Bixler added. "We don't even have any government yet, exceptin' that which we set up ourselves."

Mayor Bushman peered intently at Chaney. "As you know, liquor is illegal here at this time. Despite some people's attempts to change that.'' He looked pointedly at Sada, then turned back to Chaney. ''It'll be your job to uphold that law.''

''If I may, sir, I'd like to point out that moonshining falls under federal jurisdiction.''

''Yes, yes, we know that.'' Royce Henry waved a bony hand dismissively.

''Then I don't understand why you think a sheriff—''

''Mr. White,'' Mayor Bushman interrupted. ''No offense intended to Marshal Needles or Deputy Marshal Thomas, but since the Land Rush last year, there are just too many cutthroats and thieves and downright outlaws for them to be able to see to everything.''

''What Jeremiah is saying is that he'd like to clean up our little town, Mr. White,'' Sada Pickins added kindly.

''Not everyone agrees that it needs to be cleaned up.'' Bonnie Bixler cut a sharp gaze to Royce Henry, then added, ''Although I do like the idea of having a lawman around.''

''All the little towns around here are setting up their own government and we'd like to do the same. At least until Congress gets around to establishing these lands as some part of the United States.'' Mayor Bushman exchanged a look with his fellow council members, then looked at Chaney. ''So, Mr. White, I've got a proposal for you.''

''Yessir?''

''You've got a lot to prove, considering who your daddy is.''

''Yessir.'' Chaney's heart sank. Was there not one place on earth where his father's reputation *hadn't* reached?

''How about a trial period? We'll give you three

months to clean up this town, then we'll talk about a permanent job.''

Chaney frowned, tamping down the excitement building inside him. Before he said yes to anything, he wanted to clear up the finer points. If Heck Thomas couldn't take care of the problem, could Chaney? ''You mean shut down every still? How many do you have? How do I know they can all be shut down in that period of time?''

Respect gleamed in the mayor's eyes. ''All right, how about this? You close down what you can in three months, then we'll talk.''

Chaney considered for a minute. ''All right, but I have a condition, too.''

The mayor's eyebrows raised and Sada grinned. A slow smile spread across Bonnie's face while Royce stared flatly at him.

''I do it on my own terms. No interference from anyone.'' Chaney let his gaze lock with each one of theirs. ''If you have a problem with the way I do things, you're welcome to talk to me about it, but I don't hold with interference.''

''Sounds fair to me,'' Sada said briskly, scooping up her parasol.

''You still gotta answer to us.'' Royce Henry waggled a bony finger at Chaney.

''If you have complaints about my results, then I'll be willing to discuss it.'' Axel had always taught him to lay things out directlike from the beginning. ''We do it my way or you can find yourself another man. I've had no complaints about my work so far. I don't expect to get any here.''

Mayor Bushman nodded, a slow smile forming on his square-jawed face. ''I don't have a problem staying out of your business, White. As long as you—''

"You willing to arrest whoever you have to?" Royce Henry squinted at him, his coffee black gaze probing. "No matter what?"

"I suppose, if it comes to that. I reckon I'll first try to find another way to shut them down."

Mr. Henry eyed the Colt revolver at Chaney's hip. "You know how to use that hardware?"

"I prefer to use force only when necessary and I would hate to have to take anyone to court in Muskogee."

Sada nodded approvingly, her eyes warm. "I like the way you think, Sheriff."

"He ain't sheriff yet," Royce grumbled. "We'll see what he can do about them Huckabees."

"Huckabees?" Chaney glanced around the room.

Royce spat, "Spawn of the devil, every one."

"They certainly are not!" Sada and Bonnie defended in unison.

Chaney glanced questioningly at the mayor, who shuffled his feet and cleared his throat, looking everywhere except at Chaney. Irritation spiraled through him, but he pursed his lips and counted to ten, as Axel had taught him.

Chaney's horse had come up lame two days outside of Scrub and he'd only ridden in this morning. He was wearing a thick layer of sweat and grime, his eyes burned from fatigue, and he was hungry. He'd had no chance to clean up or even see the town. But he did want this job so he tried to be patient.

He liked feeling he contributed to people's safety. Besides, he didn't know what he would do if he couldn't be a sheriff. He wasn't much trained for anything else, except maybe farming. And he preferred the feel of a gun in his hand to a plow.

The mayor took off his spectacles, cleaned them with

his shirt, and slid them back onto his beaked nose. He threw an uncomfortable look at Chaney. ''It makes us look bad because we can't catch them at it.''

Chaney noticed that Sada and Bonnie both pursed their lips disapprovingly. ''Are you sure they're guilty?''

''Their daddy was the biggest runner of moonshine in these parts,'' Royce Henry wheezed. ''I know good and well those kids are doing the same.''

Mayor Bushman leveled a flat stare at the other man. ''No, I'm not sure, but it's a pretty good bet.''

''You know good and well they're supplyin' liquor to every town around here and over the Kansas border!'' Royce exclaimed. ''It's shameful, those kids takin' up their daddy's profession as casual as if he'd been a farmer or a minister.''

''So Mr. Huckabee operates a still?'' Chaney made a mental note to check out this family first since the mayor had mentioned them.

Sada shot Royce a perturbed look. ''E. Y. Huckabee passed on some months ago, just after the Run.'' She clucked her tongue. ''A pity.''

''Weren't no more'n he deserved,'' exclaimed Royce, turning to Chaney. ''Fell and hit his head on a tub of moonshine.''

''That was never proven!'' Sada whirled on him.

Bonnie echoed, ''Certainly not!''

In an effort to forestall yet another argument, Chaney stepped in. ''How many children did he have?''

''Four.'' Sada straightened her bodice with a huff. ''Two boys, two girls. Quite charming and well mannered, most of the time.''

''Don't be taken in by 'em,'' Royce warned. ''They're moonshiners, all right.''

"I guess my job will be to prove it," Chaney said firmly. "So, I'd best get busy."

"There's a house out behind the jail. The whole town pitched in and we had it built." Sada Pickins smiled warmly at him. "You're welcome to it. It needs a good airing out, but it's clean."

"Thank you, ma'am." Chaney doffed his hat to her, then reached around to open a door that opened onto the side of the bank building. "If that's all for now, I'll report for work early in the morning."

"That will be fine." Mayor Bushman stood, extending his hand. "Good to have you, White. I think you'll do a splendid job."

"Hmmph! We'll see how many of them moonshiners you can catch," Royce muttered darkly.

Though he could tell Royce Henry was going to be a royal pain in the backside, Chaney offered the man a polite smile, then turned, holding the door for Mrs. Pickins and Mrs. Bixler.

A planked walk ran the length of the building and cut around to the front. The thud of boots on the wooden sidewalk carried around the corner to Chaney. Horses clip-clopped down the street, partnering the sounds of creaking wagon seats and wheel rims.

Mayor Bushman glanced at his pocket watch, then snapped it shut. "I guess you'll have to give special attention to the Huckabees, but we can talk about that more tomorrow. I've got another meeting."

"Jeremiah, why don't you let Sheriff White decide who he's going to investigate?" Sada asked sweetly, swinging her parasol by one finger.

He pushed away from his desk and walked to the door. "I like them, too, Sada, but the fact remains that they're probably carryin' on illegal business." Stepping forward, he shook Chaney's hand. "Mr. White, I'll see you in the morning. If you'll excuse me?"

After a guarded good-bye, Mrs. Bixler hurried off around the back of the building. Sada moved out the door behind the mayor and Chaney followed, intending to thank Mrs. Pickins for the warm welcome.

They rounded the corner of the bank and made their way past the front door. "Mrs. Pickins, thank you—"

"Noooooo! Noooo!"

The screeching wail made Chaney want to clap his hands over his ears.

"Oh, dear!" Sada muttered, her eyes widening.

Chaney stopped when she did and followed her gaze out into Main Street. A young woman darted past, chasing a young boy with dark red hair. She caught him by the shirt collar and yanked him to her.

"She's killin' me! She's killin' me!" the boy yelled.

"Billy Jack, you hush up right now," the woman ordered sharply. She grabbed him by the ear and spun him neatly back toward Chaney.

Marching determinedly past him and Sada, the young woman slammed to a stop in front of an elderly lady.

Chaney shifted to get a better view. The boy was squirming and carrying on like a jackrabbit on coals, but the girl simply held him firmly by the ear.

"Now, you tell Miss Clara Sue that you're sorry."

Beside him, Sada chuckled. Chaney listened to the commotion, but he was more interested in the woman in front of him. She was as fresh and pretty as the first spring flower and his blood stirred.

She was only an inch or two taller than the boy, probably wouldn't even reach Chaney's chin, but her shoulders and back were proudly straight. She didn't look old enough to be the kid's mother.

His brief glimpse of her features had shown peach-toned skin and dark brows, but it was her hair that caught his attention. It was the most glorious, unusual shade he'd ever seen, of hammered gold and flame. She had a fringe of bangs over her forehead and the length of her hair, thick and wavy, was taken up tightly and wound in a bun on top of her head.

Sunlight wound through it with glittering fingers, turning it first a pure blond then a fiery auburn. His hands itched to touch the satin thickness of it, to measure its length.

The boy twisted around behind her and in front of her, manipulating her arm to awkward angles. She strengthened her hold on him and gripped him by the shoulder. "*Now,* Billy Jack. Apologize."

The boy stilled, mumbling at the dirt as he scuffed his shoe at the ground.

She leaned down to him and whispered.

He snapped as straight as an arrow. "I'm sorry, Miss Clara Sue. I most humbly beg your pardon."

Chaney grinned. Whatever the young woman had said to him had certainly done the trick. Beside him, Sada chuckled and shook her head.

At that moment a young girl, closely favoring the boy in looks, ran up. "Sister, Sister, we're gonna be late."

The older woman nodded and turned slightly, only then seeing Chaney and Sada on the porch.

"Hello, Sada," she said with an exasperated smile.

"Hello," Sada stepped forward, smiling at the two younger ones. "At it again, Billy Jack?"

The boy grimaced, eyeing Chaney curiously.

The older girl shook her head, tugging at the boy's ear fondly. Even the consternation on her features did nothing to dim the light in her eyes. "I think someone has some chores waiting at home."

Her voice sounded like honey and whiskey and Chaney's pulse kicked. He stepped forward, removing his hat. "Do you need any help there, ma'am?"

For a moment she looked confused, then glanced at her brother. She laughed. "No, but thank you."

Sada gave him a sideways glance, but he paid her no mind. He was too fascinated by the play of sunlight on that golden red hair and now he could see her eyes. They were a vivid green, wide and fringed with dark lashes.

Up close, her skin looked like creamy velvet. She had a light dusting of freckles all over her face and though he'd never even thought such a word, he found her *enchanting*.

"You're new, aren't you?" the little girl asked quietly, staring up at Chaney in wonder.

He nodded.

"My name's Katie Jo." She eased closer to him, her gaze never leaving his face as she pointed over her shoulder. "That's my brother, Billy Jack."

"Nice to meet you, Katie Jo." Chaney's gaze went to their sister. "My name's Chaney."

"I'm Morrow Beth," she said quietly, her eyes sparkling like wet emeralds. A faint blush stained her neck, but she didn't look away.

Billy Jack scowled and muttered something under his breath.

Morrow Beth sighed and looked down at him. "I know you think it's funny to get Miss Clara Sue turned around, but it isn't. What if something dangerous happened to her?"

Morrow Beth glanced back at Chaney. "Miss Clara Sue isn't very good with directions. Some people—" She looked meaningfully at Billy Jack. "Like to confuse her."

"That was Miss Clara Sue. She has three sisters," Katie Jo supplied, sidling up beside him and tilting her head back. "Miss Cholly Sue, Miss Davie Sue and Miss Carolyn Sue. See, they're all named Sue."

"Yes, I see that," Chaney murmured, trying to keep from staring at Katie Jo's older sister. "It's a good thing there are only four of them."

Morrow Beth laughed, a light full sound that made Chaney smile.

"And they're all named Warner 'cuz they all married brothers," Billy Jack put in, his sullen expression disappearing. "But the Warner brothers are dead now. There was Big Jim—"

"—and Ray Don," Katie Jo put in.

"—and Leroy M.—"

"—and Ronald T."

Chaney blinked, his gaze shifting between Katie Jo and Billy Jack so many times he was dizzy. Finally he shot a helpless look over their heads at their sister.

"You're overwhelming the poor man," she said softly.

He smiled at her, feeling a pull of want low in his belly. "They are indeed, ma'am. And I'm feeling a little left out since I only have one name and everyone around here seems to go by two."

She grinned. "We can call you by your full name, if you'd like."

"Well, I've only got a first name and a last name. It's Chaney White. My mama didn't put stock in a fella having a name that was bigger than he was."

"That sounds like a smart thing to me." Morrow Beth's gaze stayed locked on his.

Chaney was vaguely aware of Sada's interested silence, but he was more aware of the woman in front of him. He didn't want her to go. "Does everyone around here have two names?"

Morrow Beth smiled. "Not everyone."

"We all do," Katie Jo pointed out, staring up at him adoringly. "You're very tall. And handsome."

Sada laughed outright and Chaney chuckled.

"Katie Jo!" Morrow Beth grasped her sister by the shoulder.

"We gotta go now, Morrow Beth." Billy Jack tugged on her hand. "John Mark will be worried."

She didn't move. "Yes, you're right."

Chaney wondered if John Mark was another relative. Or a husband or beau. It would be discourteous to ask since he'd only just met her.

As if Katie Jo read his mind, she leaned closer and said in a low voice, "John Mark's our brother. He's the oldest of us all."

"I see." Chaney smiled at Morrow Beth, his skin prickling as if he'd just faced a wild bullet. He doffed his hat to her, hearing someone come up behind him. "Nice to meet you all."

"It was nice to meet you—" She broke off abruptly, her gaze flickering to a spot over his shoulder. The welcoming light in her eyes dimmed.

Before Chaney could turn around to see what had caught her attention, she hustled the children down the street.

"Hmmph, don't let yore eyes pop outta yore head over that girl." Royce Henry's voice grated over Chaney's shoulder.

Chaney slid a glance at the other man. Had Royce caused that guarded look to come into Morrow Beth's eyes? He could understand if she didn't like Royce. Chaney wasn't too sure he liked the man either.

Chaney's gaze never wavered from the golden flame of her hair or the gentle sway of her skirts. "She's very pretty."

"She's a dang *Huckabee* is what she is." The other man leaned into Chaney's face. "And you cain't be forgettin' that."

A Huckabee? Chaney blinked, staring after her. One of *the* Huckabees? A moonshining Huckabee?

She hadn't seemed like the type of woman to be involved in something as . . . furtive and dangerous as moonshining.

But he knew appearances could be deceiving. Still, he couldn't reconcile Morrow Beth's angelic face with anything illegal.

Now sinful, that was another matter. He could picture Morrow Beth doing all kinds of sinful things with that generous mouth—to him, on him, with him.

"Think you're going to have a problem doing your job or you gonna be panting after that girl everytime you see her?"

Chaney snapped to attention. "I'll have no problem doing my job," he said briskly. But he fervently hoped he wouldn't have to do it with regard to her.

Royce slapped a tin star in his hand. "Best see that you don't. Or you won't last three months."

❖ 2 ❖

HE WAS LOOKING at her. As she walked away, Morrow Beth could feel Chaney White's gaze stroking over her, eliciting a spark of warmth low in her belly. It was all she could do not to look over her shoulder.

His black eyes seemed to twinkle with humor and yet there was seductive intensity to them. His walnut-dark hair was neatly trimmed to well above his collar, revealing a corded neck that hinted at the strength of broad shoulders and chest covered by the muslin of his white Sunday shirt.

His eyes crinkled at the corners when he smiled and judging by the creases on either side of his kind mouth, he smiled a lot. *His kind mouth?*

Honestly, Morrow Beth, you have no idea if he's kind or not. But she would sure like to find out.

"He's watching us." Katie Jo craned her neck, looking behind her. "Oooh, I could just melt."

"Katie, straighten up." Morrow Beth tried to be firm, but she knew exactly what her sister meant.

As soon as his dark gaze had locked on Morrow Beth, her legs had gone as weak as water and a funny knot unraveled in her belly. Right now, she wanted to turn around just like Katie Jo and look.

Even though she didn't need to. She could feel Chaney White's gaze sliding over her body like warm rainwater. And she liked it. Her shoulder blades prickled in anticipation.

As much as she liked knowing that he watched her, she was also afraid he might see something he shouldn't. She glanced over her shoulder, telling herself it was to be sure that no one watched as she and her siblings slipped behind the livery. That was partly the truth, but she also wanted to see Chaney one last time.

He lifted his hat slightly and she blushed, turning quickly around. She spared one grateful thought that Royce Henry, the old grouch, was nowhere about, but her attention was focused strictly on the handsome man she'd just met.

Her heart pounded like a broken windwheel, her blood hummed, and she couldn't quite get a full breath in her lungs. She became aware of her body in a way she never had before.

How the flare of her thigh differed from the hard plane of a man's. How the soft curve of her waist complemented the brawny strength of his torso. How the swell of her breasts would cushion the tempered steel of his chest.

Astonished at her thoughts, she pushed them away, her skin heating. Rounding the corner of the livery, she shooed Billy Jack and Katie Jo in front of her and gave one last cautious glance around. Assured they were alone and no one could see them, Morrow Beth stomped three times on what looked to be a patch of ground.

In a few seconds a muffled thud resounded and she stepped back, still watching over her shoulder. A creak whispered up from the ground as the dirt moved, revealing that the ground was actually a small square trapdoor leading into the earth.

She helped her brother and sister down the small ladder, then climbed down herself, closing the dirt door behind her. It took a few seconds for her eyes to adjust to the murky light.

In the tunnel beneath Scrub, it was cool and pleasant. The walls were made of smooth packed dirt. Timber posts, extending from buildings aboveground, marched the length of the tunnel. Every hundred feet sat a lantern, ready for use. She picked one up now and found a match tucked away in the hollow of a rock just above her head.

Lantern light shafted through one of the tunnel pockets. Many people knew about the tunnel system underground that ran the length and width of the town.

There were two stories as to its origin. The first, and most popular with young boys, was that outlaws had built the mirror image of the streets aboveground to save themselves from the law. Another was that early settlers had devised the plan as a way to hide from the Indians.

Morrow Beth wasn't sure which, if either one, was true. It had certainly been here since they had arrived during the run of 1889. Several people still used the tunnel for the same reason her brother did—to transport and deliver moonshine.

Just as she was about to call out for John Mark, a tall, broad shadow appeared and she recognized the silhouette of her brother.

He held up a lantern, spilling golden light through the dark passageway. "I was starting to get worried. Trouble?"

"No, we just—"

"Ran into Chaney," Katie Jo interrupted Morrow Beth with a breathless sigh.

"Chaney?"

Morrow Beth and the twins drew abreast of her older brother. "He's—"

"He's new in town and very handsome," Katie Jo supplied, a dreamy look on her face.

Morrow Beth rolled her eyes and John Mark grinned.

"He was makin' eyes at Morrow Beth," Billy Jack announced.

"He was not!"

"He was," the younger twins crowed in unison.

John Mark grinned. "Don't need another suitor, Morrow Beth. You can't choose as it is."

"Hush, all of you. I met him only briefly—"

"But he's going to be around for a while. He said so." Billy Jack grabbed up a stick and stabbed it into the dirt wall behind John Mark. "What are you doing down here, John Mark? Can I help?"

Morrow Beth gave her older brother a warning look, but he well remembered the pact they'd made not to involve their siblings.

"Thanks for the offer, Billy, but I'm doing okay on my own."

"I don't think it's fair that I can't do something to help out."

"If you want to make some money, you could pick apples for the Warner sisters," Morrow Beth suggested. "Or sweep for Mayor Bushman."

"Them's jobs for kids," he grumbled, picking up a loose chunk of rock and tossing it into the dark pockets that stretched beyond their arc of light. "If I helped John Mark, I could ride out with him sometimes. I could kill snakes and bobcats and what needed killin'."

John Mark grinned. "Haven't come across any snakes lately so I'll just keep hopin' my luck holds."

"I guess you called us down here because you have to leave?" She tried to keep the resentment out of her voice, but could tell by the tensing of John Mark's jaw that he knew her feelings anyway.

Well, he should know them. She'd had them since the day her father died. She didn't resent John Mark; she could never do that, but she did resent that he'd taken up Pap's moonshining operation and no amount of talking could change his mind.

John Mark's eyes warned her not to start in on him. "I've got to make a run into Kansas tonight. Just wanted you to know."

Change was won by small persistent steps, not big leaps, and Morrow Beth had learned to be persistent and patient. "I wish you'd get another job."

"Ain't nothing else I can do, Morrow Beth, and you know it."

"That's not true! You're smart and good at figures—"

"Nobody wants to pay me for watching women," he teased.

She frowned. "You know I mean numbers."

"Can't read nor write. What kind of job am I going to get?"

"You could make deliveries from the mercantile. You could work at the livery. You're good with horses."

"Seems to me I do all those things now." His handsome features hardened. "Now, quit trying to change me. I make a good living for this family and there's nothing wrong with doing it the same as Pap did."

"What if you end up like Pap?" Morrow Beth asked, aching.

"He tripped and hit his head. I'm not clumsy like that."

"You could get shot going into Kansas. It's happened

to other people. Just last winter Lemuel Baker got shot.''

''Lemuel Baker makes more noise than a steam engine,'' John Mark said flatly. ''They coulda heard him in Kentucky. Now, quit your worryin'. You do the job you do and I'll do mine.''

Her job at the local restaurant contributed to their household money and Morrow Beth had never stopped hoping that her brother would follow her example and find a job that paid honest money. But so far he had refused.

She knew it was useless to argue. And she hated arguing with him. Running moonshine was about the only thing they ever argued about.

It *was* against the law, despite the fact that John Mark didn't think there was anything wrong with it. Morrow Beth couldn't bear to think about him going to prison any more than she could bear to think about him getting shot.

''Be careful and be quick.'' She brushed a kiss across his cheek.

''I will.'' He squatted down in front of the twins, holding out his arms. Katie Jo flew into them, but Billy Jack hesitated, eyeing his brother as if he were too old to be hugged.

John Mark swept him up in a bear hug. ''You two be good and mind Sister.''

They nodded.

''I'll bring you something when I come back.''

''Licorice?'' Katie Jo suggested.

''Maybe.'' John Mark kissed each of them, then loosed them with a swat on the rear end. ''See you in the morning.'' He straightened, grinning at Morrow Beth. ''Don't fret. I'll be fine and I'll be back before you can shake your tail at that new man in town.''

''Oh, stop that! I have certainly never shaken my tail at anyone.''

"No need." Affection warmed his eyes and he tapped her on the tip of the nose. "They all swarm around you like ants on sweet molasses."

"Ugh!" She wrinkled her nose.

"Y'all go on down to the other end of town. You'll have a better chance of not being seen that way."

It wasn't as if Morrow Beth hadn't been in the tunnel enough to know that, but John Mark was acting in his role as man of the family now. She kissed him on the cheek and herded the twins down the street laid out beneath the city.

As always when John Mark left on one of his trips, Morrow Beth worried. Most people in town didn't see anything wrong with moonshining and were clamoring to have it legalized. But the new lands opened last year in the run were still under the jurisdiction of Indian Territory.

The soldiers and marshals assigned to keep the peace took their jobs very seriously and Morrow Beth had heard of moonshiners who'd been shot and killed upon being caught. She was becoming increasingly afraid as John Mark continued moonshining.

At the last town meeting, Lemuel Baker had even pulled out his gun and threatened any peace officer if they tried to stop him. That's when Mayor Bushman, whom Morrow Beth had never seen lose his temper, had exploded and vowed to get a sheriff. They'd never needed one before now, but even Morrow Beth had to agree after that meeting.

But a sheriff would be obligated to lock up moonshiners, including her brother. She hated to have John Mark put himself at risk like that, but she had been unable to convince him to get another job. Still, that didn't stop her from trying again.

She didn't like or approve of what her brother did to provide for their family, but neither would she expose him. Her secrecy could mean the difference between having John Mark and losing him.

Keeping such a secret chafed at her innate honesty, but she wouldn't put her brother at risk. He would be careful; he always was. And Morrow Beth would keep her mouth shut, praying they hadn't been seen going into the tunnel.

She climbed up the ladder behind her brother and sister, coming aboveground inside a small shed behind Sada's newspaper office.

They stepped out of the shed and Morrow Beth turned back to latch the door.

"Miss Huckabee?"

At the deep masculine voice, she squeaked and whirled. Chaney White stared at her wonderingly, puzzlement dancing in the black depths of his eyes.

"You startled me!" She pressed a hand to her throat, feeling the rapid flutter of her pulse.

He turned and looked down the long stretch of street, then back at her, a small frown marking his forehead.

She forced herself to smile, trying to ignore the way his presence startled her. Surely he hadn't seen anything?

"How'd you get down here so fast?"

"What are you doing here?"

The questions tangled and Morrow Beth laughed, her mind racing for an explanation that wouldn't arouse suspicion.

He removed his hat, grinning. "Ladies, first."

"Oh, we were just—"

"Talking to John Mark," Katie Jo supplied.

Morrow Beth gripped her sister's shoulder and pulled her close, squeezing a warning. "Yes, that's right. We finally found him."

Chaney's gaze scanned the shed and the waving prairie grass beyond. "I guess I just missed him then?"

"Yes." Morrow Beth licked suddenly dry lips. "Um, yes. What did you say you were doing?"

"Just taking in the sights, trying to get my bearings. Maybe you could show me—"

"It's been so nice to see you again, but we've got to get home. Chores and all." She smiled lamely, hoping he would let them leave without further questions. Finding him here unsettled her.

Surprise sparked his eyes, but he settled his hat back on his head and nodded. "Of course. Don't let me keep you."

"Excuse us, please." Morrow Beth clutched at Billy Jack's arm and steered her brother and sister in front of her.

"It was nice to see you again," Chaney called.

Katie Jo squirmed around. "We'll see you tomorrow, okay, Chaney?"

"Okay."

Morrow Beth's heart pounded and sweat slicked her palms. Calm down. He didn't see anything.

"Good day, Miss Huckabee."

"Good day." She flashed him a smile and hurried her siblings back toward the schoolhouse where the wagon was waiting.

Her heart gradually slowed, but she couldn't quite dismiss the uneasy sense that she might have given something away, perhaps jeopardized John Mark. Nonsense, she told herself. Chaney White was new to town; he knew nothing of the underground tunnel.

She glanced back, relieved to see that he'd gone. He'd seen nothing. And even if he had, she doubted he'd be inclined to do anything about it. Chaney White seemed

like a man who would rather court a woman than solve
the pieces of a puzzle.

Anticipation curled through her. Right after services
were over, she was going to ask him to Sunday dinner.
She'd never done anything so forward. The next morning, Morrow Beth sat in the scarred, creaky church pew,
trying to keep her gaze and her attention on Reverend
Titus, but she was too aware of the man who sat across
the narrow aisle from her.

A space the width of a horse separated them, yet she
was as aware of his clean masculine scent, his curving
lips as if Chaney White were right next to her. The congregation belted out the words to "Beyond This Land of
Parting" and Morrow Beth stole another glance across the
aisle.

Yes, he was just as handsome as he'd been yesterday.
Chaney glanced her way and grinned. She bit her lip and
quickly averted her gaze, folding her hands in her lap and
fiddling with her fingernails. She could feel his gaze on
her, furtive and frequent.

Pleasure wound through her and she shifted on the seat,
anticipating the end of services so she could speak to him
again.

Beside her, Katie Jo leaned forward and rested her hand
in her chin, staring blatantly at Chaney with that drowning
look of adoration on her face.

Morrow Beth glanced at him, noted that his gaze was
locked on her lips, and flushed. Looking away, she lightly
thumped Katie Jo on the arm.

"Quit staring," she whispered.

"You're doing it," her sister whispered back indignantly.

Morrow Beth rolled her eyes and tried to concentrate

on Reverend Titus's sermon about Daniel and the lion's den. But she could feel the weight of Chaney's gaze and her skin tingled.

She was going to invite him to Sunday dinner. After all it was the hospitable thing to do, considering he was new in town and all. She knew it had more to do with the excitement tingling through her than any Christian charity, but Morrow Beth didn't care.

Just looking at him caused a knot to lodge in her chest. Yesterday in denims and a worn Sunday shirt, he'd been ruggedly handsome. Today in fresh Sunday clothes he appeared quiet and mysterious, and slightly, charmingly uncomfortable as if he didn't quite fit in a church, but was willing to try.

His eyes gleamed as if he knew a secret and it unleashed in Morrow Beth a desire to learn everything about him. She glanced at him again, flushing when her gaze crashed into his.

Their eyes locked and for a moment, Reverend Titus's voice disappeared. Chaney stared at her with a mixture of hunger and speculation, as if trying to see into her thoughts.

Morrow Beth was only vaguely aware that Katie was swinging her legs with enough force to vibrate the pew and Billy Jack shifted constantly, making a crude song from the creaking wood.

Caught in Chaney's intense gaze, a weakness washed through her. Yes, she was definitely asking him to Sunday dinner.

Though she was still concerned that he might be suspicious about finding her at the opposite end of town yesterday, he appeared very much the gentleman and Morrow Beth doubted he would ask about that. Why would he care to?

They rose for the invitation song and Morrow Beth's gaze cut to him. He grinned, his eyes dancing mischievously as he looked at a point beside her.

She glanced down to find Katie Jo hanging over the pew and leaning around Morrow Beth, wriggling her fingers flirtatiously at Chaney.

Morrow Beth pinched her.

"Ouch!" Katie Jo snapped to attention.

Morrow Beth nodded toward the reverend. "Straighten up. You're making a spectacle of yourself."

She glanced over to see Chaney staring straight ahead, his lips pursed as if trying not to laugh. A small smile eased across her face. After the song, they sat once again as the reverend made announcements. Tolah Neal was still ill at home with a broken foot and Morrow Beth made a mental note to take her one of the lemon pound cakes the old woman loved so much.

Feeling the heat of Chaney's gaze, she glanced at him again. He smiled broadly and she couldn't help smiling back.

Katie Jo pinched her arm. "You told me to stop that."

Morrow Beth gave her sister a look. "Hush."

Reverend Titus cleared his throat. "I've just been pleased to learn that the new sheriff is with us today."

Morrow Beth stiffened. Drat, Royce Henry had gotten a new sheriff after all. He had probably also already dictated that he wanted all the moonshiners closed down.

In theory, Morrow Beth didn't disagree with Royce's opinion of the evils of drink, but in reality she had to consider her family. As much as she hated John Mark's involvement, neither did she want to see her brother threatened. He did provide for the family, even if it wasn't in a way she preferred.

"I'd like for him to stand so we can all meet him proper after the services."

Morrow Beth glanced behind her, looking for an unfamiliar face, one that was craggy and unforgiving and old.

"Sheriff White, would you stand, please?"

White? Dread gripped her insides and as she silently screamed a denial, her gaze moved across the aisle. Had the reverend said . . . *White?*

"Oh, my," Katie Jo breathed beside her.

"Holy cow," Billy Jack whispered loudly.

Dimly Morrow Beth reminded herself that she would have to wash Billy Jack's mouth out with soap once they got home, but right now dread washed through her in a sickening wave.

No! No! He couldn't be the sheriff. Chaney White, whom she'd been eyeing all during services, couldn't be the new sheriff of Scrub.

But he rose slowly to his feet, smiling kindly. Her stomach plummeted as his lean, muscular legs unfolded from the pew and he raised a hand in greeting to the congregation.

Morrow Beth swallowed, feeling embarrassed and angry and shocked.

"Hello, folks." Chaney's voice was kind, courteous, and sent a chill down her spine.

She'd been planning to invite to dinner a man who could take her brother away from the family. She couldn't believe it.

A murmur of greeting went through the church and Chaney nodded, then sat down.

"Everyone make it a point to meet the sheriff after services."

Morrow Beth didn't hear another thing the preacher

said. Swamped with shock and a burgeoning panic, she sat completely still.

At last the final verse of "Nearer My God to Thee" penetrated her shocked mind and as soon as the last word faded on the air, she sprang up off the hard wooden pew and reached for Katie Jo's hand.

"Let's go." She pulled her sister down the aisle, giving Billy Jack a sharp stare that meant he'd better follow and fast.

"Hey, what're you doing?" Katie tugged at her hand.

"We're leaving."

"But I want to see Chaney." Katie Jo glanced sadly back at the new sheriff.

"I'm sorry. You'll have to see him another time." Morrow Beth kept her voice low, glancing around to make sure no one overheard her sister.

They threaded their way around the Warner sisters and dodged Sada Pickins, but Morrow Beth wasn't quick enough to make it to the door before Royce Henry.

The storeowner plugged up the doorway like a cork in a bottle. Morrow Beth slid to a frustrated stop and cast a quick glance over her shoulder.

Surrounded by a small group of people, including Sada, Chaney White stared at Morrow Beth. He smiled, questioning, tentatively.

She turned away, catching the frown that crossed his features. She couldn't become involved with him. He was a threat to John Mark and despite her disapproval of John Mark's moonshining, she would never do anything to jeopardize her brother. Anything.

"Morrow Beth?" Chaney's voice came from only a couple of pews behind her and spurred a quick flare of panic.

But she couldn't ignore him. Squeezing her eyes shut

briefly, she turned, managing to keep her voice level. "Yes?"

"Hi, Chaney!" Billy Jack and Katie Jo chorused.

"Hi, you two." He smiled warmly at them before his gaze moved again to Morrow Beth. "How are you today?"

"Fine, just fine." Urgency wound through her and she felt suddenly suffocated. Now that she knew who he was, she very much feared he would somehow know, just by looking at her, what her brother was doing at this very minute. "I don't mean to be rude, but we've got to get home."

"What for?" Billy demanded, looking up at Morrow Beth with a frown.

Chaney watched her, speculation and a hint of hurt in his eyes. "Of course," he said quietly. "Don't let me keep you."

Shame pricked at her, but she couldn't soften. He was the new sheriff! Giving him a weak smile, she latched on to Katie Jo and Billy Jack and steered them out of the church.

She squeezed and elbowed her way around Royce Henry and picked her way down the steps, dragging her siblings like bouncing ragdolls.

"John Mark ain't gonna like this," Billy Jack predicted glumly. "I wish the new sheriff weren't Chaney."

"*Isn't* going to like it," Morrow Beth corrected automatically, trying to calm her racing heart. "I wish he weren't either."

Disappointment bit at the realization and she realized how attracted to him she had really been.

The new sheriff.

She forced herself to repeat the words over and over, reminding herself why she couldn't like him, why she couldn't encourage that frank interest in his eyes.

As they climbed into the wagon, she caught a movement from the corner of her eye. She took up the reins, glancing over to see Chaney White standing at the bottom of the rickety church steps, staring after her with a combination of hurt and puzzlement.

Guilt twinged at her rude behavior, but she couldn't become involved with him. She couldn't allow herself to be a means for Chaney to get to her brother. John Mark!

Horror crawled through her as she remembered coming up out of the tunnel yesterday and running straight into Chaney. What if he became suspicious of how quickly she'd gotten to the opposite end of town? What if she had contributed to Chaney learning about John Mark's moonshining?

She would never forgive herself. She slapped the reins against Chester's rump and the old bay jerked into a lumbering gait. She could still feel Chaney's gaze boring into her back and Morrow Beth wished she could urge the horse into moving faster, but she knew pressing him would only make the animal stop stubbornly. And she couldn't risk that.

She had to get away from the new sheriff. And she had to stay away, from now on.

❖ 3 ❖

MORROW BETH HUCKABEE'S deliberate snub-
bing still bothered Chaney the next day. And it made him
suspicious as all get out. Why should learning that he was
the sheriff put that frosty look in her beautiful green eyes?

Unless she—or her family—had something to hide.

He didn't like the suspicion worming through him, but
he couldn't dismiss Royce Henry's claim, not after Morrow Beth's abrupt change of manner.

Drinking a cup of coffee, he stood in the doorway of
his little frame house. Morning stretched around him in
brilliant glory, spring sunshine glittering off the grass that
was starting to green. Cool air nipped at him.

He gazed out over the rolling hills and the town of
Scrub nestled in the thick-treed belly of the hills just to
the north of the town site of Stillwater. The headwaters
of Stillwater Creek spun from the hills and ran behind the
town, only a few hundred yards from the little house
where Chaney was staying.

Wind plucked at the thigh-high grass, rippling it like a
green velvet canvas. A hawk spiraled overhead and the
occasional quack of a duck sounded.

He would start this morning by introducing himself to

all the business owners in town and try to learn who else, besides Royce Henry, had suspicions about moonshiners in this town. Moving back into the house, Chaney set his coffee cup in the dry sink, strapped on his Colt, and settled his hat on his head.

The house was small, but comfortable. White eyelet curtains fluttered at the two windows looking into the small living room and kitchen. The wooden floor was clean; the bed's mattress was stuffed thick with clean straw. As Chaney glanced around, he felt the pull he'd felt so many times before.

To have a place to call his own. A place to put down roots where his daddy's name didn't chase him. Maybe Scrub was that place.

"Yoo-hoo!" A feminine voice called.

Chaney paused in the act of settling his hat on his head and turned. Four older women, each dressed in a pastel floral or stripe, made their way up the faint path to his porch.

He strode to the door. "Good morning."

"Are you the new sheriff?" The woman in the front had vibrant auburn hair and sparkling blue eyes. She looked vaguely familiar.

Ah, yes. Chaney remembered seeing her yesterday in front of the bank. Billy Jack Huckabee had been apologizing to her. "Yes, ma'am. Chaney White."

He walked onto the porch, tipping his hat to the four women. There was a family resemblance and Chaney realized these must be the Warner sisters about whom the Huckabee twins had told him.

It was hard to tell their ages, though he would have guessed them all to be around the age of fifty. They all wore gloves, except one taller brunette standing slightly in the back. Her hands were bare and she wore a bonnet, though it hung down her back.

The redhead gestured to the other women. "I'm Clara Sue Warner. These are my sisters, Carolyn Sue—"

She pointed to a slender blond woman who smiled but said nothing.

"Davie Sue."

A thin brunette inclined her head with a shy smile.

"And—"

"I'm Cholly Sue." The brunette with the bonnet stepped up beside Clara Sue. She had mischievous green eyes. "It's nice to meet you, Sheriff White."

"It's nice to meet all of you."

"We thought we'd come by to welcome you to Scrub. And see if there's anything we can do for you." Clara Sue clasped her glove-clad hands and smiled beatifically at him.

He grinned. "Thank you, ladies, but I think I'm settled for now."

"We brought you some of our remedy." Cholly Sue thrust a jar of peachy brown liquid at him, its neck tied with a calico ribbon.

Chaney took it, wondering what the remedy was. It looked like tea. "Thank you."

Cholly Sue and Clara Sue nodded. Davie Sue and Carolyn Sue exchanged a surreptitious glance.

"And you'll need some of our muscadine preserves," Cholly said firmly, with a stifling look at Carolyn Sue and Davie Sue.

"Yes, the preserves are quite fine," Carolyn acquiesced.

Cholly Sue batted her eyelashes and Chaney bit back a smile. "That would be nice, Mrs. Warner."

"Pooh!" Cholly Sue waved her hand in dismissal.

"You'll be all day calling us all Mrs. Warner. Just call us by our first names."

"Both of them?"

All four ladies laughed at that.

"No," Clara Sue said. "Just Clara or Cholly will do."

"Very well."

"Wonderful!" Clara Sue adjusted her straw hat and turned, eyeing the same hills Chaney had admired just before they'd walked up.

"Good-bye, Sheriff." Cholly Sue stepped up next to Clara Sue and the two of them started across the hills, away from town.

Chaney thought about calling them back, then realized they were probably going to make some other calls.

"Sisters!" Davie called, hurrying after Clara and Cholly. "That's the wrong way."

Clara and Cholly turned, both looking down their noses haughtily. "Nonsense, Davie. We've walked these hills for many years."

"And you must always argue," said Carolyn, following Davie. "But it really is this way."

She took Clara's arm and Davie took Cholly's, steering them back toward town and the direction they'd come.

Chaney stifled a laugh. He could see now the appeal Billy Jack Huckabee found in sending the Warner sisters off in another direction. He tipped his hat as the four women passed by in front of his house.

Clara looked sheepish, but Cholly simply shrugged. "We always manage to get back home."

"Good day, ladies." Chaney couldn't keep the laughter from his voice.

They didn't seem offended. They all smiled and waved, then walked down the hill. He grinned as he closed up the house and followed them, intent on introducing himself around town today.

And to try to learn something about Morrow Beth Huckabee's strange reaction to learning he was the new sheriff.

An hour later, Chaney had walked the length of the town twice. He had said hello to Sada and Royce and the banker. He'd met Utive Olen, the dressmaker. And Tom Parmsley, the blacksmith.

It had taken Chaney a good ten minutes, at an easy pace, to walk from one end of town to the other, so he couldn't for the life of him figure out how Morrow Beth Huckabee had arrived at the other end of town without running.

He walked back to the spot where he'd talked to her and eyed the footprints in the red dirt. Frowning, he hunkered down, staring blankly at a crack in the hard dirt. He ran his finger across it, not certain what he hoped to find, but testing anyway.

He stood, shifting his weight and pressing with his boot. A piece of ground gave beneath his feet and he barely caught himself from stumbling.

He glanced down and froze in surprise. What he thought was the ground was really a dirt encrusted wooden cover and it had opened up into the earth. Chaney blinked and looked around. The street was nearly empty and no one was paying a bit of attention to him. He looked back down at the hole in the ground and knelt.

Squinting into the dark hole, he thought he saw a crudely made ladder. Leaning closer, he made a sound of surprise. There *was* a ladder.

With another glance around to ensure he was alone, Chaney moved the cover aside and lowered himself into the hole. Feeling his way with his feet, he climbed down and landed on solid ground. Light filtered into the hole from aboveground and Chaney saw a lantern hanging on the ladder.

He removed it and reached in his pocket for a match. Lighting it, he touched it to the wick and turned up the kerosene.

Holding the lantern in front of him, he made out a long passageway. He glanced up, measuring his position in town and started down the earthen corridor.

As he walked, he was astonished to realize that the tunnel down here mirrored the street aboveground. This would be Main Street and two arms shooting off the middle would be A and B. Amazing. What was it for?

Dirt shifted above him, trickling onto his hat, making soft pitter-patters of sound. It was cool and earthy, mixed with mold and the pungent scent of earth. But he could smell nothing else. He could hear no sounds alerting him to the presence of anyone else. Above him he could make out the muffled sound of a wagon passing, feel the vibration of a horse, but that was all.

Lantern light arced in front of him and he spied something at the far end. He reached it, astonished to find a wooden cart. What were these tunnels used for? It was obvious they *were* used.

Something gleamed in the light and Chaney reached down, plucking a metal lid from the ground. It looked like the lid to a jar. What would that be doing down here?

Suspicion snaked over him and he straightened, staring intently at the lid. Were moonshiners using this tunnel? What would they do here—meet prospective clients? They didn't make the stuff here or Chaney would surely have found evidence of that.

He knelt, eyeing the clear footprints in the soft dirt. He

counted at least four different sets and wondered if any of these could belong to Morrow Beth Huckabee and her twin siblings. Well, there was one way to find out.

He measured the length of one of them, which fit perfectly in his hand. That could belong to a child. Or a young woman. Nodding in satisfaction, now more curious than ever about what Morrow Beth had been doing down here, Chaney started back up the tunnel.

He walked slowly, trying to gauge his position if he were aboveground. Lifting the lantern, he was surprised to see a pattern of square holes that ran the length of the ceiling and the sight of wood was unmistakable. The holes had been dug and wood pushed through, almost as if he were looking at a floor.

Or a door. Could he be looking at doors leading into the tunnel?

Chaney decided right then he'd better find out. He glanced around, spotted another short ladder leaning against the far wall and brought it over to stand beneath one of the wood squares.

He hung the lantern on the ladder, then climbed up and pushed against the wood.

At first, he was met with resistance, then the door creaked and groaned, slowly opening. Fresh air rushed over Chaney's face, followed by the scents of apples and salt pork and fragrant soap. He had to be in Henry's Mercantile.

Just then something whacked against his head.

"What the devil are you doing down there?"

Chaney raised his arms to ward off the blows. What in the Sam Hill was Royce using to hit him? "Mr. Henry!"

Whack! "Come up outta there!" *Whack!* "How'd you get in here?"

"Mr. Henry!" A stiff piece of straw gouged Chaney's

cheek and he realized Mr. Royce was whacking him with a broom. "Royce! Royce, it's me, Chaney."

"Huh?" The storekeep leaned down into Chaney's line of vision. "Sheriff? What the devil are you doin'?"

Chaney rubbed at his stinging head. "Let me get out of here and I'll tell you."

Royce gave him a hand up and Chaney straightened, dusting off his hat and rubbing the back of his neck, which still stung from Royce's straw broom.

He explained to Royce what he'd found, hoping the storekeep would know for what purpose the tunnels were used.

"It's them moonshiners, I tell you." Royce shook his head portentously. "I bet they use it to make moonshine down there."

"I found no evidence of that." He hadn't found much of anything in the tunnel, but he couldn't deny it would be a perfect place to meet if one wanted to purchase liquor.

Royce pursed his fleshy lips. "Well, then I bet they use it to make deliveries. There's lots of people in this town who buy liquor, you know."

"Like who?"

"Well . . . well." Royce rubbed his head. "I just know there is."

Chaney sighed in frustration. So far, his wonderful discovery of the tunnels had turned up nothing. "Well, maybe I'll just explore a little more."

He turned back toward the trapdoor and levered himself back into the tunnel.

"You're going back in there?" Royce demanded.

Chaney shrugged. "Seems the best way to find out what they're used for."

"I done told you."

"I need more than hearsay, Mr. Henry." Chaney
stepped down a couple of rungs and reached for the trapdoor overhead.

"See ya, Sheriff."

Royce's voice faded as he closed the door. Chaney
climbed down the ladder and walked a few more feet into
the tunnel. Small square holes just like the one he'd
climbed through into Royce's store spotted the ceiling. It
looked as if there were access to every business from
down here.

Chaney paused at the spot where he thought Sada's
newspaper office might be and climbed up the ladder
again. Her door was easier to open, and quieter than
Royce's had been.

Chaney wondered if Sada's reticence to clean up the
moonshiners might be due to the fact that she imbibed a
bit herself. Or perhaps even made the stuff.

Sada Pickins didn't seem the type, but Chaney had
learned that criminals didn't always look evil.

He found himself in a small back room. A tiny cot was
shoved into one corner and a pile of ink-stained rags in
the other. There were no jars or jugs or anything that
resembled a still.

Chaney opened the door and spied Sada hunched over
a small desk, scribbling furiously.

As quietly as he could, he said, "Sada?"

She screamed and leapt out of the chair, knocking over
an inkwell and sending her quill flying across the room.
Backing into the small area between her desk and the
wall, she faced him with one hand pressed against her
throat.

When she recognized Chaney, her hand fell limply to
her side and she dragged in a deep breath. "You scared
the daylights out of me."

"I'm sorry, Sada. I didn't mean to." He walked over, stooping to pick up her quill.

She pushed away from the wall, curiosity burning in her eyes. She glanced at the front door, then back at him. "I didn't hear you—how'd you get in here?"

"Through there." He motioned behind him to the small room he'd just exited and pointed to the trapdoor in the floor. "Did you know this was here?"

She walked over and peered into the room. "Well, actually I did, but I forgot, I guess. I never use it. Neither does anyone else," she said pointedly.

"Sorry again for scaring you." He noted the stiff set of her shoulders, the way she suddenly wouldn't meet his gaze. "Are you sure no one else uses it?"

"Not to my knowledge. Can I get you some coffee?" She turned and swept back into the front office, stooping to pick up her inkwell. Grabbing an ink-stained rag from beside her press, she knelt to clean up a splatter of ink.

Chaney followed, wondering at Sada's reticence when she had been so forthcoming with him the day before.

"I found a tunnel underground, Sada." He watched her carefully.

"Is that right?"

"You don't seem surprised."

She drew in a breath, paused, then turned to look up at him. "Well, of course I knew it was down there, but as I said, I never use it."

"Does anyone?"

"Why would someone use it to come in my newspaper office?"

He stared hard at her.

She frowned. "What do you think you've found, young man?"

"Royce thinks the moonshiners use the tunnels and maybe these doors to make deliveries."

Her eyes widened. "Oh, pshaw! What does Royce know? He and his nasty old suspicions. He probably told you I was a moonshiner!"

Chaney didn't believe Sada was a moonshiner, but he had to start somewhere. The more people he could eliminate the better. He watched as she poured a cup of coffee and raised it to her lips.

He couched his question with a grin. "Are you?"

She sputtered into her coffee. "I certainly am not! Why, of all the nerve!"

"Calm down, Sada. I had to ask." He grinned. "Forgive me?"

She pursed her lips, considering him, then a reluctant smile warmed her eyes. "Chaney White, you're a rascal. Don't be thinking to charm me with that grin. You should show more respect to your elders."

"I certainly should." He walked to the door and stepped outside. "Thanks for your help, Sada. I'd appreciate it if you'd let me know if you learn of anyone using the tunnel."

She canted her head, curiosity bright in her eyes. "What are you going to do if someone is using it? It's not against the law, is it?"

"No, it's not. But if there's moonshine involved—"

"All right." She agreed with a brisk nod. "I know you're just trying to do your job and I'll help you if I can, but I've never seen anyone use the tunnel. No matter what Royce Henry says."

Chaney touched the brim of his hat in farewell. "Thanks, Sada."

He closed the front door and continued on his way

down the street, into the dressmaker's shop, the black-smith, the doctor, the land office.

Three hours later, Chaney stood on the porch of the sheriff's office and planted his hands on his hips. No one in this town would even admit to knowing about the tunnel, despite Chaney telling them all that he'd just come from there.

But there was one person who couldn't deny knowing about it. Chaney himself had seen Morrow Beth Huckabee coming from it. And he was going to have to ask her what she'd been doing down there.

Frustration mingled with anticipation. He wanted to see Morrow Beth, but after her abrupt departure yesterday, he doubted he would be welcome.

He shouldn't care about that. He should care only about doing his job. And that's what he would do. Morrow Beth was just going to have to cooperate.

That afternoon, Morrow Beth wielded the hoe with a vengeance. Chaney White was the new sheriff! Shock and disbelief still rocked through her. She was glad, *glad,* she'd walked away from him yesterday at church.

For an instant, she saw again the hurt in his eyes at her deliberate snub and shame pricked her, but she forced herself to ignore it. She couldn't soften toward him. She couldn't. Chaney White had the ability to destroy her whole family, to knock her world from its foundation.

Still, she couldn't deny an inexplicable sense of loss, as if she'd thrown away something precious, something that she might need. Which made no sense. She hardly knew the man. How could she lose anything?

Memories of his gentle smile, the twinkle of laughter in those dark eyes ambushed her. She didn't want to re-member. Not the warm immediate connection she'd felt to him or the way his wide shoulders strained at the seams of his clean but worn white shirt.

She attacked the weeds in the next row, breaking up clods of earth in preparation for planting. So immersed was she in trying to push away thoughts of Chaney White, that she wasn't aware of a visitor until a hand settled on her shoulder.

"Morrow Beth?"

She started, spinning around to find none other than Chaney White staring solemnly at her. *Sheriff* Chaney White.

Flustered, she pushed back a stray wisp of hair and gripped the hoe as if it were a weapon. "I didn't hear you ride up."

He smiled, his black gaze flicking over her, stirring up a latent heat low in her belly.

A breath shuddered out of her and she forced herself to remember exactly what he was. "May I help you, Sheriff?"

His smile faded at her cool tone and he removed his hat, fingering the brim as though uncomfortable. "I hope I haven't done something to offend you, Morrow Beth."

His kind tone sparked a flash of guilt at her coldness. The wind had settled down a bit and the sun was almost warm on her back. She suddenly felt tired and vexed. By way of apology, she offered, "Would you like a drink of water, Sheriff?"

"I would, thank you."

She gripped the hoe tightly and walked to the side of the house, dipping the bucket into the well. Turning, she offered him a ladle full of water.

He took it with a smile and tilted it to his lips, those strong generously curved lips. He closed his eyes, pleasure easing across his rugged features. Helplessly, Morrow Beth's gaze traced the strong aquiline nose, the carved cheekbones, the square jaw.

His neck was thick and strong, cording as he swallowed, and she bit nervously at her lip. She didn't want to notice how gently his big hands held the ladle. How bronze his skin was next to the stark whiteness of his shirt. The dark curl of his lashes.

He returned the ladle to her and she dropped it back into the bucket. Annoyed now, she walked back to the garden. "Paying a social call today, Sheriff?"

"I don't mind if you call me Chaney."

The low seductive rasp of his voice skittered along her nerves, tempting. "That doesn't really seem appropriate."

"You mean because I'm the sheriff? Or because we don't know each other that well?"

"Yes."

"I see." Speculation narrowed his eyes. His gaze tracked over the yard, the barn, the chicken house, then moved back to her. His tone grew brisk, more business-like. "Are you alone?"

"No. The twins are here and John Mark's around somewhere. Out back, I think." She stiffened. What did he want? "Surely you didn't ride all this way just to take roll call of my family?"

He smiled, lighting that lick of fire down in her belly. "No, I need to ask you something."

"Ask away," she said breezily, her stomach tightening in apprehension. He was here as the sheriff, not as a neighbor. And she didn't like it.

"Remember yesterday when I saw you at the other end of town?"

Her breath froze in her chest. Had he seen John Mark? Had he discovered something about the moonshining? She nodded.

His gaze traced her features, lingered on her lips. "I was wondering how you managed to get there so quick, when I'd just seen you at the north end."

She wished he would quit looking at her as if she were exactly the thing to whet his thirst. She licked her suddenly dry lips, her mind racing for an explanation.

"That's okay, Morrow Beth. You don't have to work so hard for an answer. I figured it out today."

"Oh, you did?" She kept her voice haughty, yet she could hear nervousness in the husky edge of her voice.

He leaned closer as if confiding in her, his breath brushing her cheek. "I found a tunnel system underground. Suppose you tell me about it."

❖ *4* ❖

SHE SWALLOWED AND gave a nervous laugh. For a moment, she considered lying. "Well, of course I know about it. I've lived here all my life."

"Ever used those tunnels?"

"Obviously I used them yesterday," she said coolly, pushing past him and attacking the bean row.

"What for?"

She whirled, intending to tell him it was none of his business.

Just then Flower raced around the corner, toward her and through the row Morrow Beth had just hoed. The white rooster dodged and staggered. Morrow Beth's gaze swerved to follow him. She knew by looking at his wide unblinking eyes exactly where he'd been and what he'd been doing. He was as drunk as Lucifer. Again.

Chaney's jaw dropped. "What's wrong with that rooster?"

"Sometimes he has these . . . spells." She refused to look at Chaney and dropped the hoe to hurry after the bird.

"Spells? What kind of spells?"

"This kind," she said impatiently. "He's been our pet for years. It just comes over him."

Flower scrambled over the rows marked for beans and peas, circling dizzily next to the carrot row.

"Flower! Stop!"

"You've got a pet rooster? Named Flower?" Chaney's eyes widened in disbelief. "I've never heard of such a thing."

Morrow Beth barely registered the scornful disbelief in his voice. She was too busy trying to catch Flower. If Chaney got too close to the animal, one whiff would tell the sheriff why the bird was staggering around, about to topple over on his head.

Flower saw Morrow Beth coming and made a beeline across the carrot row, heading around the back of the house.

"Flower, come here!" She chased after him, desperate to catch him before Chaney did.

Chaney darted up the fence to head off the rooster and Morrow Beth quickened her pace. She couldn't let Chaney catch him.

Chaney raced across and blocked Flower's way. The rooster screeched and swerved in a sharp circle, heading back toward Morrow Beth.

He was slowing, his head bobbing and his wings fluttering awkwardly as though heavy. He squawked again, zigzagging dizzily toward Morrow Beth and then he fell, just plopped face-first onto the ground.

He shuddered, rolled over and jerked, his scrawny twig-thin legs sticking straight up in the air. A hoarse *paaauck* croaked out of him and he lay still.

"What the heck. . . ." Chaney skidded to a stop beside her, looking totally confused. "What's wrong with him?"

"I told you, he has these spells."

His voice turned deep and reverent. "Is he . . . dead?"

"No." She gently scooped up the rooster, knowing he would sleep for a while now. "He'll be fine."

Relieved that she'd finally caught him, she carried the rooster into the empty henhouse, laid him on a nest of hay, and walked out, latching the door.

Chaney stared in disbelief at the henhouse. "I've never seen anything like that."

"Most people haven't." She picked up her hoe and walked toward the barn, determined to get rid of Chaney White one way or another.

She hoped he would get the hint that she had work to do, but he hurried after her, straight into the barn.

"You didn't answer my question, Morrow Beth."

She grimaced, hoping he would have forgotten the questions he'd asked before Flower showed up. "Oh?"

"What were you doing in the tunnel?" His breath burned her ear.

She tensed, shocked that he stood so close to her. His chest nudged her shoulders. His heat wrapped around her, a faint scent of bay rum humming through her senses until she could feel her will wavering.

She turned, using the opportunity to step away from him. Meeting his gaze, she defiantly refused to show that he affected her. "Am I suspected of something?"

He looked surprised. "Well, no."

"Then why are you asking?"

"I'm trying to figure out why people would use the tunnel. Some people in town think it's used by the moonshiners."

"Royce Henry, no doubt," she muttered.

"Well?" He folded his arms, his brawny thighs braced as if he would stand there all day.

And he probably would. It seemed only the truth would

get rid of him. Or at least part of the truth, which she had to tell before Flower woke up or John Mark came back to the house. "Not that it's any of your business, but I was chasing Billy Jack and Katie Jo."

"Is that all?"

"What else could I be doing down there?"

He eased closer, trapping her with that deep drawl, that broad chest. His voice rumbled out seductively. "Moving moonshine?"

For just a moment, she considered moving closer to him, letting that seductive heat web around her and . . . Her knees wobbled and the realization angered her. Had he discovered something in the tunnels, some link to John Mark?

She spun away. "If I were moving moonshine, do you think I'd tell you?"

He pressed up against her back, his breath tickling her neck. "I hope so, Morrow Beth. I surely do hope so."

"Well, I wouldn't—"

"Sparking in the barn, Morrow Beth?"

"John Mark!" She whirled around, bumping noses with Chaney, her breasts brushing his chest.

Ignoring the sensation that burst up her arm, she pushed past the sheriff. Her eyes pleaded with her brother to leave, quickly.

John Mark dragged a shovel behind him. He frowned and looked over her head. Warmth twinkled in his green eyes and he said with the easy charm she'd always envied, "Don't believe I've had the pleasure."

Desperate, Morrow Beth blurted out, "This is Chaney White, *Sheriff* White."

Chaney came forward, a curious smile on his face. "So, you're the other Huckabee? I had the pleasure of meeting your sisters and younger brother yesterday."

John Mark wiped a greasy hand on his homespun trousers and held out his hand to Chaney. "Sheriff, it's a pleasure."

His voice was warm, welcoming, and Morrow Beth inwardly groaned. John Mark liked everybody, but she didn't see how even he could charm the sheriff, who was proving to be as determined as a snake hunting eggs.

The two men shook hands, Chaney still measuring her brother. John Mark crossed one ankle over the other and leaned indolently against the shovel he held.

"So, you're the new sheriff? You're pretty young."

"About your age, I'd wager." Chaney's voice was polite and pleasant, but Morrow Beth had the uneasy feeling that his mind was searching for a way to trip up John Mark.

Which wouldn't be easy, she thought with a surge of fierce pride. Her brother might not be able to read or write, but there was nothing wrong with his brain.

"How long have you been running the farm?"

"Since Pap passed on last year." John Mark glanced at Morrow Beth, compassion flitting across his features. "Sister doesn't like to talk about it much."

"I guess not." Chaney glanced at Morrow Beth apologetically.

Outside the chickens squawked and fussed. Morrow Beth could hear Katie Jo squealing at Billy Jack and she knew it wouldn't be long before they spotted Chaney's horse and came bursting inside.

"Well, I'm sure the sheriff has work to do." She wanted him to leave, before he discovered that John Mark had just this morning cooked up a fresh batch of lightning.

John Mark eyed her curiously and straightened. "Do you fish, Sheriff?"

Chaney seemed surprised at the question, but nodded

easily. "Sure do. I haven't had a chance to try the creek yet, though."

"You're welcome to come along with me and Billy Jack anytime you want. In fact, we might be going tomorrow."

"Isn't the water still a little cold for that?" Chaney's gaze plainly weighed John Mark.

Her brother shrugged. "We'll start to get a little warmth here pretty soon and the fish are starting to circle up. You're welcome to join us."

"Well . . . thank you." Chaney seemed stunned and Morrow Beth felt a surge of perverse satisfaction.

He had been all set to dislike her brother, or at least to mistrust him, and John Mark had surprised him. She liked that Chaney looked taken aback and she couldn't halt a grin.

"You wanna come, Sister?"

Morrow Beth realized both John Mark and Chaney were staring at her. "Me?"

Chaney's gaze warmed and flicked over her.

"Oh, no. Thank you." The farther away from Chaney White she stayed, the better.

She could still feel the soft mist of his breath on her neck and didn't want to give him a chance to do that again. She might like it, but that didn't mean it was prudent.

And if Morrow Beth had learned anything from having a moonshine runner for a daddy, it was to be prudent.

Chaney White's steady, hot gaze made her uncomfortable. She noticed how he eyed everything in the barn and she knew he was looking for something to tie her brother to the tunnels he'd found.

She was reassured to know that there was nothing incriminating nearby, except Flower, and she had locked him in the chicken house. She hoped the new sheriff didn't know the difference between an addled rooster and a drunk one.

A sudden burst of squawking erupted in the henhouse, a sure sign that Flower had woken. It wouldn't be long before the twins let the rooster loose and she intended to be well rid of Sheriff Chaney White by then.

She walked toward the barn door, dismissal plain in her voice. "I'd best get supper on the table."

"You're welcome to stay, Sheriff," John Mark offered.

Morrow Beth spun in surprise and she silently tele-graphed an urgent *no* to her brother.

Chaney's eyes widened and a grin tugged at the corner of his lips, as if he knew the protest she was about to offer.

Was John Mark crazy? Didn't he know why Chaney was really here? Of course he did. So what was her brother up to?

John Mark clapped Chaney on the shoulder. "Well, Sheriff?"

Chaney's gaze shifted to Morrow Beth, challenging, teasing, weighing.

She held her breath, forcing her face to remain blank, trying not to give away the panic tripping through her body.

Finally Chaney shook his head. "I'd better get on back to town, but I appreciate the invitation."

"Anytime, Sheriff. Anytime at all." There was no mis-taking the sincerity in John Mark's voice.

Morrow Beth wanted to kill him for scaring her like that. Standing beside her brother, Morrow Beth smiled until her face ached as Chaney rode away.

Then she turned on John Mark. "What were you think-ing?"

Her brother stared after the sheriff as Chaney disappeared over the rise. "I was thinking we might need to make a friend of the new sheriff." He slid a sidelong look at her. "*All* of us."

She definitely wasn't going to pursue that. It would simply be another of her brother's harebrained ideas.

"Looks like he's smitten with you."

She gaped at her brother. "Nonsense! I've only met him the one time."

"Don't matter." He shook his head, his eyes narrowed in contemplation. "You should think about getting to know him."

Morrow Beth slanted a look at her brother. "Since when did you care so much about my social life?"

"Since the sheriff seems interested in you."

"Trying to marry me off?" she asked archly.

"No, not that." He rubbed his chin. "It could help us to have a sheriff on our side."

"You want me to flirt with him so that if he finds out about the moonshine, he won't take action? He doesn't seem like the type of man to be swayed by a woman."

"You may be right. On the other hand, you might not be." He stared off into the distance, following the dust of Chaney White's horse. "I'm just saying a body can't ever have too many friends."

"Well, maybe they can," she tossed at him, walking out of the barn.

Inviting the sheriff fishing! Good heavens! She stomped through the gate and up to the house. "Supper will be ready in an hour. Don't forget to wash up."

She stepped onto the porch. "Oh, and let Flower out of the henhouse. He's been in your moonshine again."

* * *

What in the Sam Hill was he supposed to do now? Chaney had gone out to the Huckabee homestead to find out if Morrow Beth knew the purpose of those tunnels. Well, she'd admitted to being down there and that was all.

He hadn't expected it to be easy, but neither had he expected to be his own worst enemy. Just breathing in that sweet clean scent of her tangled his purposes. And he couldn't resist flirting with her, to see if she was as drawn to him as he was to her.

Which didn't matter at all because he was investigating her family. He hadn't thought about a formal investigation until now, but there it was. Frustration plowed through him. Not only at his inability to learn anything about the moonshining, but because of his undimmed attraction to Morrow Beth.

He was supposed to be gathering information about her brother and all he'd been able to think about was tasting those sweet lips. He imagined, just for an instant, kissing her. Tasting the warm velvet of her mouth—

She would have slapped him sideways. Chaney shook his head, trying to dismiss the provocative image. He wanted to be friends with her. Heck, he wanted more than that, but any friendship with her should be out of the question.

He couldn't get involved with someone he suspected of moonshining. He shouldn't get involved with any of them.

As friendly as her brother was, Chaney suspected John Mark's easy charm hid a cunning and quick mind.

And what about Morrow Beth? He wanted her, couldn't deny that. Wanted to melt that glacial look in her eyes, wanted her to smile at him again.

He had learned nothing except that she had indeed been down in the tunnels. She had admitted only to chasing her siblings down there, but was it the truth? And that rooster . . .

He grinned. The Huckabees were definitely a colorful family. John Mark's friendliness, Morrow Beth's open, winning smile? What did that hide?

Maybe he was wrong about the Huckabees. Maybe Royce Henry and Mayor Bushman were, too. Sada seemed to think so.

Chaney decided to ask around town. Maybe people would be more willing to talk about Morrow Beth's father since he was no longer around. But Chaney found, to his growing frustration, that no one would talk about the man at all.

After three hours, he had learned exactly nothing about E. Y. Huckabee. So he went to the one woman who might help him.

Sada Pickins was just locking her door for the evening when Chaney stepped up on the porch of the newspaper office.

"Hello, Sheriff." The older woman smiled warmly at him, looping her reticule over one wrist. "I'm glad you're not sneaking up on me this time."

He grinned. "I wonder if I could ask you something, Sada?"

"Certainly."

"It's about E. Y. Huckabee."

"What about him?"

Her voice sounded strangled and Chaney noted that her smile tightened. "Not to speak ill of the dead, but how did he die?"

She glanced away, nodding at Utive Olen, who passed them on the street. "No one's quite sure."

"What about you? What do you think happened?"

She shifted, unease sliding across her features. "I don't

like to speculate. And that's what I'd be doing.''

"I'd appreciate it, Sada. It seems no one in this town will tell me anything about the Huckabees.''

She stepped into the street, walking toward the east end of town. "This is a tight-knit community, Sheriff. Surely you've realized that by now?''

"Sada, I think you're stalling." He followed her, sensing she didn't want to tell him anything.

She stopped abruptly and Chaney did, too. "Sheriff, I don't feel comfortable talking about the dead. I'm sorry I can't help you. I really don't know how E. Y. died. There were rumors, of course, but I don't set much store by them.''

He could tell he was going to get nowhere with her so he tried a different tack. "I was out at the Huckabees today.''

She lifted one eyebrow.

"Do you think they run moonshine?''

Sada blinked. "I'm sure I have no idea.''

"Sada—''

She laughed nervously. "Sheriff, I could spin tales all day about what I *think*. What good would that do?''

"I just want your opinion.''

She cleared her throat, her fingers fiddling with the broach at her throat. "I simply don't know. I certainly wouldn't like to think so. Morrow Beth is in church every Sunday and brings those kids. John Mark is a delight. He's a hard worker and—''

"I met him today, too.''

Sada eyed him consideringly. "And what did you think?''

"I think—'' Chaney figured he shouldn't be discussing this kind of information with someone outside of the law. "I think the Huckabees are quite a bunch of people.''

"Yes, they are." Sada chuckled and continued down the planked walk.

Chaney walked beside her, his hands clasped behind his back. "Have you ever met their rooster?"

"Flower?" Sada grinned. "Oh, yes. Most people around here know Flower."

Chaney shook his head. "I've never seen such a thing."

As much as he liked John Mark and Morrow Beth, too, Chaney couldn't afford to dismiss the idea that they might be involved in moonshining. His job depended on cleaning up this town and he fully intended to do just that.

If no one in this town would talk to him, then Chaney would just go to the source. John Mark came across as earnest and easygoing, but Chaney suspected there was a sharp shrewd mind beneath that charm.

Gut instinct told him he should focus on getting answers out of John Mark and stay away from Morrow Beth. Chaney planned to do just that. Tomorrow, he was going fishing.

It was easier to stay away from Morrow Beth than to stop thinking about her, Chaney realized, but he was determined to do both. The next morning dawned clear and pleasantly cool. He whistled tunelessly, skirting the back side of Scrub as he headed for Stillwater Creek.

He carried a cane pole over his shoulder and hoped that John Mark Huckabee and his younger brother were indeed fishing.

Walking up the hill, he halted at the top, impressed with the view. The creek spun out of the hills on the other side and wound its way through the foothills to flow over a natural rock dam into the sandy-bottomed bowl.

Fringed thickly with oaks, cottonwoods, redbuds, persimmon trees and a stately magnolia, the water glittered like gold dust in the early morning light. Though the trees were still bare, it didn't diminish their grandeur.

Knee-high grass, turning from winter drab to green, crunched under Chaney's boots as he started down the hill. A rabbit scampered across in front of him and another animal rustled in the brush beyond. From here, he could see that John Mark and Biily Jack were on the creek bank.

The elder Huckabee reclined against the base of an oak tree, his pole resting between his massive thighs. Billy Jack sat on the ground, peeling off his socks. His sturdy shoes lay to one side; the legs of his overalls were already rolled up to his knees.

"Good morning," Chaney called.

Billy Jack leapt up and darted toward him. "Hey, Sheriff!"

"Hey." Chaney shook the little boy's hand, noting that his eyes were the exact shade of his older sister's. Annoyed, he pushed the thought away. He wasn't here about Morrow Beth Huckabee.

He was here to find out something about her father, and her brother if things went well. He reached the edge of the creek.

"Morning," John Mark offered affably, doffing his limp slouch hat. "Pick a seat. Looks to be a nice day."

Chaney eyed the edge of the creek, seeing a spot on the other side of John Mark that curved down a steeper incline.

"Guess you changed your mind about joining us?" John Mark asked easily, settling back against the tree.

"Yes." Chaney grinned. "The day turned out to be too pretty to waste."

John Mark grinned. "Amen to that."

Chaney wondered how often John Mark came fishing.

If he did so too often, how could he support them on the farm? Chaney moved in front of John Mark and hopped down a small incline onto the bank.

Billy Jack snatched up his pole and skipped over to Chaney. "Can I sit by you?"

"Sure." Chaney smiled, eyeing the ground for the best place. Situated next to the tree where John Mark sat, the edge of a boulder poked out of the bank.

Chaney sat on the rock and eased his pole down beside him. The river was up from the recent rain, and he would have no trouble casting here.

"Do you fish very often?" He pushed his hat farther back on his head and set his pole in the ground, grabbing the line to check his hook.

John Mark pulled his line up and checked it, then tossed it back out again. "Seems to be just enough."

Which was no answer at all, Chaney realized. He tossed his own line out and watched the tiny cork bob. Settling himself back against the rock, he adjusted his hat to shade his eyes. "I just wondered if the farm kept you too busy to do much fishing."

"Depends on the time of year. We're busier in the fall. I've got a little time right now since everything's been planted."

Chaney felt John Mark's gaze wander over to him. He kept his attention on the shimmering water. It wouldn't do for John Mark to guess Chaney's intention and shrink up tighter than skin on a snake.

"Yahoo!" Billy Jack splashed into the water, yanking up his line. But when he saw there was nothing on the other end, his shoulders slumped. "Dadgum it!"

Chaney smiled. "Isn't that water a tad cold?"

Billy Jack grinned. "It's not too bad . . . now that I'm in here."

He pulled a worm out of his pocket and wiggled it onto the hook before dropping his line back into the water. Noisily he trudged back to the bank. "I thought I had a durn fish."

Chaney grinned. "Looks like he got lunch and you got nothing."

"Gotta give it some time, Billy." John Mark stretched lazily.

The boy eased down beside Chaney, speaking in a loud whisper. "Morrow Beth says they can hear you if you're too loud, and they won't come."

"Might be true." He didn't want to be reminded of Morrow Beth, but couldn't stem his curiosity about her. "Does your sister come with you often?"

"Nah," John Mark offered. "She's too busy with the house and her job at The Golden Goose."

"But when she does," Billy Jack said, "she likes to wade."

"She works at the restaurant?" Perhaps that was why John Mark was able to go fishing in the middle of the week instead of doing chores at the farm.

John Mark nodded, settling his hat over his face. "She does."

Chaney let the sunlight slide over his face, trying not to imagine Morrow Beth with her stockings off and her skirts above her ankles wading in the water. "So, it's just the four of you, huh?"

"Yep." Billy Jack nodded emphatically. "Me, Katie Jo, Morrow Beth and—"

"He's met all of us, Billy," John Mark said patiently. "Haven't you, Sheriff?"

"Yep." Chaney smiled at Billy Jack. "It's good you have each other. I don't have any brothers or sisters."

"Well, sisters can be right vexing sometimes," Billy

Jack said as if in confidence. "Katie Jo ain't as bad as some. Morrow Beth's all right, too, 'cept she makes me wash my mouth out with soap all the time."

Chaney grinned. "Is that right?"

"Says I swear too much. Dang, I only do it when I need to make a point, ya know?"

Chaney chuckled. "I think so."

John Mark laughed softly. "Trouble is, Billy, you think you need to make a point with every sentence."

"Do not," Billy defended with a grin. He tossed a pebble into the water then dug into the soft mud with a twig. "You have a pa, Chaney? Our pa died last year."

At last, the subject of fathers, though Chaney wasn't too eager to talk about his. "My pa died, too."

Beside him, John Mark straightened. "They're sayin' in town that your pa was Clarence White. Is that right?"

"Afraid so."

"Well, I'll be." John Mark's eyes narrowed speculatively. "How'd you get to be a sheriff?"

"Who's Clarence White?" Billy asked impatiently.

Chaney preferred to talk about the Huckabees' father, not his. But maybe he would get some information in exchange for giving some. "He was a horse thief."

"Beggin' your pardon, Sheriff, but he wasn't just a horse thief." John Mark's eyes warmed with admiration. "He was the slipperiest, most daring horse thief in three states."

Billy Jack's eyes grew wide as quarters. "Well, I'll be danged."

"They almost never caught him, ain't that right?" John Mark pressed.

"It is," Chaney admitted, feeling the same resentment and loneliness he felt every time he talked about his father.

The other man slanted a look at him. "You have anything to do with him getting caught?"

"Me?" Chaney barked in surprise. "I didn't even know where he was."

John Mark's gaze weighed him for a long moment. "Didn't think so. A fella would have to be one cold-hearted son to help catch someone he loved."

Chaney met the other man's gaze. He hadn't said he loved his father, though perhaps some part of him still did. But he sensed that John Mark was trying to determine how Chaney would handle a case if it ever became personal.

"How *did* you get to be a sheriff?"

"My pa left when I was twelve. A good man took me in. He was a lawman and I learned from him."

"Didn't you want to steal horses, like your pa?" Billy Jack asked earnestly. "Pap taught me to do the things he knew."

"Like what?" Chaney's shoulders tightened in anticipation of learning something.

"Like fishin'." Billy Jack shrugged.

John Mark's lazy words were underlined with steel. "And plowin' a farm."

Billy Jack leaned against the bank of the river, using a twig to gouge a deep hole in the mud beside him. "Our pa wasn't just a farmer."

"Oh?" Chaney waited expectantly.

"He was the best farmer around," John Mark answered before Billy Jack could. "That's what he means."

There were no visible signs of tension in the man's body or voice, but Chaney felt the air between them shift.

"I understand he passed on last year," Chaney said quietly.

"Yeah, he did." Billy Jack stared down at the ground.

Chaney squeezed the little boy's shoulder. His own father had come in and out of his life so many times, Chaney had never been sure if he would ever see him again. It appeared E. Y. Huckabee had been around for his children. "How did it happen?"

He looked over his shoulder at John Mark, who sat staring out across the water. His handsome features were pulled tight, a poignant look on his face. His gaze slid to Chaney's and he grinned sheepishly. "He was drunk."

Chaney's pulse leapt. Was John Mark about to give him what he wanted, just like that?

"And he fell into the water trough." The other man shrugged. "He drowned."

Chaney couldn't stifle a pang of disappointment though he chastised himself. John Mark was talking about the death of his father and Chaney couldn't callously ask if E. Y. Huckabee had been drunk on his own moonshine. "I'm sorry to hear it."

And he was. He hated to hear about anyone losing family. He could understand that, because he'd lost all he'd had and that hadn't been much.

"Our ma's been dead for years."

"Since me and Katie Jo were born." Billy Jack wiped surreptitiously at a tear.

It was no wonder the Huckabees were close. And if they were involved in moonshining, it was a good bet that they would all protect each other.

"Me and Morrow Beth do the best we can. The farm provides for us and Morrow Beth's job does, too."

It seemed to Chaney that the farm was too small to provide much besides food for the family, but he didn't say so. He'd learned nothing, except how the elder Huckabee had died. And, he admitted uneasily, that he was coming to like these Huckabees.

It was difficult not to like John Mark, who'd never met a stranger. And Billy Jack. Or any of them, especially their pretty sister.

Chaney tried to put further thoughts of Morrow Beth out of his head, but he just kept thinking about the responsibilities she'd taken on when her father had passed away. She'd probably become like a mother to the twins at the death of her own mother, and now this.

Chaney had only needed to take care of himself, not an entire family. So what if they had to make do the only way they could? But, he cautioned himself, he couldn't afford to look the other way if they were involved in moonshining.

His job, his livelihood, depended on him closing down the stills in this territory and he had given his word. Chaney had never gone back on his word and he didn't intend to start now.

Not even for a pair of green eyes, and the sweetest lips he'd ever seen.

* 5 *

MORROW BETH FOUGHT it and sidestepped it
and denied it, but finally she had to admit she liked Chaney White. She didn't want to. She told herself it would
only lead to trouble, but she couldn't get around it.

She had enjoyed his visit the day before. So much so
that she was still thinking about it the next day, especially
the way he'd followed her into the barn.

She tried to focus on the annoying questions he'd
asked, on his obvious intent to learn something about her
family, but all she wanted to remember was the way his
warm breath had tickled her neck, sending streamers of
sensation tingling in her fingertips, tickling her toes.

And, she admitted reluctantly, she wanted to feel his
lips on hers.

Astonished at the boldness of the thought, she flushed
and glanced quickly around the supper table, reassuring
herself that none of her siblings noticed her heightened
color or could read her thoughts.

John Mark stared intently at her and smiled warmly.
Sparing only a thought at her brother's obvious attention,
she flashed him a smile and looked down at her plate. She
couldn't quit thinking about Chaney's big hands or his

strong neck or the way his eyes smoldered like summer midnight.

He looked at her, really *looked* at her, and the hunger in his eyes made her feel aware of her body in ways no other man ever had. While it was exciting, it was also a little intimidating. But the thing that intimidated her most was his kind smile.

That flirty curving of his lips made her feel safe and protected and that was just hogwash. He was the sheriff, for crying out loud! He could ruin her whole life if he found out about John Mark.

As much as she had enjoyed his company yesterday, it was better to stay as far away from him as she could.

John Mark cleared his throat, his gaze still pinned on Morrow Beth. "Sheriff White went fishing with us today."

"Yeah, we had fun!" Billy Jack reached for another helping of mashed potatoes.

Morrow Beth's bite of pork stuck in her throat. She took a swallow of buttermilk and stared warily at John Mark. What had happened? Had Chaney discovered something about the moonshining? John Mark didn't look upset, but then he rarely did.

"His pa is a horse thief," Billy Jack announced excitedly. "And Chaney's a sheriff because some nice man took care of him after his pa got caught."

Nausea rolled through her stomach. Morrow Beth forced herself to forget the pleasure she'd felt at Chaney's attention and remember that they could very well be talking about John Mark's future in jail as easily as not.

She looked from Billy Jack to John Mark, waiting, hoping to learn more about Chaney. His father a horse thief? He'd been raised by someone other than a parent? Did he have brothers and sisters? What about his mother?

She stanched her thoughts with a firm resolve. She shouldn't want to know more about Chaney White than she already did.

"He's a good marshal," Katie Jo said, picking at her plate and staring off dreamily.

Morrow Beth didn't even correct Katie Jo about Chaney's title.

"Oh? How do you know that, Katie?" John Mark asked with a smile.

" 'Cuz he's handsome and nice and—"

"Dang, Katie Jo, that don't make a good sheriff."

"Billy Jack," Morrow Beth warned automatically, though her mind was fully occupied with Chaney.

"What makes a good sheriff is somebody who's fast with a gun and mean and don't let nobody walk all over him. Heckfire, sheriffs don't go around being nice to people."

"Billy Jack, that's twice." Morrow Beth's stomach dipped strangely at the prolonged discussion of the sheriff.

"Well, he's smart, I'll tell you that," John Mark observed casually. Too casually.

Morrow Beth looked up, a small finger of dread working through her. What exactly had gone on today at the creek?

"Of course he's smart," Katie Jo said indignantly. "Anybody can tell you that."

Morrow Beth ignored her sister's obvious fascination with Chaney and focused instead on her older brother. *Something* had happened.

"And he looks to have the persistence of a mule that don't want to be turned around."

Dread thumped at her and Morrow Beth's chest grew tight.

"Chaney was asking questions about Pap."

At John Mark's fatalistic tone, Morrow Beth sucked in a breath. "What kind of questions?"

"Wantin' to know how he died," John Mark said with a thoughtful look on his face. "I think I was right before."

"Right about what?" Katie Jo reached across Morrow Beth for another biscuit.

Foreboding drummed through her. She hoped John Mark wasn't talking about what she thought he was talking about.

His gaze sliced to Morrow Beth. "I think we all need to make friends with the sheriff."

She looked down at her plate, counting peas, trying to block out her siblings' voices.

John Mark droned on. "Be neighborly and all."

"I'm already friends with him," Katie Jo said enthusiastically. "He is so handsome."

"I like him, too," Billy Jack said with a mouthful of potatoes. "Don't you like him, John Mark?"

"Yep. What about you, Sister?"

Morrow Beth counted faster, her mind racing. She needed to gather eggs and check on Flower. He hadn't been seen today. Or heard from.

"Morrow Beth?" John Mark's insistent voice penetrated her rambling thoughts. "I've been thinking."

She groaned and covered her eyes with one hand. "I hate it when you do that."

"I've got a plan. This new sheriff needs a distraction and I know just the perfect one."

"What?" Billy Jack asked with a biscuit in his mouth.

"You said he liked to fish," Katie Jo put in.

Morrow Beth could feel John Mark's heavy gaze on her and dread puddled in her stomach.

"The perfect distraction for the sheriff," John Mark said slowly, "is your pretty sister."

Her head came up slowly and she levelled a gaze on her brother.

Katie Jo swiveled her head toward Morrow Beth and her small mouth formed a perfect O.

"Hmph," said Billy Jack. "I think fishin' would be better."

"Trust me, Billy Jack," John said with a grin.

Morrow Beth shook her head, dread and anticipation curling inside her. "No, no, no."

"It's for the good of the family, Morrow Beth."

"I won't do it. You're asking me to—" She had this sudden image of Chaney White kissing her, touching her. Her brother couldn't be asking her to do *that,* could he? "Exactly *what* are you asking me to do?"

"I want you to cozy up to him. Be friendlier. You were as chilly as November to him before."

"He's the sheriff, John Mark. You know what he wants," she said pointedly. "And if he proves it, you'll go to jail."

"Chaney would never put John Mark in jail," Katie exclaimed indignantly.

"Why would he do somethin' like that?" Billy Jack demanded.

"It's his job," Morrow Beth said impatiently, glaring at her older brother.

"I think men are more likely to go easy on people they consider friends, don't you?"

She sank back in her chair, wishing she could disappear. "I won't do it. I won't."

"What would we do if John Mark got sent to jail?" Katie Jo wailed, dropping her chin to her hand.

Billy Jack's voice rose. "We can't let John Mark go to

jail. Chaney never saw his dad after he went to jail."

Morrow Beth covered her face with her hands.

"You can't let Chaney send John Mark to jail, Morrow Beth," Billy Jack declared.

She shook her head, hating the guilt worming through her. Hating the little voice that nagged *All you have to do is be nice to him.*

"We're a family. We have to stay together," Katie Jo piped up. "Pap said."

Morrow Beth dropped her hands to her lap and glared at John Mark. "I won't encourage him to take liberties."

"Never said you had to." He leaned back in his chair, looking content. "Just be nice to him."

She rolled her eyes.

"There's no one you can't charm when you set your mind to it, Morrow Beth."

"Oh, stop it!" She pushed away from the table and snatched up her plate. "If I do this, you will all do the dishes for a month."

"Done." John Mark nodded.

"And sweep."

"Okay," said Katie Jo.

"And hoe the garden." She looked pointedly at Billy Jack.

He firmed his lips, looking stubborn.

John Mark's deep voice rumbled out in warning. "Billy Jack."

"Oh, all right." He blew out a loud breath. "I hate that dang ol' garden—"

"That's three." Morrow Beth walked over and reached above the dry sink.

Her younger brother groaned and closed his eyes.

Morrow Beth held out the tin of soap. "Here you go. And wash it out good."

Billy made a face, trudging over to the pump handle and working up a good stream of water before he stuck his fingers in the soap and thrust them quickly into his mouth. "Ugh!"

Even Morrow Beth laughed as Billy coughed and sputtered his way through another mouth washing.

Despite the good humor that had been restored to the household, Morrow Beth didn't like for one second what she had agreed to do. Not only because it was dishonest, but because she feared she would like it way too much.

Chaney forced himself not to think about Morrow Beth, about the way the sun gilded her skin to the color of peaches and cream, about the way her eyes crinkled at the corner when she smiled, about the way those sweet lips parted to reveal white, even teeth. He wanted to feel her lips on his, taste her.

He had swept both jail cells and polished the windows until they gleamed. He'd checked and double-checked the chain across the five rifles his gun rack held and he'd polished his desk.

He'd found a stack of wanted posters in the desk along with a blank ledger. Chaney left the ledger where it was, but pinned the wanted posters to the wall behind his desk. Reading about horse thieves, murderers, and bank robbers should have wiped his mind clean of Morrow Beth Huckabee, but she lingered in his thoughts like smoke from a fire.

He didn't expect to get information from her. He certainly hadn't gotten any from her brother. But he could hide out in the tunnel, conduct his own surveillance.

Yes, he would wait down in the tunnel and see who used it, and what they used it for. He pinned the last poster to the wall. That was the best way to get answers about the moonshiners. He sure as heck wasn't getting any information from anyone in town.

He grabbed his hat and plopped it on his head. Tucking the keys to the cells into his leather vest pocket, he turned for the door. Just as he put his hand on the knob, it opened and he took a step back in surprise.

Morrow Beth Huckabee stopped abruptly in the doorway, her gaze going to his hat. "Oh, I'm probably late."

"Late?" He couldn't believe she was standing here in front of him. If possible, she was even prettier than his numerous musings.

Her long thick hair was pulled into a low chignon. She wore a pale green dress and in her delicate hands, she held a tray.

Chaney reached belatedly for it. "I'm sorry. Let me take that for you. Is everything all right?"

"Yes. Well, except I'm late with your lunch." She ignored his offer of help and swept around him, setting the tray down on his desk.

"You brought me lunch?" A grin split his face before he could stop it.

She turned, eyeing him strangely. "Well, not me. The restaurant. Bonnie always provides the sheriff with lunch and dinner. You haven't been in your office any of the other times she's come by, but today you are."

"Yes, I am." Disappointment swept through him that it hadn't been Morrow Beth's idea to bring him the meal, but he chided himself. The last he'd seen of her, she was trying to stay as far away from him as she could. And hadn't he told himself to do the same?

He shifted, watching her closely. There was something different about her today. She seemed . . . nervous. Was she remembering that moment in the barn, the energy that had hummed between them?

She turned back to the tray and lifted up a thin towel. "There's steak and potatoes, carrots, bread baked this morning, and apple pie for dessert."

"Sounds delicious." His trip to the tunnels could wait for a little while. "Would you like to join me?"

"Me?" she said sharply, then gave a small laugh. "Oh, no."

But she hesitated next to the desk. The savory aroma of bread and meat wafted to Chaney. Morrow Beth smiled tentatively and Chaney smiled back, wondering why she wasn't hightailing it out the door. Yesterday she hadn't been able to get rid of him fast enough.

"How are you liking Scrub?" Her voice sounded forced, but she smiled warmly at him.

Chaney wondered at her interest. "Very well, so far. Everyone's been real friendly."

"Have you met everyone now?"

"I think so. There may be a few I haven't met."

"The Warner sisters?"

He grinned. "My first day here. They paid me a visit, brought me some of their preserves and something they called a remedy."

"Oh?" Morrow Beth's lips twitched. "Have you tried that yet? They have quite a reputation."

"No, I haven't." He didn't know what was different about her, but the smile on her face made him want to smile, too. Mostly he wanted to know why she was suddenly so all-fired interested in *anything* about him. "I took it that the remedy was to be used if I got to feeling poorly."

She nodded, stepping toward the cells and running a finger across the bars. "You've cleaned up in here. It looks real nice."

He hadn't noticed before, but she had a soft drawl that

curled invitingly around plain words. "Thank you."

He stepped closer, coaxed by the soft scent of her, by the growing urge to feel her heat mingle with his.

"John Mark told me you went fishing with him and Billy after all."

Ah, John Mark. Perhaps he had something to do with this new, friendlier Morrow Beth. "Yes, I did. I enjoyed getting to know them."

"They said the same about you."

Had he passed some kind of Huckabee test? Did that make him fit company for her now, he wondered? Or was she here at the request of her brother, similar to invading an enemy camp?

Denial surged through him, but Chaney refused to dismiss it completely. Morrow Beth's sudden friendliness, while not overt, did cause a niggle of suspicion. "John Mark told me about your pa. I'm sorry to hear it."

He watched her carefully, looking for anything in her pretty face that might give him some hint as to what was going through her head.

Sadness darkened her eyes to moss green and she gave a wan smile. "It doesn't sound like you had a pa at all."

"No. No, I didn't." He tensed. Generally people made assumptions about him based on what they knew of his father and two people couldn't be more different.

She canted her head, studying him thoughtfully. "I'm sorry. I guess you don't want to talk about it."

"I don't really like to."

She nodded. "I can understand that. People probably think you're like him or something."

"Yes." Amazed, he stared at her, adding perceptive to her list of qualities.

"I don't think people mean to be hurtful by doing that,

but sometimes it is," she said quietly, her slender fingers curling around one of the bars.

He nodded in agreement. "I don't much like being compared to him."

"I know what you mean. I wouldn't want to be judged by my folks either."

Chaney tensed, though he tried to keep his voice casual. "Oh? Why's that?"

She stared into his eyes for a long moment, then shrugged and looked away. "We're just all very different people."

He had a feeling she'd been about to reveal more than that and he wanted to draw her out. He told himself it was strictly in order to get information, but the fact was she fascinated him.

She shook her head then and started for the door. "I've spent much too long here. Enjoy your lunch. Someone will come by later to get the tray or you can drop it off if you're down by the restaurant."

"Will you come?" Maybe he shouldn't have asked, but he wanted to know if he would see her again.

She hesitated in the doorway, glancing at him. "Probably."

"I'd like that," he said, cursing himself even as he said it.

Her gaze moved to the street and indecision crossed her features. Then she looked at him. "So would I."

Chaney smiled and she smiled back, the first full smile she'd given him. Heat trickled through his body and he reflexively took a step toward her.

He became aware then of the heavy thud of boots, coming up the steps toward the jail.

A short barrel of a man peered around Morrow Beth and stuck his head in the door. "You the sheriff?"

"Yessir." Chaney stepped up to the door, close enough now to Morrow Beth that their arms touched. She swallowed, shifting away from him. He wondered if she suddenly felt as nervous as he did.

The man jabbed his thumb toward a spot behind him. "Got some people here I think you'll want to see."

"Who's that?" Chaney frowned, trying to see past the man's broad bulk.

"I'm Marshal Hayes. Been working the Kansas border, especially up by Baxter Springs."

"Yes?"

"I caught me a couple of moonshiners and they tell me they live here. They said there was law here now and I thought you'd want to know."

"Moonshiners?" Chaney's pulse leapt. At last something pertaining to his job.

Morrow Beth glanced at him, her delicate features strained with worry.

Chaney offered what he hoped was a reassuring smile and turned back to the marshal. "Well, let's see what you've got."

"Beats all I've ever seen," Hayes muttered, backing out of the door and turning his body so Chaney could look into the street.

"Holy cow." His jaw dropped.

"Oh, my stars." Morrow Beth's disbelief echoed his own.

There, sitting double on a swaybacked mule, were Cholly and Clara Warner.

Chaney felt as if he'd been punched in the gut. He slanted a glance at Marshal Hayes. "This is who you're talking about?"

The man nodded heavily.

"We've done nothing wrong. I demand you untie us

right now.'' Cholly somehow managed to look haughty, even atop a mule.

Miss Clara nodded. "Yes, so do I."

Next to Chaney, Morrow Beth gave a gasp of horror. "They're tied up!"

"I'm sure there's been some sort of mistake," Chaney began.

The other man shook his head and stepped down to the ground. Opening a bulging saddlebag, he withdrew a jar that looked as if it contained milk. Then another. Then another.

Denial shot through Chaney even as he acknowledged the common trick among moonshiners to paint the inside of the jar to make it look as if it held buttermilk instead of liquor. He forced himself to look into the open jar that Marshal Hayes held out for his inspection. He smelled the stout liquor before he saw its amber color.

The Warner sisters moonshiners? He couldn't imagine. Then, like a sting to the backside, came the memory of them giving him a jar full of exactly the stuff that Hayes held.

Was their "remedy" moonshine? Was that why Morrow Beth had gotten such a funny look on her face when Chaney had told her about the gift from the Warner sisters?

"Caught 'em red-handed, selling to four gentlemen along the border."

"We were conducting business," Clara began.

"We didn't do anything wrong," Cholly maintained. "Those poor men simply needed some of our remedy. We are not going to turn our back on those in need."

"Yes, Sheriff. If you'll recall, we even gave you—"

"I'll handle it from here, Hayes." Chaney cut Clara off before she could inform the other man that even now Chaney had a jar of this same stuff sitting in his kitchen. Remedy indeed.

He glanced at Morrow Beth, but couldn't tell if she was trying to smother a laugh or was mortified.

Hayes nodded and approached his mule hesitantly. Cholly kicked at him and the big man jumped back in time to avoid the blow to his belly.

"I been dealin' with this for the whole trip," he muttered as he went around the back side of the mule and hauled the two women down unceremoniously.

The sisters sputtered and stomped, glaring at the big man. Chaney noted that Morrow Beth's features tightened in anger as well.

Cholly tossed her head, her bound hands jabbing awkwardly toward Hayes. "I've never been so poorly handled in my life."

"Neither have I," Clara said with a huff.

Morrow Beth hurried to the women, patting their hands and trying to calm them.

A knot coiled in Chaney's gut. What was he supposed to do with them? They'd been caught with moonshine in their possession. They weren't denying that the stuff *was* moonshine and that it belonged to them.

But he didn't see how he could throw them in jail. Certainly not all four of them, if indeed Davie and Carolyn were involved, too.

"They're not in my jurisdiction." Hayes struggled to get on his mule, pulling his heavy bulk atop the animal's back. "It's your problem now, Sheriff. I assume you'll contact the proper authorities?"

Chaney nodded, wondering what he was going to do. He would have to shut them down, but he refused to notify Marshal Needles or put the Warner sisters in jail.

He stood with Morrow Beth and the sisters as Hayes rode out of town.

Then Miss Cholly sighed in relief, holding out her bound hands. "Can you get these ropes off, Sheriff? They're chafing something awful."

Her green eyes pleaded with him and Miss Clara Sue smiled winningly, holding her hands out imploringly as well.

Chaney went inside and found a knife, coming back to cut the ropes from the women's wrists.

Morrow Beth smiled at him, turning to the Warner sisters. "There, that should be much better."

"Yes," said Clara, turning away. "Let's go home."

"Let's." Cholly took her sister's arm and they started for the east end of town. "I cannot believe the nerve of that man. Imagine, capturing us as if we were outlaws!"

Despite the fact that Cholly and Clara were going the wrong way, Chaney felt the situation rapidly slipping out of his control. "Ahem, ladies?"

They turned, their eyes innocently wide.

"Don't you mean to go this way?" He pointed over his shoulder. "I'm afraid I can't let you go home. At least not without me."

"Whatever do you mean, Sheriff?" Cholly demanded.

"Yes, what *do* you mean?" Morrow Beth planted her hands on her hips, staring flatly at Chaney.

He looked from her to Cholly to Clara. "I'm afraid I'm going to have to shut you down."

"Shut us down?" Cholly asked crisply. The two sisters exchanged puzzled looks.

Realization crept across Morrow Beth's features, then outrage. "Shut them down!"

"If you mean take away our remedy, you can't do that," Cholly burst out.

Clara Sue shook her head vehemently. "Exactly as Sister says."

"Sorry, ladies. It's my job."

"Your job!" Morrow Beth exploded. "They're not hurting a soul. How can you even think of being so mean?"

His jaw dropped. "*Mean?* This isn't mean! My job is to shut down moonshiners and that's what I'm doing."

She simply stared at him, fury gathering on her pretty features. Her eyes crackled like green fire and she whirled away from him. Miss Cholly and Miss Clara started to cry. Soft silent tears that made Chaney feel as if he'd just taken a switch to their bare skin.

Morrow Beth put an arm around each of their shoulders, speaking to them softly.

He could catch only a few phrases, but they all dealt with what a snake he was. He hadn't even done anything yet and they were wailing as if they were at a funeral.

He glanced around, shifting uncomfortably, but determined not to let their tears sway him. Every moonshiner within a hundred miles would get wind of it and Scrub would not only become the center of moonshining, but Chaney would become the laughingstock of the territory.

"Come on, ladies. We might as well get this over with."

Morrow Beth glared at him over her shoulder. "I'm coming with them. There's no telling what you'll do to the poor things."

He planned only to dump out their moonshine and get rid of their still, but what he wanted more than anything was to turn Morrow Beth over his knee.

What had happened to the tentative truce that had evolved between them only moments ago? What had happened to the understanding he'd seen in her eyes when they'd spoken about their fathers?

Judging by the way those green eyes were glaring at him, she'd rather cozy up to a snake than pass within a foot of him again.

She gently turned the Warner sisters in the right direction and steered them toward their house. Chaney heaved a sigh as he followed the arm-linked threesome down the road to the Warner sisters home.

It didn't look as if he'd be learning anything about the tunnel today. Disappointment and disgust shifted through him.

He yanked his hat down tighter on his head and muttered, "Welcome to Scrub."

❖ 6 ❖

SHE WAS OUTRAGED. Morrow Beth marched arm in arm with the Warner sisters down to their charming three-story Victorian home at the west end of town and followed them through the door.

Chaney White stayed three steps behind them the entire way. Morrow Beth struggled to hold on to her anger. The Warner sisters would never hurt anyone! Sheriff White was acting as if they were the . . . the James brothers!

So what if their "remedy" was more liquor than medicine? So what if they were trying to support themselves by making moonshine? They were widows, struggling to survive.

Still, Morrow Beth's conscience twinged. What they were doing was no different than what her brother did and she definitely didn't approve of that. Still, that didn't mean Chaney—*Sheriff*—White had to completely ruin the lives of these women.

She walked with Cholly and Clara into their airy open parlor where Davie and Carolyn sat stitching on a quilt. The three windows on the opposite wall were bare of curtains, letting early spring sunshine into the room. Two divans of worn pale green taffeta faced each other. Two sewing baskets, frothing with thread and yarn and fabric, sat at the women's feet.

Davie and Carolyn rose, their welcoming smiles fading to puzzled ones as Chaney stepped into the room.

Morrow Beth greeted them quietly and stood to one side, arms folded, foot tapping. If he so much as laid a finger on them, she would—Well, she didn't know what she would do, but it wouldn't be pleasant.

Davie looked from her sisters to Chaney. "Has something happened?"

"I should say so," Cholly huffed out, rubbing her wrists.

Clara nodded vehemently. "This awful man arrested us!"

Davie and Carolyn gasped in unison, their gazes shooting to Chaney. "Sheriff?"

"Not him," Cholly grumbled. "A Marshal Hayes."

"Ladies," Chaney began.

"The oaf!" Cholly interrupted, holding out her arms. "Look at my wrists. Just look at them!"

Morrow Beth saw the pale red circles where Hayes had bound Cholly's wrists and her temper flashed again. She noted with satisfaction that Chaney shifted uncomfortably. "Why don't you get it over with, Sheriff? Tell them why you came."

He glanced at her, his face set in stern lines. "The Warner sisters will be fine, if you need to get back to the restaurant."

"Bonnie will understand when I tell her there was an emergency."

A muscle flexed in his jaw. "I'm not going to hurt them," he said through gritted teeth.

Morrow Beth looked down her nose at him, wishing

she couldn't smell that enticing scent of his bay rum. "I should say not."

He stared flatly at her, frustration flashing across his face before he turned back to the Warner sisters. "Ladies, I'm sorry, but your still must go."

"Our still?" Davie crumpled a quilt square in her hand as she turned to Clara. "What does he mean?"

"He means the cooker." Cholly glared at him.

Carolyn turned puzzled blue eyes on Chaney. "But why?"

Morrow Beth's foot tapped faster. "Yes, Sheriff, *why?*" she asked sweetly.

He took off his hat, fingering the brim. "Ma'am, it seems your sisters have been selling something they call a 'remedy'."

"Yes." Carolyn's shoulders straightened, a tentative smile playing around her lips.

Davie nodded. "We all do."

The sheriff paled beneath his sun-weathered skin and Morrow Beth thought he looked nauseated.

"It's to help people who are feeling peaked. The way you look right now, Sheriff," Cholly added.

Clara nodded regally. "You do look as if you could use a dram—"

"Ladies." He held up one hand. "I'm afraid your remedy is really moonshine."

"Moonshine!"

"I never!"

"Landsakes!"

Davie gasped and put a hand to her throat in horror.

"Now, Sheriff, how do you know that?" Morrow Beth batted her eyelashes at him. "Have you already tried the jar they brought to you?"

Chaney turned, irritation turning his eyes to flint.

"Thank you, Miss Huckabee. No, I haven't—"

"You can't make a judgment based on something you haven't experienced." Cholly lifted a brow and stared flatly at him.

Chaney glared at Morrow Beth and turned back to the Warner sisters. "Very well. Why don't you give me a sample?"

Davie and Carolyn looked wide-eyed at Clara and Cholly.

Cholly grabbed Davie's arm. "You get a cup and I'll get the remedy."

Davie paled and looked ready to protest.

Morrow Beth spoke soothingly, "It's all right, Davie. The sheriff did ask."

He threw her a look guaranteed to curl paper and Morrow Beth felt a flutter of uncertainty about goading him. Before, he'd seemed even tempered, but now he looked . . . fierce and unyielding. The generous lines of his mouth were flattened in disapproval; the spare angles of his features were drawn taut with reluctance.

Chaney White didn't like this any better than she did! The realization took the vinegar right out of her. She struggled to hold on to her indignation. He was, after all, taking away the only livelihood the sisters had.

Cholly and Davie returned. Davie handed Chaney a cup of dark amber liquid. He glanced at all of them, then took a cautious sip. His eyebrows shot up, his eyes widened and he coughed once, twice. A flush crept up his neck.

"Whoa!" He took a deep breath and smiled at the sisters, his eyes watering as he handed back the cup. "That packs a wallop, ladies."

They all smiled as if he'd given them the best compliment in the world. He cleared his throat and said in a gentle voice, "I'm afraid I'm going to have to take your still and all your remedy."

"But it's Papa's recipe!" Cholly protested.

"What will you do with it?" Davie asked in her soft quiet voice.

Reluctance crossed his features. "I'll have to dump it out. And confiscate your barrels, your pipe—"

"After all that work!" Cholly burst out.

"I'm afraid so."

The four sisters looked at each other, then at Chaney. "Oh, Sheriff," they said in unison, glumly.

Sadness pulled at Carolyn's delicate features. "What would Papa think if he were here?"

All four of them shook their heads.

"I'm sorry, ladies. I truly am, but it's my job."

"Surely you can see they're not hurting anyone?" Morrow Beth had been quiet as long as she could stand.

He turned, his gaze warning. "They're breaking the law. It's my job to make sure people don't do that."

For all his firm words, Chaney seemed to be fighting himself as well as the rest of them.

"Are you going to put us in jail?" Cholly demanded, hands on her hips.

"Oh!" A gasp came from Clara, Davie, and Carolyn. Their stunned gazes shot to Chaney.

Regret and compassion chased across his features. "No, ladies. I don't want to do that. If I can just have access to your still, jail won't be necessary. We'll consider this a warning."

He wasn't going to put them in jail? He very well could and Morrow Beth knew it. Relief eased the tightness in her chest, yet she felt her heart clench for him. She could hear the regret in his voice when he spoke to the Warner sisters.

Oh, what was the matter with her? She shouldn't be feeling compassion for him. She shouldn't be feeling anything for him. He would do exactly the same thing to her family if he caught them.

"Ladies, if you'll lead the way, I'll get it over as quickly as possible."

The sisters exchanged glances, their features first uncertain, then sad.

Clara nodded and led the way out of the parlor and back through the foyer, stepping outside. "This way, Sheriff."

"I apologize, ladies. I wish there were another way. Maybe someday liquor will be legal."

"We're not really part of Indian Territory." Morrow Beth hurried behind him.

"We're not part of anything else, either," he said impatiently. "Until we are, we must follow their laws."

She pursed her lips, sweeping past him to catch up with the Warner sisters.

Ten minutes later, she stood in a wooded grove behind the Warner place, watching Chaney with a mixture of sympathy and trepidation as he uncovered the still. A screen of broken tree limbs and honeysuckle bushes concealed the neat circle of equipment.

The Warner sister had cleverly used a length of copper pipe to transport water from Stillwater Creek. Two large covered barrels stood to one side. The still pot, a coil of copper tubing snaking from its top, rested on a mud-chinked furnace made out of the earth. Another barrel, full of water for cooling the vapor into liquor, sat beside the furnace.

With one last reluctant look at the Warner sisters, Chaney removed the tubing from the pot and the water-condensing barrel, stuffing it under his arm. One barrel was empty, but the other one contained fermenting corn mash.

Regret pinched his features as he glanced at them. The four sisters clustered behind him like mama birds protecting a nest. Absolute silence drummed through the trees as Chaney dumped over the barrel of mash.

A strangled sound came from one of the Warner sisters, but Morrow Beth wasn't sure which one.

As he wrestled the barrel to the ground, muscles strained and his white shirt pulled taut across his shoulders. Morrow Beth frowned. If she noticed something about him, she wanted it to be the fact that he wouldn't be swayed, that he was taking away the livelihood of four women. She certainly didn't want to notice the strength in those arms.

"I apologize, ladies. I know this is hard on you."

Or the kindness in his voice.

He stuffed the copper tubes into the still pot and hefted it in his arms. The six of them moved out of the trees and back toward the house, silent except for the rustle of grass beneath their feet and the hiccup of a cricket.

They reached the house and the sisters filed up to the porch, gazing morosely at Chaney.

"What will we do?" Davie looked searchingly at Cholly.

Cholly shook her head, angry tears glimmering in her eyes. "I don't know. We'll think of something."

Chaney paused at the bottom of the porch steps. "I didn't destroy your barrels, but please don't think of trying this again. I'm afraid I'll have to be checking on you from now on and I'd hate to find out you were back at it."

"You'd put us in jail then, wouldn't you?" Cholly demanded.

"I wouldn't want to," Chaney responded quietly.

And Morrow Beth believed him. She wanted to think that he enjoyed this, that he was strutting around showing that he had the power to close down something that made four ladies happy. But she could see that he was genuinely regretful.

He could have made this so much worse. He could have made an example of them, marched them in front of the whole town to show what would happen to people who were caught moonshining. *What could happen to her brother.*

Yes, this same thing could happen at her home, to her family. Though she wouldn't miss the moonshine, she couldn't bear it if Chaney were forced to put John Mark in jail.

Morrow Beth drew in a deep breath. The last of her anger faded. Chaney White was treating the Warner sisters with dignity and respect. Would he treat her brother the same way if he learned of John Mark's even larger operation?

A reluctant admiration spread through her. What kind of man was Chaney White? Obviously compassionate. And honorable. Perhaps John Mark was right. Perhaps making friends with Chaney White would help things go easier on them if John Mark's still was discovered.

It was obvious Chaney liked the Warner sisters. And though she tried to push it away, John Mark's suggestion popped into Morrow Beth's mind. *Just be friendly to him.*

She was surprised at even thinking it, but the longer she allowed it, the more John Mark's suggestion seemed the wisest choice.

"I'm sorry, ladies." Chaney looked genuinely concerned and Morrow Beth's gaze locked on him.

"I believe you are, Sheriff," Clara sniffed. "I believe you are."

So did Morrow Beth and the realization played havoc with her determination to stay angry at him. She had come with the Warner sisters not only to offer support, but to prove to herself that she was protecting the sisters from a man bent on justice no matter what the cost.

Instead she'd seen compassion and kindness even while he'd done his job.

The Warner sisters went inside and quietly closed the door. Chaney hesitated, staring at the door remorsefully.

Morrow Beth had told John Mark she wouldn't go along with his plan. Yet she had seen how Chaney treated the Warner sisters. It occurred to her then that she was considering a friendship with the sheriff.

She'd been considering it since Chaney had admitted he might be wrong about the sisters' moonshine and agreed to taste it first. He seemed to be fair and compassionate.

Which vexed her no end. She told herself she would be friendly to the sheriff simply because John Mark might need that kind of friendship in the future. It had nothing to do with the fact that she liked Chaney White. Or that she respected the way he did his job without crushing the Warner sisters' dignity.

With the tubing stuffed under his arm, Chaney started down the hill. "Are you satisfied that they're all right?"

He wasn't being flippant, she realized. She stared up at him, amazed at the determination in those firm lips, how the strength in his face was tempered with kindness. "Yes."

He slammed his hat back on his head, his long strides carrying him quickly away from her. "Guess I'll get back to town then."

''May I walk with you?'' Morrow Beth hurried to catch up.

He slowed, looking surprised. ''If you want to.''

They walked in silence for a few moments, down the hill and through the small grove of peach trees that lined the road to the Warner place. Beside her he heaved a sigh of unmistakable relief.

Compassion tugged at her. Morrow Beth clasped her hands behind her back and looked at him. ''You were very nice to them,'' she admitted grudgingly.

''I had no intention of being otherwise,'' he said stiffly.

She flushed, ashamed now that she had acted as if, and *believed* that, he would humiliate them. Even though a little voice niggled at her to keep a distance, she said, ''I guess I owe you an apology.''

He stopped cold and eyed her warily. ''Really?''

Her gaze locked on his black eyes, wary and guarded. ''Really,'' she said softly.

His gaze shifted to her lips and a tingle shot up her arm. He wanted to kiss her! She could see it plainly in the hungry eyes, the way his gaze riveted to her lips. And suddenly she wanted him to kiss her.

Appalled at the thought, she told herself it was only because of John Mark. She'd told her brother that she would help him and if this was the only way, well, then, she would do it. But that didn't explain the nervous energy coiling in her stomach or the slow burn that inched through her.

She met Chaney's gaze and waited, hoping. He looked suddenly uncertain and she glanced down, astonished at her boldness.

Then he leaned toward her.

She looked up, saw the hunger, the question in his dark eyes and she tilted her face up to his.

His lips touched hers, at first testing. They stood in the shade of a peach tree, surrounded by the sweet scent of fruit nectar and sunshine and new grass.

His hand settled at her waist as he pulled her closer. The tubing he held thudded to the ground. Morrow Beth steadied her suddenly shaky legs by sliding a hand up his arm. He was strong and unmovable beneath her hands, sturdy and warm.

His mouth moved over hers, more confident now, then his tongue touched the corner of her mouth. She tensed for a moment. Urged by instinct, she gripped his arm tighter, pulled him closer and opened her mouth.

Warmth flooded her and tiny pricks of feeling scattered along her nerves. Chaney pulled her hard against him. She could feel the power of his arms, the hard length of his body, his growing arousal against her belly.

Then he pulled away swiftly, his breath tearing out in ragged pants. "I . . . shouldn't have done that."

Why not? she thought fuzzily. In fact, she wanted to do it again. Her hand tightened on his arm, but he stepped back.

"Morrow Beth."

Her name was hoarse on his tongue and served to shake her out of the web of sensation enveloping her.

She dropped her hand from his arm, then touched her lips. She felt winded and breathless. No one had ever kissed her like that before. "You're right. I'm sorry."

"You're sorry? *I* kissed *you*." He looked dazed and shook his head, frustration creasing his features. "I think."

He snatched up the copper tubing and started down the small hill. Morrow Beth followed, stunned.

She kept at least two feet of distance between them, her emotions tangling. She shouldn't have kissed him.

She'd *liked* kissing him. What about John Mark?

Yes, she couldn't forget Chaney's obvious attempts to learn something about John Mark.

They reached the bottom of the hill and Chaney turned to her. "I'll take you back to the restaurant, unless you're going home?"

"No. I mean, you don't need to take me to the restaurant."

"I won't allow you to walk by yourself."

How could she tell him she wanted to get away from him as quickly as possible? "I'm sure you have things to do. You're busy and I—"

"I'm sorry, Morrow Beth. That . . . shouldn't have happened." He looked miserable and confused and contrite.

She knew he was talking about the kiss, but he certainly couldn't bear the brunt of blame. "Let's just not talk about it again."

Because if they did, she would never forget how wonderful it had been.

Chaney eyed her warily and nodded. Together, silently they walked toward the edge of town.

Despite the liberty she'd allowed him, Morrow Beth was not outraged and the admission drew her up short. Chaney was right. They shouldn't have kissed.

She'd done it for her brother's sake, she told herself desperately. And she wouldn't mind doing it again. Strictly for John Mark, of course.

What in the Sam Hill had he been thinking? He hadn't been thinking at all. At least not with his brain, he added wryly. He'd wanted to kiss Morrow Beth since the first time he'd seen her in the street and now he'd done it.

She walked next to him, her soft scent floating around

him, her skirts brushing his leg, tantalizing, teasing.

Want pounded through him and he could think of better uses than picking peaches for that grove leading to the Warner place. He slanted a glance at her, his gaze moving slowly over her cream and gold skin, the slight upturned nose. He'd wanted to touch that velvet skin, unfasten her bodice and see if she was that same peachy gold all over.

Whoa. He dragged his gaze away and shifted to put more distance between them. The silence between them was awkward, just on the edge of tense and part of him wanted to reassure her. Despite her eager participation in the kiss, he could tell she was also embarrassed.

But he said nothing. He couldn't afford to get close to Morrow Beth Huckabee in any way. He needed to be objective, uninvolved, because he had every intention of investigating her brother for the very thing the Warner sisters had been doing.

The Warner sisters. With focused effort, Chaney dragged his attention away from Morrow Beth and concentrated on the widowed sisters. Shock and disbelief still lingered. Those dear sweet ladies, making moonshine. Who would have guessed? Not him, obviously.

They'd even given him some of the stuff. What an idiot that made him look. He'd have to throw that out as soon as he got home. He could do that before he headed into the tunnel. He'd drop off this tubing at his house, too.

The tunnel. The sun slanted gold and fire streamers over the western roof of the bank. Yes, he could still make it to the tunnel before dark.

If it hadn't been for that unfortunate incident with the Warner sisters, Chaney would already be in the tunnel. And perhaps he would have a lead on John Mark Huckabee. Or whoever else was running moonshine out of this charming little town.

The Warner sisters. Chaney shook his head. Who else could be right under his nose, doing the very same thing? Sada? Royce? Bonnie? He immediately dismissed them, then reminded himself that he would never have guessed about the Warner sisters either.

He and Morrow Beth rounded the corner of the mercantile and he noted absently that the streets seemed rather empty for the middle of the day. Automatically he moved to Morrow Beth's outside elbow. As he did, he glanced toward the jail.

"What the—" He slammed to a stop. A throng of people clustered in front of the jail like ants on honey, so thick he could barely see the barred windows on the jail.

Morrow Beth glanced at him and followed the direction of his gaze. "Something's happened."

She took off at a fast clip and he followed, holding tight to the tubing. Concern wove through him. He searched the crowd, recognizing Will Bell and his wife, Polly. Elda Mineberry, the schoolteacher, elbowed her lanky body through to the front of the crowd. Bonnie Bixler stood at the foot of the stairs, her wide hands planted on ample hips.

Chaney spied Sada at the top of the stairs, in front of the door. Squeezed between Royce and Mayor Bushman, she was gesturing frantically, but Chaney couldn't hear a word she said.

A dim roar sounded as he and Morrow Beth reached the fringe of the crowd.

"Here he is!" Will Bell hollered, standing head and stooped shoulders above most of the crowd. "Let's ask him."

"Excuse me. Pardon me, ma'am." Aware that Morrow Beth was somewhere behind him, Chaney worked his way up to the jail, eyeing the group of people who clustered around the narrow porch and down the shallow steps.

Voices rose from the crowd in a hushed roar and the townspeople stared at him with angrily expectant looks.

He frowned, his gaze seeking Sada's. Her handsome features were pinched with concern though she gave him a tight smile. Beside her, Royce Henry beamed.

That realization dropped in Chaney's stomach like a bad biscuit. He had no idea what this gathering was about, but the smile on Royce's face made Chaney pretty sure he didn't want to know. What in the Sam Hill had happened?

Mayor Bushman shifted nervously and Royce Henry looked as smug as if he'd just overcharged everyone in town two hundred percent.

"What seems to be the problem, folks?" Chaney reached the top of the stairs, setting down the tubing behind him then glancing over the crowd.

The mutterings quieted and everyone stared mutinously at him. Except for Sada, the mayor, and Royce.

Chaney glanced at Bushman. "Mayor?"

The man blinked, shifted from one foot to the other, and glanced pleadingly at Sada.

"Oh, forevermore!" She threw her hands up in the air, meeting Chaney's gaze. "Will Bell saw the Warner sisters in front of your office a while ago. There's some kind of nonsense going around that you arrested them. Tell us it's not true so we can all get back to work."

"I didn't arrest them." Dread drummed through him. He'd spoken the truth, but somehow he figured it wasn't the truth the good people of Scrub wanted to hear right now.

Surely this crowd wasn't a result of what had happened at the Warner place? How had all these people heard about that?

"Then how come they were dragged into town, tied up on the back of a mule?" Mr. Bell stepped closer to the porch.

Chaney glanced at the crowd. Restlessness shifted through them and Chaney couldn't fathom what they might do once they learned what had happened.

Questions suddenly erupted, like a gush of water springing from the ground.

"Where were you taking them a while ago?"

"Why was Morrow Beth with you?"

"Where are they now?"

He was going to have to tell them, at least something. Chaney held up a hand, sighing reluctantly. "Folks, please."

Royce heaved a sigh and looped his thumbs in his waistband. "I'm glad you caught somebody. Now maybe moonshiners will hightail it outta here."

If Chaney was counting on support, it wasn't that kind.

"You cain't keep it from us, Sheriff."

"I'm not trying to—"

"You might as well just tell us. Else we'll march up to the Warner place ourself and find out."

Sada stepped up next to Chaney and raised her voice, waving her arms in the air. "Hold your horses for a minute and we might find out what this is all about."

Several people grumbled, but the crowd finally fell silent.

"Thank you, Sada." Chaney wasn't sure how grateful he was. He was none too eager to share news that he had tried to keep quiet for the sake of the Warner sisters.

"You cain't come here and arrest our own people."

"I was hired to do a job."

"Well, the Warner sisters ain't done anything wrong," Will Bell burst out.

The crowd murmured in agreement.

"If you'd let the sheriff speak, we could get to the bottom of this," Sada pointed out impatiently.

Again the crowd fell silent.

Royce Henry said gleefully, "Well, tell 'em, Sheriff. You did arrest the sisters, didn't you?"

"No, Mr. Henry, I did not." Chaney shot him a quelling look, but the older man only beamed as if he'd stumbled across a chunk of gold. "I did not arrest them."

"Hmmmph!" Royce grumbled. "You shoulda put 'em in jail. A night of that and they would've trod the straight and narrow path."

"I didn't think that was necessary," Chaney said stiffly.

"Why were they tied up?" Bonnie's voice was only slightly less accusing than Will Bell's.

Chaney saw Morrow Beth scanning the crowd and chewing nervously at her lip. Her gaze met his, but he couldn't read anything on her face.

He turned his attention back to Bonnie's question. "A peace officer from Kansas brought them in. He claims he caught them selling moonshine on the border."

"Moonshine!"

"You mean their remedy?"

"There's nothing wrong with that."

"Now, listen, people," Sada charged in. "Sheriff White's a good man. I'm sure he didn't do a thing to the Warner sisters at all. Tell 'em, Sheriff."

"Thank you, Sada." Chaney's head was beginning to pound. "I was hired to shut down moonshiners and that's what I've done."

"What do you mean?" Sada turned slowly, her eyes frosting.

He felt a new tension gather in the crowd and spoke

calmly. "I went with the Warner sisters, discovered they were indeed making moonshine, and I had to destroy their still."

"You what!" Sada whirled on him hands on hips, glaring. "Those poor ladies wouldn't hurt a thing!"

"Believe me, I've heard that before." His gaze shifted to Morrow Beth and she stared flatly at him. "It doesn't change the reason I was hired or the fact that I gave my word to do my job."

"How could you do that to the Warner sisters?"

"I didn't hurt them. I merely—"

"You took away their soul, that's what," Sada declared.

The crowd nodded and murmured in agreement.

Chaney gritted his teeth.

"They don't make their remedy for personal gain, but because they believe they're helping someone."

"Yes, I know. They told me." He sighed, looking at Sada, but raising his voice to be heard by the rest of them. "Look, folks, I tried to be considerate of them—"

"There ain't nothin' wrong with moonshine anyway. Just 'cuz a bunch of people in the government say there is don't make it so." Mr. Bell gave a sharp nod of his head.

Chaney felt as if he were sinking like a stone. "We're all entitled to our opinion, Mr. Bell, but my job is dictated by the law—"

"Hmmph!" said Bonnie. "That's the pot calling the kettle black, I'd say."

"That's right." Will Bell nodded emphatically. "We don't take kindly to you stirring up trouble, not when your pa was a horse thief. What makes you think you can come in here—"

"The law says I have to shut down moonshiners,"

Chaney cut in. He glanced pointedly first at Mayor Bushman, then at Sada. "So did the town council."

The mayor flushed and looked away, but Sada held his gaze stubbornly. "It's just not right hurting those poor widows."

"I didn't hurt them." Though exasperated, Chaney held on to his temper. "I didn't lay a finger on them. They came willingly. They took me to their home and they showed me the still."

"The poor dears," Sada murmured.

"What he said is true." Morrow Beth's voice was quiet, but every head turned toward her.

She stared at Chaney for a moment and he read resentment in her eyes, but her voice was even and calming. "He could've paraded them through town and completely humiliated them. Yet he didn't."

"That don't make it right," Mr. Bell spat.

Morrow Beth turned to him. "He was kind to them. He could've been cruel."

"Hmmph," said Mr. Bell. "Probably trying to sneak around so none of us would know what he did to the sisters."

"I wasn't sneaking around," Chaney said firmly.

Silence sifted through the crowd, though all eyes regarded him with accusation.

He couldn't defend his job every time he took action. He wouldn't. He had been hired to shut down moonshiners and that's what he had done. It didn't matter that he didn't like himself much at the moment either.

He pushed his way to the door and opened it. "I've told you all I can. I won't apologize for doing what I was hired to do."

"Is this supposed to serve as a lesson to anybody else making moonshine?"

Chaney looked out over the crowd, his gaze honing in on Morrow Beth. "That's not why I did it, but you may take it as a warning."

Sadness clouded her eyes and the sight tugged at his heart.

"So, now that you've caught the notorious Warner sisters, who's next?" Mr. Bell shot at him.

Chaney fought the urge to snap at the man, his gaze still locked with Morrow Beth's. "The law is plain. Anybody caught making moonshine is breaking the law and it's my duty to see that it's stopped."

Bleak realization settled on her pretty features and Chaney fought back the urge to go to her, reassure her.

"See, now. The sheriff is just doing his job." Royce Henry clapped Chaney on the shoulder.

With great effort, Chaney kept from flinching. He did not particularly want Royce Henry's support.

"The Warner sisters were wrong and they shoulda paid," Royce continued. "Ain't no call for moonshine, no matter how nice you think the people are."

"Oh, shut up, Royce." Sada turned to the crowd. "I don't like it much, but Morrow Beth's right. He could've been mean to the Warner sisters, and I, for one, appreciate that he didn't arrest them."

"Thank you for that, Sada."

She nodded and pushed her way through the crowd gathered around the steps. "Come on, people. We've got work to do and so does the sheriff."

"Who's he gonna arrest next?" Mr. Bell grumbled, turning away with his wife.

"He didn't *arrest* anybody, Will." His wife, Polly, gripped his arm and tugged him down the street. "For once, would you stop causing a fuss?"

The crowd broke up, moving away from the jail. Morrow Beth stood completely still, staring up at Chaney with a wistful sadness.

His gut clenched. He would do the same thing to her family, if necessary, and he could see she understood that.

She turned away then, her shoulders stiff, her jaw tight. Slowly she walked toward the restaurant.

Chaney watched her trim back and an ache spread through him. *Turn around, Morrow Beth. Just once.*

She glanced over her shoulder and he could read the disappointment, the sadness on her bright features. Chaney had the sense that something precious and rare had just slipped through his fingers.

Hogwash, he told himself, but he couldn't dismiss the heaviness that settled over him. For the first time, he wondered exactly what this job would cost him.

✦ 7 ✦

STREAMERS OF GOLD and red rippled across the lush hills behind him. As the sun dipped low in the sky, Chaney slipped around the back side of town and down to the covered hole he'd found a few days ago. Making sure he was unobserved, he lifted the cover and slipped inside.

Dim light closed around him, and for a moment he stood poised on the second rung of the ladder, trying to get his bearings. Cool musty air swirled through the tunnel. The odors of damp wood and tree roots and animal droppings rose up around him. He pushed his hat farther down on his head and with his feet, felt his way down the crude wooden ladder.

After the crowd had dispersed in front of his office, he'd written an account of what had happened at the Warner place. Just in case he would need to remind anyone that he had actually done his job.

He grimaced. Somehow he didn't think he would have to remind anyone about what had happened today.

He had focused determinedly on writing the report, trying to keep thoughts of Morrow Beth out of his mind. Then he had gone to his little house and emptied out the jar of "remedy" the Warner sisters had given him.

Chaney's eyes had watered at the potent odor flowering out of the jar. Even if he hadn't discovered the Warner sisters' secret today, he would have known at his first whiff of their "remedy" and been forced to take action.

The town's blatant lack of support nagged at him, but not nearly as much as the bleakness in Morrow Beth's face as she walked away. And so he'd worked hard to keep the thoughts of her at bay.

But down in the tunnel, surrounded by silence and the scent of earth, he could no longer dodge the images that chased through his mind. He recalled the regret in her green eyes and wondered if it was the same regret he felt. A regret that whatever was between them must be squelched before it even got started.

He kept replaying the velvet slide of her lips against his, the tentative touch of her tongue. Want pulled tight in his gut. Annoyed, he shoved the memory away.

It was only one kiss, White. But it felt like more than that in his soul.

He shouldn't be thinking about her. He should be trying to catch more moonshiners. He had only a little over two months remaining to prove he was the man for this job. He wouldn't be waylaid from his purpose.

So he'd come down here, fiercely determined to find something in the tunnel tonight. He moved slowly but surely, staying close to the wall of earth, but not touching. He didn't want to risk knocking over one of the ladders or one of the several lanterns hanging about.

From his previous trip, he remembered the layout of the tunnel and how the path mirrored that of the street above ground. A noise floated toward him and Chaney froze, straining to listen.

He closed his eyes, honing in on the distant sound. A

muffled hum, like a voice? A soft laugh. And then a definite *clink*. It could have been the clink of glass or crockery.

Anticipation surged. Opening his eyes, Chaney slowly moved forward. From memory, he counted six paces, then curved slightly to the left. He miscalculated and bumped the dirt wall with the toe of his boot.

Clods of dirt and pebbles rained down, making soft plopping noises on his boot. The voices at the opposite end stopped, cut off as abruptly as if someone had jammed a cork into a bottle of sound.

Chaney winced, cursing silently. For long seconds, he remained motionless, listening, hardly daring to breathe. Not a sound came from the end of the tunnel.

Above him he heard the scratching of something in the dirt—a mouse perhaps, or an insect. He remained perfectly still. Then a slight whisper carried to him.

He couldn't make out the words, but knew it was a human voice. Suddenly a weak silver light crept through the tunnel and Chaney blinked, trying to adjust his eyes.

The unexpected twilight seemed bright in the thick darkness. Startled by the sudden appearance of light, Chaney didn't realize at first what it meant.

They're leaving. He hurried forward, dodging a hole in the earthen floor and as he rounded the slight curve in the earth, he saw someone poised on the ladder. A man?

The body was big, angular and strong, with no hint of feminine curves. He wore a dark shirt and pants and a hat pulled low over his head. Chaney sprinted after him.

The man bolted up the ladder and disappeared aboveground. Cursing, Chaney followed. Because of the man's hat, Chaney hadn't even been able to see the length of the person's hair or even if they had any hair.

He pulled himself to the top of the ladder and vaulted

outside, coming up next to the bank. After the darkness of the tunnel, even the dim light of fading day burned his eyes and for a couple of seconds, his vision blurred.

His gaze scanned the street, his focus sharpening. People meandered down the boardwalk. Royce Henry swept his porch with abrupt punctuated movements. A candle flared in the window of Utive Olen's dress shop. A lantern flickered at the newspaper office.

Chaney's gaze targeted a long wagon moving slowly down the street. John Mark Huckabee raised a hand in greeting to several people and clucked to his team. Had it been John Mark in the tunnel?

He looked to be the same height as the man Chaney had seen. John Mark wore dark clothing and a dark hat lay on the seat beside him.

Chaney scanned the street.

As if to prove it could have been any number of people in the tunnel, Will Bell shuffled past on his way to the restaurant.

"Evenin', Sheriff," Will grumbled.

"Good evening." Chaney tipped his hat, his gaze following the man.

Bell, too, wore dark pants and a dark work shirt. His dark hat was pulled low on his head, obscuring his hair.

Frustration rolled through Chaney. He glanced down, spying fresh footprints in the dirt right in front of his own, but they, too, could have belonged to anyone. Hell, they could have belonged to him.

Irritated, he snatched off his hat and threw it down. Exhaling heavily, he swept the town with one last look and bent to scoop up his hat.

Except for the Warner sisters, he'd caught not one moonshiner. He did not want his reputation or his future to be decided by the fact that he had managed to bring to justice four of the sweetest women he'd ever met.

He climbed back down in the tunnel. But after pains-takingly searching the area for thirty minutes, Chaney was forced to admit that he wasn't going to find anything. At least not tonight.

He was still exactly nowhere.

Morrow Beth stood in the kitchen, absently kneading another batch of biscuits. She kept reliving the gentle strength of Chaney's arms around her, the heat in his kiss, his broad chest pressed against her breasts—

"Ouch!" She yanked her hand away from the hot stove, chiding herself to pay attention.

Carefully she rolled the dough and cut out the biscuits, haunted by the look of confusion and hurt on Chaney's face as they had reached his office.

The people of Scrub had hired him to do a job, yet when he'd done it, they'd acted as if they wanted to lynch him. Morrow Beth understood how they felt, yet after seeing how Chaney handled the Warner sisters, she also felt sympathy for him.

He had handled the crowd well, too, she admitted re-luctantly. He hadn't lost his temper, yet neither had he defended himself or asked them to understand. He had simply pointed out that they had hired him to do a job.

Despite the unease caused by that job, Morrow Beth couldn't deny she was impressed by the man. Popping the pan of biscuits into the stove, she reached over and stirred a pot of peas.

She thought again about John Mark, who had left a couple of hours earlier with a wagon full of moonshine packed in hay. He'd told Morrow Beth he would be at the tunnel, making deliveries. What if Chaney White dis-covered John Mark down there?

Despite the respect she'd developed for the sheriff today, she knew she couldn't continue with John Mark's idiotic plan. She had become *very* friendly with the sheriff today, friendlier than she had planned.

She liked his kiss and though warmth glowed inside her at his obvious interest, she also knew she couldn't lead him on the way John Mark wanted. It wasn't right.

She also didn't think she could completely ignore him. Something had changed between them today. His compassion toward the Warner sisters reached deep inside Morrow Beth and warmed her.

John Mark stepped into the house, tossing his hat into a corner. He sprawled down in one of the chairs at the kitchen table and eyed her with a broad grin.

She frowned and turned back to open a jar of peas.

"Just saw the sheriff."

Morrow Beth spun, splashing water on her hand. Absently blotting the liquid with her apron, she stared at her brother. "He didn't catch you?"

"Dang near."

"Oh, my." She closed her eyes, nausea rolling through her.

John Mark drummed his fingers on the table. "It's all right. He didn't."

"This time," she said grimly, turning back to the stove.

Her brother's chair shifted, scraping across the floor. "Heard there was some excitement in town today."

Morrow Beth tensed. "Yes, the Warner sisters had their still destroyed."

"That's a shame." Her brother sounded appropriately concerned, but also preoccupied. "What else happened, Sister?"

What else had he heard? She had no intention of telling

him about the kiss she'd shared with Sheriff White. "Nothing, really."

"I spoke to Will Bell."

Morrow Beth's heart sank.

"He said the town had a little talk with the new sheriff. He said you were there and that you stood by Chaney. That's good."

"I didn't do it because it would look good, John Mark." She set a steaming plate of biscuits on the table and looked at him, feeling tired.

"No, no, I didn't think you would." He pushed his chair back on two legs, eyeing her speculatively. "You seem to be getting right friendly with the sheriff—"

"I'm not." Immediately a memory flashed of that kiss and she flushed at her quick response. Her brother didn't know about that kiss and she meant to keep it that way. She marched to the table, slapping down a bowl of peas. "I mean, I'm not going to do what you asked."

John Mark's chair slammed to the floor. "Why not?"

Morrow Beth looked at him, assaulted by guilt and determination and resentment. He *was* her brother, but she simply didn't believe his plan would work. And she couldn't make herself deceive Chaney. "My being friendly with the sheriff might help you if you're discovered. Or it could just be the reason you are discovered."

"Now, how do you figure that?" Her brother watched her closely.

She sat at the table across from him, staring at him earnestly. "I don't want to be the means Chaney uses to get to you. If we've planned something like this, don't you think he might have, too?"

"Well, no, I hadn't." He scratched his nose. "But you might be right. I still think we stand a good chance this way, though. At least he didn't throw the Warner sisters in jail.''

''I don't think he would throw anyone in jail, unless they put up a fight.''

John Mark stared hard at her and a broad grin split his face. ''Are you getting sweet on him?''

''Of course not!'' She pushed away from the table and moved to the stove. ''I just don't feel right about this plan of yours.''

''What if it keeps me out of jail?''

She threw him a sharp look. ''The one thing that *would* keep you out of jail is if you'd quit moonshining.''

''We've been all through this, Morrow Beth. I can't quit.''

Katie Jo and Billy Jack's excited voices sounded from the porch.

Morrow Beth set her jaw. ''I'm not going to argue with you again. Why don't you take no for an answer and quit hounding me about it?''

''I just can't believe you'd let your older brother go to jail if it was in your power to change it.''

''My being friends with the sheriff isn't going to make any difference. It certainly didn't today. He still closed down the Warner sisters, even though I argued with him.''

''I still think my plan's better than taking a chance.''

''Your plan *is* a chance, John Mark.'' She tried to keep her voice down so the twins wouldn't hear. ''It's too risky.''

Frustrated that her brother couldn't or *wouldn't* admit to the dangerous line they trod, she turned away. ''You're willing to take the risk, but I'm not. I'm sorry. I just can't do what you want.''

After a long pause, he rose from the table and grabbed a biscuit. ''That's all right. I'll figure something out.''

Morrow Beth turned, her eyes narrowing in suspicion. John Mark never, *ever*, let something drop. He always worried it until it was chewed to bits. "What are you planning now?"

He smiled benignly at her. "Not a thing, Sister. Not a thing."

She didn't believe him for a minute, but it didn't matter. She'd made her decision and she intended to stick by it.

She'd seen that look of hard determination in Chaney's eyes, his unapologetic response when the townspeople had backed him into a corner. Why would he react any differently if he discovered John Mark's still? Certainly not because he might be "friendly" with John Mark's sister.

No, Morrow Beth told herself firmly. No more visits to the sheriff, no more apologies and certainly no more kisses. The more distance the better.

"Supper? Tomorrow night?" Chaney eyed John Mark with suspicion. What had brought this on?

Morrow Beth's strapping older brother nodded. "Just caught a mess of fish. Thought you might enjoy it."

"I would." He bit off the urge to ask John Mark what his sister thought about the invitation. "But I'm not sure if *everyone* at your home would welcome me."

"Oh, you mean Morrow Beth." John Mark grinned and settled his hat on his head, turning for the door. "I thought y'all were gettin' on better. I heard she was with you during that fray in town yesterday."

"She was, but I think that was her way of keeping an eye on me. She thought I was going to hurt the Warner sisters."

Chaney rose from his chair, intending to refuse the invitation. He had managed to keep a fair distance from Morrow Beth the last two days. It wouldn't be wise to spend the evening at her house. "So, you've been doing some fishing?"

"Well, a fella can't fish all the time. There's the farm to consider."

Chaney followed the other man out the door, squinting against the midmorning sun. "How *is* the farm doing?"

John Mark gave him a sly look, lifting a hand in greeting as Elda Mineberry passed. "We're doing pretty well. The corn's coming in and if we get another good bout of rain, should have a banner crop of hay."

Chaney nodded. "Saw you in town yesterday. Making some deliveries?"

John Mark's affable expression never changed, but he turned a sharp look on Chaney. "Yeah, I was. Had to bring some eggs to Bonnie. Morrow Beth forgot 'em."

His gaze met John Mark's and they exchanged an even stare. John Mark's eyes were friendly yet sharp with the knowledge that he knew what Chaney was up to. He didn't look offended or even guilty, but Chaney sensed that the other man considered the questions a challenge, victory belonging to the one who could stay a step ahead.

There was no dirt or odor of liquor on John Mark to indicate he'd been the one Chaney had seen in the tunnel yesterday. There was no guilt on his face, no hurried stutterings about his whereabouts.

In fact, John Mark hadn't denied that he'd been in town and the man had to know Chaney would certainly check out his story about delivering eggs to Bonnie. If Chaney could just get something on John Mark—

Realization hit him. If he accepted Huckabee's invitation to supper, Chaney could snoop around, try to find something that would prove John Mark had been the person Chaney had seen in the tunnel yesterday.

He felt a twinge of guilt at his plan, but he pushed it

aside. He had a job to do and it wasn't as if he were using Morrow Beth to get to her brother. He was simply taking his opportunities where he found them.

"So, how about supper?" John Mark eyed him expectantly, his eyes glinting with amusement.

Chaney had the feeling that the other man was extending the invitation for his own purposes. The two men eyed each other, silently acknowledging the fact that each knew the other was up to something.

"If you're worried about Morrow Beth, don't be."

Chaney arched a brow. "No, I'm not worried about her."

"Good," John Mark murmured. "Good."

The mention of Morrow Beth brought a flashing memory of petal-soft lips and the shy touch of her tongue on his. Chaney hadn't forgotten that kiss, though he'd managed to keep it shoved to the back of his mind. He wondered if John Mark knew about that, then decided he didn't. Surely the man wouldn't have been so friendly.

John Mark stepped to the ground. "So, can we expect you for supper tomorrow night?"

"Yes, I'd like to come. Very much."

The other man grinned. "Let's say six o'clock, then."

"Six o'clock." Chaney watched as Huckabee climbed into his wagon and slapped the reins against the mule's rump.

He had an open invitation to the Huckabee homestead. And while these people were extending hospitality to him, he had every intention of snooping around, finding some incriminating evidence on John Mark.

Guilt rushed back and Chaney fought it. He didn't like taking advantage of them, but he couldn't let that stop him. Nor could he allow his attraction to Morrow Beth to get in the way.

John Mark was up to something; Chaney felt it in the hum of his blood, that prickle up his spine. Tomorrow night would be his chance to get some evidence on Huck-abee.

Morrow Beth was quite proud of herself. She'd managed to avoid Chaney White for almost two days. Bonnie had agreed to take lunch to the jail and Morrow Beth had come into the restaurant through the back door instead of the street entrance.

Still, just because she hadn't seen him didn't mean she'd been as successful at erasing him from her thoughts. It wasn't just the kiss. It was the kindness he'd shown the Warner sisters. It was the dignity with which he'd treated them.

Just the memory of how he'd gently informed them that he would have to destroy the still caused Morrow Beth's heart to clench. She didn't want to think about Chaney White; she especially didn't want to think *kindly* of him.

She'd meant it when she'd told John Mark she wanted no part of his harebrained scheme. Even so, she found herself wondering what Chaney was up to, if he thought about that kiss as often as she did, what he would do if he discovered her brother's still.

Though she was careful to keep to the restaurant and go straight home, the whole time Morrow Beth was in town her nerves were drawn tight. Yesterday, when Bonnie had returned from taking Chaney's lunch, she told Morrow Beth that Chaney had asked some questions about John Mark.

Bonnie knew nothing to tell him and Morrow Beth had sighed in relief, thanking her employer again for taking the food so she wouldn't have to. But every time the tiny bell above the door jingled, she feared it would be Chaney coming in for more questions. Whenever a knock sounded on the back door, Morrow Beth tensed, holding her breath until she saw it wasn't Chaney.

At least she didn't have to worry about seeing him at home. That evening, Morrow Beth pressed a hand to the small of her back and stretched. Being on constant alert for the sheriff just plumb wore her out.

John Mark wanted to cook up the fish he and Billy Jack had caught. They were in the barn now, cleaning the fish. She had watered the corn and was now in the chicken house.

Evening sun slanted into the little shed. She placed the eggs in her deep-bottomed basket and thrust her fingers into the next nest.

As she stepped outside, Flower strutted past her, squawking indignantly because she wouldn't let him into John Mark's still. She shooed the rooster away. He flapped his wings at her in a snit and hopped over the potato row to the row of carrots.

She wished she could forget Chaney White, but she kept remembering the true reluctance in his dark eyes as he'd discovered the still at the Warner place.

She kept remembering the stoic set of his jaw, the intense way his gaze had locked on her mouth, that first gentle press of his lips against hers.

Her skin flushed and she shook herself out of her musings. She shouldn't be thinking of him at all. He was the sheriff. He was not her friend. Or her beau.

"*Squaaaaawk!*" Flower belched out a grating screech. Morrow Beth looked up, finding him on top of the chicken house. "Get down off there, Flower."

"*Pauuuuwk.*" He bobbed his head at her and teetered on the steep edge of the roof. "*Pauuuwk.*"

Morrow Beth rose, heading for him. "Come down from

there, you silly bird. You're supposed to crow at dawn.''

He gave an abrupt squawk and strutted across the top of the chicken coop.

If she didn't get him, he would fall off and knock himself unconscious. She reached up and just as she touched his chest, he fluttered his wings in her face and flew to the opposite end.

''Ugh!'' Morrow Beth rubbed her nose, fighting the urge to sneeze. ''Flower, get over here!''

''Pauuwk! Pauuwk!'' He bobbed and dipped, then hopped clumsily to the ground.

Morrow Beth lunged for him.

He flapped his wings and tore off around the back of the chicken coop—straight for John Mark's still. She grabbed up her skirts and ran after him.

She was already annoyed, thanks to those taunting memories of Chaney White. She did not want to be chasing around a big stupid rooster.

''Flower! Get over here right now!''

The bird dodged a blackberry bush, ducked under some scrub and rounded a cluster of cottonwood trees. *''Squaaaawk! Squaaaawk!''*

Morrow Beth bypassed the bush and ran straight past the cottonwood trees, around the dense cover of honeysuckle and bois d'arc bushes toward the still. Flower trotted past her and Morrow Beth grabbed for him.

She grabbed at his wing and tucked her other hand around his breast, holding him gently but firmly. Her hair tumbled into her face and a bead of sweat trickled down her forehead. Cradling the rooster to her, she plopped down on the ground, breathing hard.

''Someday I'm gonna make chicken and dumplings out of you,'' she threatened softly.

His wide eyes stared unblinkingly into hers and he squawked a protest.

She shook her head and got to her feet, keeping careful hold of the bird. Clammy now from chasing the bird, her bodice stuck to her. Dirt and grass stained the apron she wore over her blue-and-green calico. She puffed out a breath, trying to move the strands of hair that tickled her nose. She didn't dare take one hand off Flower.

As much trouble as Flower was sometimes, she would rather deal with him than with the sheriff. At least she knew what to expect with the rooster.

She rounded the corner of the chicken coop and tapped the rooster on the head. "No more stunts, Flower. I'm tired of chasing you all over kingdom come."

"Hi, Sister."

"Hi, John—" Morrow Beth looked up and froze.

Chaney White stood in front of her, his gaze raking over her.

Her arms went limp and Flower fell to the ground.

He squawked in outrage, hopped up and shook his feathers, then marched off to the barn.

"What's happened?" Automatically her hand went to her hair, pushing the tousled mess out of her eyes, smoothing it behind her ear. She was acutely aware of her disheveled state, the dirt stains on her clothes, the sweat sticking to her body.

Morrow Beth licked her suddenly parched lips, tearing her gaze from the sheriff to stare at her brother. Had John Mark been found out? Had Chaney come to destroy the still? Would he take John Mark to jail?

Fighting to keep the fear from her voice, she focused on her brother. "Is something wrong?"

He grinned as if he'd just lassoed a bear. "Nope. Chaney's agreed to have supper with us tonight."

A buzz sounded in Morrow Beth's ears. She heard what John Mark said, but it didn't register.

Chaney tipped his hat to her, his gaze skipping over her bodice, then meeting her eyes. "Thanks for the invitation, ma'am."

John Mark clapped him on the shoulder. "Let's go wash up."

Chaney gave her one last long look and went with her brother.

Morrow Beth's breath rushed back with a knife edge. *John Mark had invited Chaney to supper?*

He'd invited Chaney to supper!

The feeling returned to her arms and legs; her brain clicked in realization. She turned, staring after the two men. John Mark wouldn't have to worry about going to jail. She was going to kill him!

❖ 8 ❖

WELL, WELL, SHE hadn't known he was coming. Chaney glanced at Morrow Beth as he took another helping of boiled potatoes. Again he wondered what John Mark was playing at.

It was quite obvious that Morrow Beth knew nothing of John Mark's supper invitation. Chaney's appearance had caused first startlement, then astonishment, rendering her speechless. And even while she gaped, Chaney had seen anger flare in her eyes. But since then he'd seen nothing on her face. Not anger, not joy, nothing.

Her features were calm, but still flushed. She had combed her hair, gathering the thick curls into a low chignon. She'd changed her dress and her apron, wearing pale yellow gingham that looked as if it had seen better days. The high-necked bodice sleeked over her breasts the way his palm itched to do.

He forced his mind away from the temptation of Morrow Beth and catalogued his surroundings. The Huckabee cabin was composed of crudely fitted logs and though it looked rough on the outside, it was homey and comfortable inside. There was a large front room divided into sections that served as kitchen, dining area, and parlor. Its wooden floor was cleanly swept.

The other two rooms in the cabin were bedrooms, one for the twins and one for Morrow Beth. John Mark, Katie Jo had informed Chaney, slept in the barn loft except during the coldest winter months.

The twins had given him a quick tour of the small house. Chaney wasn't oblivious to the little girl's adoring gazes, but he was totally captivated by her older sister. Morrow Beth was quiet, her face flushed, and she wouldn't look at him. He wondered if that was because of the kiss or because she was furious with John Mark for bringing him.

She hadn't uttered a cross word, but he could tell she wanted to strangle her brother. Chaney brushed away his own unease at being an obvious surprise and tried to surreptitiously study the cabin.

He could find nothing suspicious in the books that were stacked in the corner, nothing curious about the wooden crate that held firewood and twigs and chips for the stove. A small jar graced the middle of the table and brimmed with sunflowers and wild daisies and tiny purple flowers.

Across from Chaney a sideboard sagged beneath the weight of age and held innocuous things like food and dishes and pots. The sink was to his left, outfitted with a pump handle. A spring room sat just off the kitchen. He should probably try to have a look in there, as well.

A potbellied stove, pulsing with heat, stood in the corner. The two windows at Chaney's back were paned glass, their oilskin shades rolled up neatly to allow in the setting sunlight. Dainty crocheted curtains fluttered at the windows.

However he'd made a living, E. Y. Huckabee had done well by his children. The front door stood open to offset the heat from the stove and the soft sounds of settling night drifted through to Chaney. The frantic chirp of crickets, frogs, and locusts mingled with the soft bawl of the Huckabees' milk cow. The chickens gurgled and that silly rooster trumpeted a hoarse call every few minutes.

Morrow Beth politely joined in the conversation, but did not speak directly to him. If he asked her a question, she either smiled her answer or one of the twins rushed in to speak for her.

She had stared with absent interest at his chin and smiled vaguely at a spot over his shoulder, but not once had she looked him in the eye.

He should be glad. He should stay as far away from Morrow Beth Huckabee as a horse thief from a noose. He had come for answers, not to moon over a green-eyed girl who obviously didn't want him here. He knew he should concentrate his efforts on snooping around, though it would be a challenge to break away unobserved from this group.

Especially seeing as how Katie Jo hadn't quit staring at him all night and Billy Jack had at least ten things he wanted to show Chaney.

Katie Jo rested her chin in her palm, her wide gaze locked on his face. "Your badge is so pretty, Marshal. Do you have to shine it every day?"

He glanced down. "I probably should, Katie, but I don't."

"I bet you clean your gun every day," Billy Jack asserted, wagging his head emphatically.

"Well, a man needs to keep his gun in shape," John Mark drawled. "Never know when you'll need that."

"That's right," Chaney agreed.

Morrow Beth glanced around the table and rose to pull another batch of biscuits out of the oven.

Chaney's mouth watered at the drifting scents of fresh-baked cinnamon and raisin cake.

Morrow Beth set fresh hot biscuits on the table and took her seat.

Chaney reached for the bread. "These are the best biscuits I've ever had."

"Thank you." Her voice was like silk, yet he could feel the tension simmering inside her like boiling water.

Was it because of him or John Mark?

"I kilt a snake today, Sheriff," Billy Jack announced, beaming. "It was trying to get at the chickens."

Chaney tried to look suitably impressed. "How big?"

"About this long." The boy stretched his arms as far as they would go and Chaney bit back a smile.

"That's one big snake."

"Bigger than you, kid." John Mark ruffled Billy Jack's hair.

"You can come see it. It's tacked up on the wall of the barn."

"All right. How about after supper?"

Morrow Beth made a face, but said nothing.

Chaney told himself to stop paying so much attention to her. He didn't stare at her, but he was aware of her on every level. Beneath the aroma of skillet-fried fish and biscuits and cake, Chaney could pinpoint the slight hint of soap on Morrow Beth.

Every time she shifted in her chair, he caught a whiff of her clean pure scent. Every time her generous mouth lifted in a smile, his gut cinched tight. Every time her gaze turned in his direction, his skin prickled in anticipation, but she never looked at him. He determined she would before the night was over.

"I can shine it for you if you like," Katie Jo offered.

Chaney shook himself, trying to figure out what the

little girl was talking about. Oh, yes, his badge. "I appreciate that, Katie Jo, but I think it looks just fine."

"Well, if you change your mind," she breathed with a giddy smile.

He bit back his own smile. She was a cute kid and he didn't have the heart to tell her he was much too old for her.

"I got a turtle, too, Sheriff." Billy Jack spooned in another helping of boiled potatoes. "Maybe you'd like to see that?"

"Sure." He watched as Morrow Beth's delicate hands buttered a biscuit and passed it to Katie. He felt again the glide of her fingers against his neck, the heat of them in his hair.

Whoa, White. You're here to snoop, not spark Morrow Beth Huckabee.

"Do you look for there to be any trouble at the Easter celebration this year?" John Mark pushed his chair back from the table and hooked his thumbs in his belt loops.

Frowning, Chaney wiped at his mouth with a napkin. "What kind of trouble?"

"So, Royce Henry didn't tell you everything," Morrow Beth murmured.

Chaney glanced sharply at her, but she was eyeing Billy Jack with a stern warning on her features.

John Mark grinned. "Don't pay her any mind. It's just that we usually get a rowdy bunch in from Kansas during our picnic. I'm sure you'll be able to handle it."

Chaney put down his napkin and shifted in his chair. "Why do they come to Scrub?"

Billy Jack leaned forward, his eyes bright. "To get drunk—"

"To sell moonshine," John Mark interrupted easily.

Chaney's gaze sliced to the other man, who smiled openly. "Is that right?"

He glanced at Morrow Beth, but her face was set in graceful stone. He could read nothing on her delicate features.

She eyed her younger brother and sister, then settled her gaze on John Mark. "Time to clear the dishes."

He grimaced and threw a halfhearted smile at Chaney as he lumbered out of his chair. "Come on, you two."

Billy Jack and Katie Jo groaned, but rose and picked up their plates.

Chaney observed the affection between the Huckabees with a combination of warmth and regret. He'd never cared much that he was an only child. He'd simply wanted a parent, just one.

His mother had died when Chaney was born and he'd never known when or if his pa would return. The few times his father had spent time with him Chaney had busted his backside trying to make his father see that he was no trouble, that he could do all the work and make things easier for his father, but his father had never seen that.

Clarence White had always left again. Finally one day he'd been captured and hanged shortly thereafter. By then, Axel had become Chaney's guardian as well as friend, but Chaney had never really had a family of his own.

A thought occurred to him, followed by a flash of stark disappointment. If he were successful and did discover that John Mark operated a still, Chaney might have to separate the Huckabee family.

Reluctance and resentment sheared through him. He didn't want to do that. A family should be able to stay together. But his conscience, his sense of duty argued that

the law was the law and must be upheld. Which was why
he had to look around.

"We can take coffee on the porch, if you'd like." Morrow Beth spoke to the plate in front of her, but Chaney
assumed she referred to him.

"I'd like that." He rose from his chair and moved to
stand behind hers, waiting.

She stiffened, but allowed him to move her chair as she
rose, throwing John Mark a look Chaney couldn't decipher.

Leading the way, she preceded him to the porch. The
sun had disappeared behind the horizon and a smoky gold
light settled over the land.

Chaney waited until she sat down, then decided this
might be his only opportunity. "I need to be excused for
a moment."

She frowned, then flushed as she understood. "Oh, yes.
It's just around back."

Chaney nodded and stepped off the porch, walking
around the house. The privy stood several yards away and
Chaney walked there, opening and closing the door just
in case Morrow Beth was listening.

Then he moved behind the outhouse, wrinkling his nose
at the pungent odor. Quickly he walked toward the woods
and a cluster of cottonwoods that formed a natural line.
He doubted the still would be in the barn, but he couldn't
afford to double-check that right now.

He wanted to see if he could find anything out here.
Off in these woods would be the perfect place, hidden by
that tangle of honeysuckle and thorn bushes.

But before he reached the screen of bushes, a twig
snapped behind him. Footsteps rustled through the grass
and Chaney froze.

Someone was coming.

*   *   *

She shouldn't follow him. She wouldn't. Even as she said the words, Morrow Beth walked to the corner of the cabin, hesitating. A frustrating awareness of Chaney stroked up her spine, but there was also suspicion.

What was he doing back there? Why was he here in the first place? Was she supposed to believe that he was becoming friends with John Mark? Not that her brother was hard to like, because he wasn't, but Chaney White was up to something. Morrow Beth could feel it.

And what was she going to do if she discovered that he was? She chewed on her lip, uncertain about following him, but deciding she had to. John Mark had gotten her into this, drat his hide.

She didn't want to see Chaney White. She certainly hadn't wanted to have supper with him. And she especially didn't want to be alone with him out here on the fringe of the woods.

The sounds of her siblings' voices floated outside and John Mark laughed heartily. Morrow Beth hauled in a deep breath and went to find the sheriff.

Streamers of golden light rimmed the outhouse. She stopped a few feet away and tilted her head, but she heard nothing.

Turning slowly, her gaze drifted over the knee-high prairie grass, the clump of cottonwoods, the bulk of honeysuckle and bois d'arc which hid the still. A chill skipped up her arm and her gaze moved back to the cottonwoods. She could see nothing, yet she felt as if someone stood there in the deepening shadows, watching.

Frowning, she glanced again at the outhouse. Maybe he really was—

"Miss me?"

His voice reached out through the trees and his rich

baritone rasped along her nerves. Morrow Beth stiffened so quickly her teeth snapped. "Hardly."

He stepped out of the cover of the cottonwoods, his broad chest dappled by a mix of setting sunlight and beginning shadow. She couldn't see his eyes, but knew his gaze was fixed on her face. She fought the urge to lick suddenly dry lips.

Lifting her chin, she took a step toward him. "Lose your way?"

He chuckled, a low soft sound that sent a shower of warmth through her. "That would be difficult, wouldn't it?"

Frustration seized her, not only at his obvious caginess, but also because she wished for one fierce instant that they were meeting in secret for another purpose.

Her gaze moved pointedly to the outhouse and back to him. "What are you doing in the trees?"

"Can't you even give me a minute of privacy, Morrow Beth?"

She didn't like the way his tongue curled around her name, like heat over cool flesh. "It doesn't look like you needed any privacy."

He strode toward her, stopping only inches away. His gaze traced over her with unnerving thoroughness, touching on her eyes, her lips, her breasts.

Her breath wedged in her chest and she took a reflexive step back.

He stepped forward, closing the distance she'd created. His breath floated against her cheek, making her want to lean into him, touch him.

She lifted her chin, determined not to let him see that he rattled her. "What are you doing?"

"Just admiring the view."

His words jolted her. She searched his eyes, looking for

the same need that shifted through her, the same uncertainty.

Hunger flared in the midnight darkness of his eyes. She told herself not to believe what she saw there.

His gaze dropped to her lips and tension etched his features.

She shifted, her lips burning, but she didn't look away and she didn't move. She didn't think she could. She tried to tell herself she was keeping him occupied, bungling any attempt he might be making to snoop around their place. But that reason was distant in her mind.

Chaney crowded her senses. She was too aware of the breadth of his chest, the thick forearms revealed by the rolled-back cuffs of his shirt, the woodsy, warm-flesh scent of him. His black gaze peeled through every layer of clothing and flesh to the untapped feminine soul of her and her hand rose protectively to the neck of her bodice.

His heavy-lidded gaze drifted over her as if he were lazily savoring a sweet. "If you didn't miss me, then why follow me out here?"

"I don't trust you." Was that rusty squeak *her* voice? Trying to ignore the awareness spinning between them, she cleared her throat. "How did you get my brother to invite you to supper?"

His gaze shifted over her, stroking her breasts, her waist, her skirt before returning to her eyes. "Didn't."

His voice was coarse and achy, just the way she felt. Need flared through her.

"*He* asked me, out of the clear blue."

Her eyes narrowed, but she didn't argue.

"So, is that the only reason you followed me?" He caressed the words as if he were caressing her and her skin burned.

She shook her head, trying to escape the sensual trap

closing around her. "I didn't follow you. I simply came after you."

He hesitated, his eyes snapping with a fierce intensity she didn't understand. "You've been thinking about it, haven't you?"

Her breath jammed in her chest. "Thinking about what?"

But she already knew. She knew by the savage desire in his eyes, the warmth of memory burning in the black depths. Her heartbeat kicked up and she was vividly, starkly reminded of the way his lips had covered hers, the bone-melting way his tongue had stroked the soft inside of her mouth.

He moved toward her and she tensed, but didn't move. A distant voice reminded her of her brother, but it was drowned by the thunder of her heartbeat, the realization that Chaney's breath was just as ragged as hers.

This was wrong, wasn't it? She wasn't supposed to do this, but she couldn't remember why.

His gaze locked on hers fervently and he circled around her. His breath stirred her hair and she could feel his warmth against her shoulders, her backside.

Her breath caught painfully in her chest and some un-named instinct caused her to stiffen. Gently, very gently, he reached up and fingered a stray wisp of hair at her neck.

A delicious lethargy seeped through her and she shuddered, feeling caught in a tangle of right and wrong. She knew this wasn't why she'd followed him. She knew she didn't want to distract him in this manner, but it suddenly became about more than what she wanted.

Remember his job, she ordered herself. Remember that he's bound by the law.

Remember what could happen to John Mark.

His finger traced the rim of her ear and a soft warm breath tickled her neck. She whirled suddenly, her heart thundering. "What are you doing?"

The movement brought her breasts against his chest, her arm bumping into his.

Before she could step back, Chaney's arm locked around her waist and he pulled her to him. "I think I'm about to do this."

"No—"

"I can't stop thinking about it, Morrow Beth." He lowered his head.

She made a tiny sound in her throat, part protest, part want. She should pull away. She should slap him. Yet she stood there, her gaze locked with his, waiting for that breathless touch of his lips on hers.

He nuzzled her cheeks, her nose, her chin, before moving to her lips. Weakness washed through her legs and she found herself gripping his biceps. Her breasts teased him, soft and full and growing heavy. She wanted him to touch her. She wanted . . . him.

His lips covered hers and her world tilted. There was no conscience, no family, no moonshine to hide. Only a rush of sensation at the glide of his lips on hers.

She melted against him, her arms moving tentatively around his neck, then locking there.

He drank her in, his lips gently demanding on hers. She met him, greedy to taste him, to feel again the stroke of his tongue on hers. It came, the glide of velvet against her tongue. Strong and sure and devastating. Her knees buckled and she latched on to him with a surprising desperation.

Something nagged at her, some sense of wrong, but swept into a maelstorm of sensation, she couldn't focus and didn't care.

Chaney made a sound against her mouth, more of a grunt than a groan of passion. Morrow Beth pressed closer to him.

He yelped and jerked away.

She stared up at him, lost in a fog, watching dazedly as he looked down.

"Ouch!"

Struggling against the wave of desire moving through her, Morrow Beth fought to focus. He was in pain, saying something about . . . Flower?

"*Pauuuwk! Pauuuwk!*"

She looked down. The rooster stood between them, his beak poised over Chaney's boot like a loaded gun.

"That rooster damn near pecked my toe off!"

Morrow Beth blinked, realizing now where they were, what they'd done. Oh, my stars! She'd just kissed him again.

Flower glared at Chaney, his wide eyes unblinking, and Morrow Beth stared down at him, still shaking off the desire that weighted her bones.

The rooster drew back again and Chaney jumped out of the way.

Morrow Beth moved this time, scooping up Flower. The rooster squawked angrily and lunged for Chaney. Morrow Beth caught him to her. "No."

Chaney hopped on one leg, rubbing at his foot. "What is wrong with that crazy bird?"

Memory flooded back—why he was out here, how she'd caught him snooping. She bristled, tightening her hold on the bird. "He thought he was protecting me."

"You weren't acting as if you needed protecting." He glared at her, wincing as he massaged his foot.

The truth of his words stung, reminding her that she

had tumbled right into his arms. She glared back, hoping his toe fell off. "Hmmmph!"

She swept past him and toward the house, mortified that she'd kissed Chaney again. And loved every second of it!

He followed, limping slightly and grumbling under his breath.

She marched toward the chicken coop and gently locked Flower inside. The bird chattered furiously. She frowned down at the bird, shaking her head. Flower had never done anything like that to any of Morrow Beth's other callers. She wondered wryly if the rooster knew that Chaney was a sheriff and could pose a threat to the family.

Turning back, she retraced her footsteps to the cabin where Chaney waited at the edge of the porch.

She stared down her nose at him, not at all sure why she felt hurt and disappointed, with a stinging sense of regret. "I guess you'll be taking your leave now."

"I guess I will," he growled, rubbing at his foot again.

John Mark stepped out onto the porch, looking from Morrow Beth to Chaney. He smiled slyly. "Where'd you two get off to? Find somethin' interesting behind the house?"

"Oooo!" Morrow Beth stomped up the steps and into the house, slamming the door shut behind her.

❖ 9 ❖

SHE'D CAUGHT HIM snooping and he told himself he'd only kissed her as a distraction. It was a bald-faced lie. He'd kissed her for one reason: he wanted to. And he wanted to do it again.

He could still taste the sweet heat of her, feel the fullness of her breasts pressed against him. She had wanted him to kiss her, just as much as he'd wanted to.

This was going to lead nowhere. He couldn't dream about the woman all night and then spend his days trying to catch her brother breaking the law.

Chaney cussed. He needed to get back to the Huckabees'. They certainly wouldn't expect him to return tonight. But if he ran into Flower, that rooster would bugle Chaney's presence at the top of his lungs. Everyone within a mile would know he was at the Huckabee place. He would have to wait for a better time.

He cussed again. What had gotten into him? Why had he thought, for one second, that he could toy with Morrow Beth?

He wanted John Mark Huckabee, if the man was guilty of moonshining, but Chaney didn't want to use Morrow Beth to get to her brother.

Guilt shifted through him. He shouldn't have kissed her, but once his lips had touched hers, he couldn't even remember his own name.

He should probably apologize. Certainty settled over him like a heavy blanket. Yes, he should definitely apologize.

The next morning, regret pushed through the guilt for how they'd left things last night, but he pushed it away. Morrow Beth was just a distraction, one he didn't need. The words rang hollow. He couldn't dismiss his feelings about her. He felt something more for her, something that made him feel as if he belonged.

He scowled, walking around the corner of the jail and up to the porch. He had an obligation first to the job. Besides, his three-month trial period didn't include finding a woman.

"Sheriff! Hold up a minute."

Chaney inwardly groaned. The last person he wanted to see this morning was Royce Henry. He opened the door to his office and turned, waiting for Royce.

His eyes widened in surprise as he spied the mayor climbing the steps behind the store owner.

"Good morning, Mayor." Chaney eyed the two men warily. Why were they both paying him a visit?

He invited them inside and closed the door. Taking off his hat, he hung it on a peg and strode to his desk. Thoughts of Morrow Beth hovered at the edge of his mind and Chaney forced his attention to the men in front of him.

Mayor Bushman cleared his throat and shifted from one foot to the other, giving him a weak smile.

Royce Henry settled his lanky frame into a chair across from Chaney. "We were wonderin' what you've discovered on Huckabee."

"Nothing yet." Chaney didn't want to be reminded that last night, while he'd been trying to discover something incriminating on John Mark, he had been completely distracted by the man's sister. "I'm not so sure they're moonshining at all."

"Oh, they are, I can tell you that." Royce leaned forward in his chair, his face flushed with conviction. "I've seen John Mark delivering that devil juice myself."

"Royce, Sheriff White can't do anything about it unless he sees it."

Chaney started in surprise that the mayor had actually defended him. "Mayor Bushman's right. I haven't seen anything like that and until I do—"

"Yeah, yeah. I know. You cain't do nothin'."

"No need to look so disappointed, Mr. Henry," Chaney said drily. "Why do the Huckabees bother you so much anyway? They don't seem to bother anyone else."

"It's because of E. Y. and—"

"They're breakin' the law, that's what." Royce cut off the mayor and surged out of his chair, crumpling his hat in his hands. "That's all it is."

Chaney glanced at Mayor Bushman, who pursed his lips and stared across the room at the iron bars of a cell. Chaney looked back to Royce Henry. Did Mr. Henry have some kind of vendetta against the Huckabees? If so, why? He knew he would get no answers from Royce. But maybe the mayor . . .

Royce flung the door open. "We expect you to make some progress, White. Your days are slipping away."

"I know how much time I have left, Mr. Henry." He rose, following the two men to the door. "I wonder if y'all might tell me something?"

"What's that?" Mayor Bushman glanced uncertainly at Chaney.

"Do you expect trouble on Easter?"

"Oh, you mean those cowboys from Kansas?" Bushman asked.

"Yes. I'd heard they like to visit during the festivities."

"They certainly do," Royce exclaimed. "And I'm sure you can guess why."

"I was told it had to do with moonshine."

"And where do you think they get it?"

"I don't know, Mr. Henry," Chaney said evenly. "But if things go well, perhaps I'll find out."

"Hmmmph! You better hope you do, boy." Royce jammed his hat on his head and walked outside.

Mayor Bushman eyed Royce uneasily, then turned to Chaney. "I think you're doing a fine job, Sheriff. I have no complaints."

"Thank you, Mayor." Chaney paused. "I wonder if you'd be willing to tell me why Royce is so all-fired eager to see the Huckabees brought to justice?"

The mayor hesitated, watching as Royce threaded his way between a wagon and two men on horseback, striding toward his store. "Well." He made a soft clucking noise with his tongue. "E. Y. Huckabee was sweet on Royce's wife."

"There was a Mrs. Henry?" Chaney couldn't disguise the astonishment in his voice.

Mayor Bushman nodded. "Real nice lady. E. Y. had a soft spot for her and some people in town thought she had one for him, but she never acted on it. She passed on a few weeks before E. Y. and Royce has never gotten over it. He hasn't forgotten that E. Y. liked her, either."

Chaney's gaze swept the street, watching Royce Henry as he disappeared into his store. "Well, that doesn't give me any kind of reason to arrest the Huckabees."

"No, sir, it doesn't. It's really not much of a reason for

Royce to be so bitter either, but I suspect he misses his wife."

Chaney nodded, surprised at the mayor's understanding tone. "I suspect so."

The mayor said good-bye and walked down the shallow steps to the street.

"Thank you, Mayor."

Bushman lifted a hand. "You're welcome."

The man walked up the street to his office and Chaney gazed after him absently. Royce Henry had no good reason to suspect the Huckabees of anything, nor to want such comeuppance for them.

At this point, neither did Chaney. He felt guilty about the way he'd left things with Morrow Beth last night. He didn't need to apologize for doing his job, but he did need to apologize for . . . for what? Kissing her?

The sad truth was that as long as Morrow Beth was vexed with him, Chaney stood a better chance of concentrating on his job. But what about this gnawing unease in his belly, this heavy certainty that he owed her an apology?

He'd tried to push thoughts of her away, but he knew he wouldn't be able to concentrate on anything until he'd apologized to her.

Closing the door to his office, he walked down to the livery for his horse. Now that he'd decided to see her, he wondered if she would even talk to him.

"I'm telling you this is dangerous." Morrow Beth glared at John Mark, but her brother barely glanced up from the batch of moonshine he was making.

The old still pot, handed down from Pap, simmered over a furnace fire. The condensing barrel, filled with water from a carefully hidden length of pipe that ran from the creek, stood to one side. Dull copper tubing, the "worm," spiraled between the barrel and the pot, spilling over to drip into a mud-colored crockery jug.

Dipping a cup full of fermented mash from another barrel, John Mark poured it into the battered copper cook pot. He eyed the fire critically before he shoved in another log.

Morrow Beth stamped her foot. "John Mark, ignoring me will not change what happened. Chaney White was out here snooping around last night. I caught him in the cottonwoods." She gestured wildly to the trees over her left shoulder. "How much closer do you want him to get?"

"You kept him from finding anything," John Mark pointed out calmly, leaning close to the tubing, listening as the corn mash bubbled into steam and rose through the thin pipe where it would cool into pure corn liquor.

She wanted to throttle her brother. "I don't know that for sure."

She refused to think about the way in which she'd stopped him. She'd spent all last night and this morning pushing away the memory of that kiss. Her legs still felt like air and her lips still tingled from the feel of his.

No, she didn't want to be reminded. Frustration wound through her. Why couldn't John Mark see how close they'd come, how dangerous Chaney White could be to their family?

"I'm sure you stopped him or he would've shown me what he found and proceeded to shut me down," John Mark said matter-of-factly.

"I don't see how you can be so calm about this."

"Sister, you need to do some calmin' down yourself. For one thing, if the sheriff saw you now, he'd know something was wrong. You've got guilty written all over your face.''

Aghast, she looked down, plucking at an invisible speck on her apron. Her guilt had nothing to do with moonshining and everything to do with a certain broad-shouldered, black-eyed sheriff whose kisses took the starch right out of her.

"Now, why is that?"

Morrow Beth looked up, eyeing her brother warily. "Why is what?"

"Why do you have guilt all over you?" John Mark settled more comfortably on his stool, his eyes narrowing in speculation. "You weren't kissing the sheriff, were you?"

She gritted her teeth. John Mark was trying to make her lose her temper and she wasn't going to.

"Now, that's mighty interesting," her brother crowed. "I bet he forgot all about what he was looking for."

"John Mark!" Heat seared her cheeks and she stared openmouthed at her brother.

He grinned and her thin hold on control broke. "You should be worried about defending my honor," she huffed. "Not sitting there with that stupid-mule grin on your face."

His grin grew broader. "Well, well, sounds to me as though you liked all that attention the sheriff was giving you."

Morrow Beth bit off a scream. She knew her brother was goading her, but it didn't make it any easier to calm down.

He poked at the fire under the still pot, eyeing the coiled tubing that snaked from the lid. "I think you should take advantage of his obvious interest. And it's obvious he's interested."

She ignored that. "I still say he could use me to get to you."

"Doesn't really matter." He folded his arms behind his head and stared up at the crisscross of tree branches above him, the glimpse of clear blue sky through the leaves. "Pretty soon liquor will be legal and we can do as we please."

"And what about until then?"

"I'm trusting you to take care of it, Sister." A protest bubbled up, but in the end, she sighed loudly. It was no use. She would never convince John Mark that his idea was ridiculous.

She wanted to believe that Chaney had kissed her because he was interested, but cautioned herself against it. He was a smart man, perhaps as sly and cunning as her brother, and could be using her for exactly the reason she feared.

Her heart sank and Morrow Beth gave a little sigh. Sometimes she wished she were an only child.

Moving out of the thick wall of bushes, she walked toward the house. She couldn't put that kiss out of her mind and she desperately wanted to. Not so much to forget Chaney as to forget what he'd obviously been doing last night.

She tried to tell herself that kissing him had distracted Chaney from finding the still, but Morrow Beth didn't care.

She liked him and she wanted him to like her, not because she could help him get to her brother, but because of *her*.

But as long as he was after her brother, there was no chance of exploring that and she'd do well to keep her distance. She rounded the corner of the house, intent on skirting the new yellow flowers that pushed up through the ground.

"Morrow Beth?"

She jumped, clapping a hand to her mouth to prevent a shriek.

Chaney White stood on the front porch, hat in hand, his steady gaze boring a hole into her.

She threw a wary glance toward the screen of bushes that hid her brother. "What are you doing here?"

He stepped toward her, his gaze tracing over her. "I came to see you."

Pleasure burst inside her, but was squelched by a startling thought. *Oh, my stars! What if he discovers John Mark?*

Morrow Beth's gaze shot again to the bushes, then she looked back at Chaney, trying to steady her voice.

"What did you want to see me about?" She eyed him warily, unsure if he were telling the truth or if this visit might have something to do with John Mark.

He walked down the steps and stopped a few feet away, removing his hat.

Did she smell like corn mash? Alcohol? What if he smelled something on her? She reflexively backed up a step.

At her movement, confusion passed through his eyes and she realized she'd hurt his feelings. Her heart twinged at that, but she didn't move forward. She couldn't risk it.

"Yes?" she asked coolly, her hands smoothing over her apron, hoping to dislodge any evidence of corn or anything else that might make Chaney suspicious.

His gaze met hers, earnest, searching. "I'd like to apologize. For what happened last night. I was out of line—"

"For snooping?" She kept her voice strong though she

wanted nothing more than to forgive him immediately and send him on his way. "I should think so."

He winced. "For kissing you."

"Oh." Disappointment stabbed at that and she mentally shook herself.

"You didn't give me leave—"

"I believe I did." She lifted her gaze to his, reading surprise and pleasure in the black depths. She should have kept her mouth shut. He had, after all, been in the back trying to find something to incriminate her brother.

But she had participated in that kiss. And she didn't appreciate him acting as if she'd been a party with no say in the matter. "I believe it was a mutual thing."

"You were pretty mad when I left."

She pressed her lips together, eyeing him cautiously. "I was mostly mad at John Mark."

Heat flared in his eyes and she half turned away from him.

"It doesn't mean I'll give you leave again."

"I understand." His voice rumbled out.

How could he when she didn't understand herself? Her gaze darted to the back of the house and she silently urged John Mark to stay where he was until Chaney left.

"Well." He stared at her for a long moment then settled his hat on his head. "Guess I'll be going."

"Yes," she murmured, hoping he couldn't hear the roar of her heartbeat. She squashed the urge to rub her clammy hands together.

He walked through the gate and gathered his reins. Her gaze skipped over his wide shoulders, the trim waist, the lean muscular legs.

With one foot in the stirrup, he suddenly turned to her and she jerked her gaze away.

"Maybe I shouldn't have kissed you last night, Morrow

Beth, but I enjoyed it. I meant every word I said.''

Her eyes widened and her jaw went slack.

He grinned and swung into the saddle. ''Better close your mouth. You'll get lockjaw.''

He fiddled with his reins and glanced down at her. ''I've been thinking about the Easter picnic.''

Anticipation swelled through her. *Ask me. Oh, ask me.*

''I was thinking maybe—'' A flush darkened his neck as he met her gaze. ''I was thinking maybe you'd like to go.''

Yes! The word rose immediately to her tongue, then she remembered exactly what she'd said to John Mark only minutes ago. What if Chaney *was* using her to get to her brother?

His gaze locked with hers and she read the same battle between conscience and duty, the same resentment and hope that wound through her. In his eyes were the very same doubts she felt and she wondered again if he'd asked because he wanted to or because it was another chance to learn about John Mark.

She knew what her answer had to be. Disappointment tightened in her chest like a sharp knot and she forced a smile. ''I appreciate the invitation, but I'd best say no. I'll need to watch the twins.''

It was a lame excuse and they both knew it. For an instant, she thought he would protest or invite the twins along or point out, quite reasonably, that her brother could watch them.

Regret darkened his eyes for a moment but he smiled at her. ''Oh, I hadn't thought of that.''

He clucked to his horse, looking down at her from the saddle. ''I'm sure I'll see you there, though?''

''Oh, yes. We never miss it.''

He touched the brim of his hat and rode off.

Morrow Beth gripped the rough wooden rail of the fence and watched him go, her throat tight with tears.

"How come you said no?" John Mark's voice was quiet at her elbow.

Morrow Beth dashed a lone tear from her eye. "We both know he didn't want to go with me. Not really."

She turned and went into the house, feeling the weight of her brother's thoughtful stare.

She'd been right to turn him down, Chaney told himself for the hundredth time as he stared blankly at the piece of paper on his desk. Still, the fact that she was right didn't lessen the sting of rejection or the deep ache that had settled low in his gut.

His determination to nail John Mark Huckabee was starting to waver and Chaney knew it was because of Morrow Beth's sweet lips and those green eyes that turned him inside out.

He'd wanted to go with her, truly. But he'd been torn between that want and the realization that he still had a job to do. A job that Morrow Beth might be able to help with.

He'd thought about using her before, but he couldn't bring himself to do it. Whether or not anything came of these new feelings, he didn't want her to look at him with resentment.

She would never use him to save her brother. How could Chaney do the same thing to her?

He recalled again the shocked surprise in her eyes when she'd found him on the porch and the way her gaze had darted frequently to the back of the house. Did he make her that nervous? Or was her obvious unease caused by something else?

He hadn't heard anyone else around the Huckabee

place, but once he'd started talking to Morrow Beth, he hadn't been aware of anything except her anyway.

"Hey, Chaney!" Billy Jack Huckabee charged through the door of Chaney's office.

He swung around in his chair, grinning at the little boy. "Hey, Billy."

"Hi, Marshal." Katie Jo followed at a more sedate skip, her green eyes twinkling. "Whatcha doin'?"

"Trying to get a little work done." He grinned. Katie would forever insist on calling him marshal instead of sheriff. "What about the two of you?"

"We came into town with John Mark." The little girl came up beside his desk, leaning over onto her elbows.

Billy Jack moved to the other side. "Hey, look at this."

He dug into the pocket of his overalls and pulled out a rock. Black and shiny, it glittered in his palm.

Chaney examined it closely then laid it back in the boy's palm. "Very nice. Where'd you find it?"

"Down in the—"

"On the street," Katie Jo put in emphatically with a meaningful look at Billy.

Chaney raised his eyebrows.

"Yeah, in the street." Billy Jack shrugged. "John Mark says it's onyx."

"How did you like supper last night? Morrow Beth's a good cook, huh?"

Katie Jo chimed in. "Have you ever tasted biscuits like that?"

"She makes good pie, too." Billy Jack rubbed his stomach, his eyes fluttering shut in pleasure. "Apple, peach, pecan."

"Sounds good." Chaney bit back a smile.

"How come Morrow Beth was mad when you left last night?" Katie asked.

"You probably need to ask her." Chaney's gut knotted as if a twister had just landed.

Billy Jack propped his elbows on Chaney's desk and rested his chin in his hands. "When are we going fishing again?"

"Anytime."

Katie walked over to the empty cell and hopped up on the bottom bar of the door, swinging back and forth. "Have you arrested anybody yet?"

"Not yet. What's your brother doing in town?"

"He had to talk to Bonnie and somebody else," Katie Jo answered unconcernedly.

Billy Jack leaned in to whisper to Chaney. "She don't know nothing. John Mark's taking care of some business."

Chaney knew he shouldn't use two ten-year-olds to gather information on their brother, but he'd gotten nowhere with their older sister. Besides, he doubted that they knew. John Mark seemed the kind to protect these children. "What kind of business?"

Billy shrugged and grinned, exposing the gap in his front teeth. "I don't know neither."

"Chaney, you're not really going to arrest anybody, are you?"

He glanced over at Katie Jo, who was walking around the inside of the cell. "I hope I don't have to, but I might."

"I would hate staying in this little ol' room." She came out, smiling sunnily at him. "Are you going to the picnic on Easter?"

"I've thought about it."

"We think you should ask Morrow Beth."

Chaney stared, first at Billy Jack, then at Katie. "What?"

"Ask Sister," Billy urged.

"She's been kinda sad," Katie Jo whispered as if sharing a confidence. "This would make her happy."

"I'm not so sure your sister would like to go with me."

"Oh, she would." Billy Jack nodded as if he knew exactly what Morrow Beth would like.

"Every girl would," Katie said meaningfully, her braids bobbing.

Billy Jack paced in front of Chaney's desk. "You would have the best time. There's three-legged races and egg tosses and seed spitting and wood chopping—"

"You could buy her some lemonade and sit under a big ol' tree, fanning and talking and stuff," Katie suggested in a soft dreamy voice.

He looked from one to the other of them again. "What brought this on?"

"We just thought it would be so nice of you to ask her." Katie looked at him with wide eyes. "Don't you?"

"Well—"

"John Mark said you wanted to. He said the two of you would have a good time."

"I think it's a good idea." Billy Jack nodded firmly.

"Oh, you do?" Chaney felt as if he'd just had the wind knocked out of him. "Well . . . I think it sounds nice, but I don't think your sister really wants to go with me."

"Oh, she does! She does!" Katie nodded sagely.

Then why did she just turn me down?

"John Mark said the two of you should be doing a lot of stuff together."

At Billy's words, suspicion prickled Chaney's spine. "What kind of stuff?"

"Just spending time together. I said it would be better if you had something to do, like fish or kill snakes, but Brother says you'd know what to do if you got Morrow

Beth alone for ten minutes.'' Billy Jack wrinkled up his face. ''I don't know *what* you would do. Do you?''

Several images, all of them inappropriate for a ten-year-old's ears flashed in Chaney's mind. ''Well—''

''I think it would be just dandy,'' Katie Jo whispered. ''Will you ask her, huh?''

''I'll think about it.'' John Mark had to know by now that Chaney had been snooping around last night and he still wanted him to spend time with Morrow Beth?

Realization slammed into him. The Huckabees were using him, just the way he'd tried to avoid using Morrow Beth. Somehow John Mark was betting on Chaney becoming fond of Morrow Beth, then not following through if he did discover Huckabee was moonshining.

Anger exploded inside him and he could barely make out the kids' words as they rattled on about the Easter picnic.

Questions pelted him. When had John Mark come up with this idea? Only today? Or earlier, before he'd extended that supper invitation? Or before Morrow Beth had made that tentative truce with him just before the Warner sisters' fiasco?

Exactly what was John Mark doing in town anyway? Talking to Bonnie, the kids had said. About what? Chaney couldn't think of a thing Huckabee might need to say to the restaurant owner, for the second time this week.

He rose, herding the kids out the door and onto the porch. ''I'll think about what you've said, okay. I'm glad you stopped by. I want you to do that anytime you feel like it.''

''Where are you going?'' Katie frowned up at him.

''I've got some business I need to finish. Do you want me to walk you over to the restaurant to find John Mark?''

''No, we can find him.'' Billy Jack shielded his eyes

from the afternoon glare of the sun. "You look kinda funny. Are you sick or something?"

"No, I'm fine. Or I will be. Now run along and tell your brother I appreciate his idea."

Billy and Katie exchanged puzzled looks, then shrugged.

"Be sure and tell him," Chaney urged.

"Okay." The twins hopped off the porch and headed up the street toward Bonnie's.

" 'Bye, Chaney," they chorused.

"Good-bye." He watched as Billy Jack turned his attention to pulling Katie's braid.

As the twins teased and tormented each other, Chaney strode to the opposite end of town. Maybe John Mark was in the tunnel right now. Maybe that was why he'd come to town.

With a sick feeling in his gut, Chaney knew he was right about the reason John Mark wanted him to spend time with Morrow Beth.

Alone now, Chaney's anger blazed through him. She'd acted so prim and proper last night about finding him snooping, making him feel guilty for taking advantage of their hospitality when she'd probably come out back to find him in order to shield her brother.

Even as Chaney let himself down into the tunnel, he tried to deny it. He simply couldn't believe that of Morrow Beth. She was honest and straightforward and he couldn't imagine that she would agree to such a plan.

If she were in on such a plan, why not accept Chaney's invitation this morning? That had been sincere, a selfish urge to spend the day with her, and she had turned him down.

The image of Morrow Beth as sneaky and manipulative just didn't fit.

He silently made his way down the tunnel, his feet moving slowly but surely. He heard no sound, no hint of another person underground. His thoughts rattled with enough force to cause their own noise.

Morrow Beth wouldn't allow herself to be a party to something so deceitful. She wouldn't. She hadn't known he was coming to supper last night. What was to say she knew about this new plan of her brother's?

And why was it so all-fired important that Chaney spend Easter with her?

Positive now that he was onto something, Chaney reached the end of the tunnel. The cover was open, indicating that someone had left recently and in a hurry.

Light drifted inside. Against the back wall something glittered and Chaney walked over, bending to pick it up. It was an empty jar minus the lid. Lifting it to his nose, he caught the faint odor of liquor.

Someone had been down here, but who? Chaney climbed up the ladder, gripping the jar. Out in the daylight, he examined it closely.

It was a different shape and size from the ones he'd found with Cholly and Clara. And it wasn't painted white. Something about the slender curve of the glass nagged at him, seemed familiar. The manufacturer's stamp on the bottom was unfamiliar to him.

Where had he seen this jar before?

❖ 10 ❖

CHANEY COULDN'T REMEMBER where he'd seen a jar like this before and as he walked toward Royce Henry's store, he mentally thumbed through his mind. Not at his house. Not at the Warner sisters'. Not at Bonnie's restaurant.

He shook his head, impatience rolling through him. *Where* had he seen this jar? He stared down at the glass in his hand, but couldn't remember.

The day had dawned clear and pleasant. Morning sunshine glittered off the windows in town, giving everything a new sparkle. He stepped onto Royce's porch, smiling as he saw the Warner sisters coming toward him.

"Good day, ladies." He doffed his hat to them.

"Hello, Sheriff," they chorused like a well-rehearsed quartet of sparrows.

They were decked out in their finery today. Each one wore a dress in varying shades of purple, a poke bonnet, and short white gloves. Each one carried a basket over their arm.

"Out shopping today?" He stood aside to let them pass.

They all smiled, but Clara spoke. "Running here and there, Sheriff."

"And what about you, Sheriff?" Even Cholly, who hadn't spoken to him since the incident at their house, smiled at him. Her gaze zeroed in on the jar. "*What* are you doing?"

"Getting a few things from Royce." He paused, not quite sure they'd forgiven him for destroying their still. He held the jar up for their inspection. "Ladies, I wonder if you've seen a jar like this before?"

All four of them looked at the jar. Davie shook her head. "It just looks like a jar."

Carolyn nodded. "A jar."

Cholly tilted her head, considering him for a moment. "Is that some special kind of jar, Sheriff?"

"No, no." He chuckled, determined not to give anything away. Especially not to the sweet, unpredictable Warner sisters.

Clara eyed him curiously for a moment, then lifted an elegant glove-clad hand. "Come, sisters. We've got things to do."

"Good day, Sheriff," they murmured as they passed him and stepped into the street.

"Good day." He watched them as they marched across the street and straight into Bonnie's restaurant. Though a grin tugged at the corner of his mouth, he couldn't halt a flare of suspicion.

The Warner sisters were cheerier than he'd seen them in a long time. Even Cholly, who hadn't spoken to him the last three times he'd seen her in town.

What exactly were they doing today? As he watched, they came out of the restaurant and walked next door to the bank. He didn't want to think that they might be up to their old tricks again, but what if they were? Would they possibly make moonshine again when they knew what he would have to do if he caught them?

He strode inside Henry's Mercantile. The double glass doors were propped open and a chime of pennies tinkled overhead. A slight breeze blew through the doors, sending the scents of cinnamon and apples and leather dancing through the store.

A blend of spices Chaney couldn't identify rolled under the scent of tobacco and cigars. He glanced toward the counter, which groaned under the weight of fabric bolts and ribbon, cans of molasses, and a sack of flour.

Mrs. Sarah Jones stood there, waiting as Royce tallied her bill. She turned, giving him a warm smile.

"Good day, Sheriff."

"Hello, Mrs. Jones." Chaney touched the brim of his hat and moved next to a barrel of apples.

He glanced outside, seeing the Warner sisters step outside the bank, confer for a moment, then tap on the window of the newspaper office. *What* were those dear ladies up to?

Royce glanced up, his forehead furrowed in concentration. "Be right with you, Sheriff."

"No hurry."

Chaney scanned the row of shelves to his left, walking in front of them. His gaze moved quickly over men's boots and belts and denim pants. No jars here.

Looking over his shoulder, he saw the Warner sisters walk down the street out of view. The certainty that they were up to something grew stronger.

Chaney's attention returned to the shelves and he catalogued dainty button-up boots for women, parasols, lace trims, small bottles of perfume. On the last shelf, he spied a box of jars and moved over to look at them carefully.

Behind him, he heard Mrs. Jones call out, "Good-bye, Sheriff."

"Good-bye, ma'am."

"Will you be going to the Easter picnic tomorrow?"

Chaney turned with a smile. "I couldn't miss that, now, could I?"

She smiled broadly, her smile disappearing into the plumpness of her face. "My girls and I will look forward to seeing you."

He smiled and nodded, but inside he grimaced. Her girls? He wanted to stay well away from Mrs. Jones's girls, who were shameless man-chasers.

Royce strode over to him, straightening a pair of pants that dangled off the shelf. "You looking for something in particular, Sheriff?"

Chaney held up the jar he'd found in the tunnel. "Do you carry these?"

Royce shook his head. "No, sure don't."

"Are you sure?" The storeowner had barely glanced at the jar. How could he tell anything so quickly?

The other man grinned, although on him it looked more like a grimace. "I know everything I carry, Sheriff, and I don't carry those jars. I could order some for you, though."

"No, that won't be necessary." Chaney turned away from the shelf, satisfied that he'd seen every jar Royce had. "Would anyone around here carry them?"

"Maybe in Stillwater or down in Guthrie. Couldn't tell you." The other man's eyes narrowed. "What's so all-fired important about this here jar?"

"Nothing." Chaney smiled, not caring whether or not Royce believed him. "I appreciate your help."

Royce eyed him suspiciously. "Has something happened? Did you find something in this jar?"

"I told you, Royce, it's nothing. Just satisfying my curiosity." Just as he was about to do with the Warner sisters.

Royce followed him onto the porch, squinting against the bright sunlight. "Well, if I can help you in any way with anything, let me know."

"I will."

"Excuse us, Sheriff." Clara Warner spoke directly behind him.

Chaney made a double-quick step out of their way and moved to the edge of the porch. "Excuse *me*, ladies."

They paraded past him, their skirts swinging slightly, their baskets dangling from their arms.

"I wonder what they're up to," Royce muttered beside him.

So did Chaney, but he kept it to himself. "I'm sure they're just out for the day."

"Hmmmph." The storekeep eyed the sisters one last time as he walked back in his store.

Chaney bid Royce farewell and stepped out into the street, noticing that the sisters had stopped to talk to Polly Bell. It looked as if Carolyn took something out of her basket and handed it to the shorter woman, but Chaney couldn't be sure.

He didn't like the direction his thoughts were taking him. Surely the Warner sisters wouldn't be so brazen as to start up their moonshining again, then parade it around town right in front of him?

Chaney couldn't imagine it, but he couldn't dismiss it either. He'd learned to expect the unexpected with these women.

Across the street, Sada stepped out of her office. She waved and walked over.

"Hello, Sada. How are you?"

"Fine, Chaney. Yourself?" Her gaze dropped to the jar.

He lifted it, angling it so she could see it. "Ever seen a jar like this before?"

She pursed her lips, her gray eyes twinkling. "Can't really recall. Is that some kind of evidence or something?"

He grinned. "I'm not sure. I've seen a jar like this, but I can't remember where. I thought maybe you might have seen one, too."

She shook her head slowly. "It looks like a plain jar to me."

"That's what everybody says." Frustrated, he stared down at the jar. If it hadn't smelled like moonshine, he never would have kept it.

Maybe there was nothing to go on here. Maybe he was so anxious to find something on John Mark that he was trying to make evidence out of something that wasn't evidence at all.

The Warner sisters sailed down the planked walk toward him and Sada.

Chaney touched the brim of his hat, saying to Sada in a low voice, "Do they seem really . . . *happy* to you?"

"Happy?" Sada stepped forward, extending her hand to Clara Warner. "Good day, ladies."

"Hello, Sada." Clara shook Sada's hand.

Cholly stepped up next, grinning irrepressibly. "Sheriff, we seem to be running into you everywhere today."

"That's so, ladies." He smiled as Davie and Carolyn leaned forward to shake Sada's hand. "You ladies are in better spirits than I've seen you for a while."

"Better *spirits*? Very clever, Sheriff." Cholly laughed, her green eyes sparkling.

Chaney grinned with them, yet he was suddenly

swamped by the feeling that they were carting around moonshine right under his nose.

"Will you be at the picnic on Easter, Sheriff?" Clara Sue smiled sweetly at him.

"Yes, ma'am. Wouldn't miss it."

"How lovely!" Cholly beamed, a little too brightly.

Chaney's gaze shifted from one basket to the other and he asked casually, "What are you ladies delivering today?"

"Delivering?" Clara asked breathlessly, her eyes wide.

"We're not delivering anything." Carolyn shook her head emphatically.

Davie agreed somberly. "Certainly not."

Cholly's eyes glinted mischievously and she held out her basket. "Would you care to take a look, Sheriff?"

Her sisters turned shocked gazes on her.

Though a little taken aback at her bold offer, Chaney wasn't about to refuse. He grinned and reached for the linen covering. "I certainly would."

"Help yourself." Cholly's grin stretched wide across her face.

Sada frowned, watching as Chaney lifted the covering. The other three Warner sisters stared blandly at him, simply waiting.

Chaney peeked inside and saw . . . nothing. *Nothing?* He lifted his gaze to the Warner sisters. He could have sworn he saw one of them remove something from the basket.

Clara offered hers to him. "Would you like to look in mine, too?"

"And mine?" Davie asked quietly.

"And mine?" Carolyn echoed.

Sada cleared her throat and Chaney fought the urge to sigh. How did they manage to make him feel like a recalcitrant schoolboy caught pulling a little girl's braid? He was only trying to do his job.

Refusing to feel guilty, he stubbornly lifted the cover on all their baskets. All were empty.

Each sister patted her linen covering delicately back into place. Clara beamed at Chaney. "Have a nice day, Sheriff."

"You, too, ladies." He doffed his hat, watching as they swept past him and marched down the street, looking for all the world as if they had just left church.

"You should see your face." Sada chuckled beside him.

Chaney shook his head. "I don't know how they're doing it, but they're at it again."

"Making moonshine?"

He nodded.

Sada laughed. "Well, look at it this way, Sheriff. It doesn't look like you'll lack for work."

He glanced at her and back to the Warner sisters, who were sashaying toward the west end of town. "I guess not."

"See you at the picnic." Sada started across the street.

Chaney stared after the Warner sisters as they disappeared up the hill. "Uh-huh."

"Things are getting out of hand."

"The sheriff is causing everyone to be afraid."

An hour after Chaney had run into the Warner sisters, they, along with the majority of Scrub, met in the back room of Bonnie's restaurant.

"No one wants to come to town for fear he'll think they're moonshining," Will Bell grumbled.

"Oh, Will." Sada sighed. "That's hardly true."

"Might as well be," the old man complained. "And

what's going to happen if the Warners pick up and move?"

"Pooh!" Cholly Sue dismissed with a wave of her hand. "We just ran right into Sheriff White in broad daylight. He didn't find a thing."

"Not for lack of trying," Sada reminded drily.

The Warner sisters exchanged satisfied smiles.

"What about the rest of us?" Bonnie pointed out. "The sheriff hasn't suspected *me* yet, but what if he does? Liquor's a good part of my business."

"What does J. T. say about it?" Clara Warner asked.

"Ooh, you know J. T. He's content to let me take care of things as long as he can go fishing."

"Don't let Morrow Beth catch you buying that stuff from her brother," Sada warned.

"We've got a system all worked out. The girl will never know," Bonnie said confidently.

"Everyone can get around it," Clara Warner spoke up. "We certainly have."

"You can't mean to say you forgive the sheriff for shutting you down?" Will Bell gaped at her.

Clara shrugged and Cholly spoke up. "It's not a matter of forgiveness. It's a matter of resourcefulness."

"Huh?"

"There's more than one way to skin a cat," Carolyn said sagely.

Davie nodded.

Will's gaze encompassed them all. "Are you saying you've set up your still again?"

Clara nodded. "If we could just get liquor legalized, there would be no need for this deception. I simply don't like it."

"Neither do I," agreed Cholly. "But we can't turn our back on people who need us."

"Thank goodness," said Polly Bell, holding up a small brown bottle. "I don't know what I'd do if you hadn't been able to give me some of your tonic. I've felt ever so much better since you started making it again."

"Well, there's got to be something we can do, some way we can distract the sheriff." Will brought them back to the business at hand. "If he gets John Mark, he'll get the rest of us, for sure."

Everyone nodded in agreement.

"What do you think, Sada?" Clara Warner asked.

Sada grimaced. "I feel an awful fraud even being here. I don't think I should be hearing this."

"You know him better than the rest of us," Polly observed. "What would distract him?"

"Chaney is a good man. He's only trying to do his job."

"His job could close down our little town," Will grumbled. "I'm not willing to let that happen—I've got an idea!"

The Warner sisters exchanged uncertain looks. Polly looked startled. Bonnie eyed him suspiciously.

Sada shook her head. "I don't think—"

"He's sweet on that Huckabee girl, ain't he?" Will Bell glanced around triumphantly. "Well, ain't he?"

All the women eyed him uncertainly.

Comprehension slowly bloomed on Sada's features, then turned to apprehension. "Now, Will, if you're thinking what I think you're thinking—"

"Well, why not?" he demanded, looking around the group for approval.

"What exactly are you thinking?" Cholly asked.

"I've noticed that the sheriff seems taken with her. She seems taken with him. Why don't we just help them along?"

"You mean play matchmaker?" Clara asked.

Her sisters' eyes grew wide. Polly gaped at her husband.

Will nodded. "Just think how happy we could make those two."

"Oh, Will, call a spade a spade," Sada burst out. "If you're going to try and use Morrow Beth to make Chaney White forget his job, then say so."

"Whatever you want to call it, I think it would work."

"What would we do?"

"How would we do it?"

"When?"

"How about tomorrow?" Polly suggested, warming to the idea. "At the picnic?"

"Yes, Easter! How lovely."

Sada paled and looked as if she might be sick. "I don't want to hear this," she said, letting herself out.

"I've got it!" exclaimed Will. "Here's what we'll do."

Chaney leaned back in his chair, surveying the jar that sat in the middle of his desk. He'd had no luck finding out who it belonged to. Or remembering where he'd seen one like it before.

After the Easter celebration, he would make a ride down to Stillwater, see if he could learn anything there.

A knock sounded on the door.

"Come in." Chaney shoved the jar into the drawer of his desk just as Bonnie poked her head inside.

She wore her usual pale blue shirtwaist and white apron. Her dark blond curls framed her flushed face. "Came to get your lunch dishes."

He stood and picked up the tray that sat on the corner of the desk. "It was very good, Bonnie. As always."

"Thank you." She beamed, her round face flushed with pleasure as she took the tray from him.

He said casually, "I guess Morrow Beth's not working today."

For a moment, Chaney thought he detected a gleam of delight in her eyes.

"Uh, no, sir. She's off today. She's such a dear, sweet girl. I don't know what I'd do without her."

Chaney nodded, regretting again that she had refused his invitation to the picnic.

"She takes such good care of her family. And she can make a pie every bit as good as mine. That crust—" Bonnie touched her fingers to her lips and blew a kiss. "Flaky, wonderful. Took me years of marriage before I could make a pie like that."

Chaney shifted, suddenly aware that Bonnie was very enthusiastically listing Morrow Beth's attributes. As if he didn't know a few himself.

"I'll tell her you asked after her."

"Oh, that's not necessary." He rose, panic flaring through him. He didn't particularly want Morrow Beth knowing that he'd asked about her. Especially when she'd made it clear they should keep a distance. And they should.

"Well, we'll be closed tomorrow. For the picnic and all."

Chaney nodded.

"I'll be back to bringing your lunch the day after." Bonnie paused in the door, holding it open with her ample hip. "Sheriff, you *will* be at the festivities tomorrow?"

"Of course." He looked up, wondering at the secretive smile playing around her lips. "I guess I'll see you there."

''You certainly will. And Morrow Beth, too, I reckon.''
With that, she let the door close.

Chaney frowned, listening to the retreating thud of her footsteps. Bonnie had seemed to make a special point of mentioning that Morrow Beth would be there tomorrow. To list some of her attributes, as if Chaney needed any reminding. He thought of the woman far too often as it was.

Pushing away the thoughts of her that tickled his brain, he struggled to focus on remembering where he'd seen a jar similar to the one he'd found in the tunnel. Again, he mentally tracked the places he'd been.

But instead of recalling those, he kept feeling the tentative touch of her tongue to his, the complete surrender in her kiss.

He'd told himself repeatedly to forget her, but he might as well have told himself not to breathe. He couldn't stop thinking about her, the rich timbre of her laugh, the shy smile after their first kiss, the warmth in her green eyes.

And he couldn't dodge this ache that had settled in his heart. He missed seeing her.

''Hello there, Sheriff.''

Will Bell's voice jerked Chaney out of his thoughts.

''Mr. Bell.'' Chaney smiled broadly, spying plump Polly beside her husband. He rose from his chair. ''Mrs. Bell.''

''Don't get up, Sheriff.'' Polly waved him back.

''We just stopped by to say hello,'' Will said. ''And to make sure you're going to the picnic tomorrow?''

''Yessir. I'll be there.''

''Very good.'' Will inclined his head. Polly beamed at him. The Bells backed out of Chaney's office and continued on their way.

Chaney walked to the window, staring absently as the

Bells walked up the street, pausing to speak to Bonnie. Why was everyone suddenly so concerned that he go to the picnic?

Sada stuck her head in the door. "Sheriff—"

"Yes, I'm going to the picnic!" he burst out.

She blinked. "How . . . nice."

He grinned sheepishly. "You weren't going to ask me that, were you?"

She shook her head. Laughter danced in her eyes as she held a copy of the *Herald* out to him. "I thought you might want your daily issue of the paper."

"Thanks." He took it from her, feeling his neck heat.

Sada nodded, backing out the door. "See you tomorrow. At the picnic."

Her laughter echoed in his ears and he laughed, too.

The sincerity in Chaney's black eyes, the earnestness with which he'd apologized for that kiss stayed with Morrow Beth all through the night.

She wished she could have accepted his invitation, but she refused to be his means to get to her brother. If he would indeed do something like that. The more she was around him, the more Morrow Beth doubted that Chaney would stoop to such manipulation.

Still, the safest thing was for her to keep a distance and that's exactly what she was doing. Never mind that she couldn't forget the hunger in his kiss or the way he cradled her against his broad chest. She had to stay away from him, as much for John Mark's sake as for her own.

Morrow Beth had many gentleman callers, but none had ever affected her in the least the way only a smile from Chaney did. And his kisses made her head spin. She knew he would be at the picnic tomorrow, probably looking for a way to catch John Mark with his moonshine.

It was that thought that finally allowed her to sleep. The next morning, Morrow Beth was up early, frustration nagging at her. She fed the chickens, watered the garden, and plucked weeds before Billy Jack and Katie Jo bounced excitedly into the kitchen.

An hour later, breakfast dishes had been cleaned and Morrow Beth tucked the last of the biscuits into Billy Jack's lunch pail then stuck it in the basket with the pecan pie.

Usually she was more than enthusiastic about the Easter picnic, but not today. She wanted to go with Chaney White. And she'd turned him down flat.

She knew she'd done the right thing. Still, regret nagged at her like a pesky mosquito.

Drat John Mark and drat Chaney's job as sheriff! Morrow Beth didn't appreciate the way she'd gotten drawn into the middle of their business, but she appeared to be the only one giving up anything.

Sawing at the ham with enough vigor to make her arms ache, she stared down at the mangled meat. "Drat!"

"Morrow Beth, did you swear?" Billy Jack's voice was sharp with disbelief as he straightened from tying his shoe.

Blast! She closed her eyes, not in the mood for a lecture from her younger brother.

"You did!" he crowed, peeking around her elbow into her face. "Wash your mouth out with soap."

"Get on with you, Billy Jack. I've got work to do if we're going to be ready by the time John Mark is."

"I'm ready now." Her older brother stuck his head in the door. "Billy, help me with the wagon.

Morrow Beth whirled, her gaze locking with John Mark's. "You're not taking—"

"Grab a biscuit, Billy and come on." John Mark gave her a warning glare over the child's head.

Morrow Beth snapped her mouth shut, fuming. Her brother *was* taking moonshine to the picnic! What was wrong with him? Was he trying to get caught? Chaney would be even more suspicious today.

She slapped the ham on a plate and covered it with a towel, dumping it unceremoniously into the box that she'd prepared for the picnic.

"Don't forget to tie that box up real pretty, Morrow Beth." Katie Jo gave her hair one last brushing. "That's how you get a fella to eat lunch with you."

"I know, Katie Jo," Morrow Beth muttered, wrapping up a dozen boiled eggs and tossing them in next to the pie. "I've been doing this a lot longer than you have."

Her sister stuck out her tongue and skipped out the door.

"Come on, Morrow Beth!" bellowed John Mark.

"Come on!" chorused Billy and Katie.

The harness jingled and the wagon rolled to a creaking stop outside the door. She whipped off her apron and closed up the box, grabbing a sunflower from the vase on the table. Using the flower as her only means of decoration, she stuck it between the slats of the crate, then she hefted up the box and walked outside.

John Mark slouched easily in the wagon seat, holding the reins loosely in his hands. His hat was pushed back on his head and his eyes glinted at her. "Don't worry, little sister. We're going to have a good time today."

She handed the box up to him. "You'd better take care how much *fun* you have," she muttered darkly.

He chuckled and helped her into the wagon. "Everything is going to be just fine."

She settled herself beside him, wishing she felt as confident. If John Mark was going to pass out the stuff right under the sheriff's nose, Morrow Beth didn't want to be anywhere near.

Yesterday had been too close for comfort. Today, Morrow Beth would make certain she stayed as far away as possible from Sheriff White. Even if it made her miserable.

The trip to town was taken up with Billy and Katie's excited chatterings about how they were bound to win the three-legged race this year. And which of them could spit seeds farther than the other.

Morrow Beth relaxed as the twins' enthusiasm washed over her. The Easter celebration was always fun and today promised to be a perfect day. Lacy clouds danced across a clear blue sky. The wind blew only enough to cool the gathering heat of the butter yellow sun.

Pushing away thoughts of Chaney, she laughed and talked with her siblings. Despite the fact that she still wished she could have accepted Chaney's invitation, she *would* enjoy today. She truly believed she would.

Until they pulled up in front of the livery.

"Hello, Morrow Beth." Chaney White smiled up at her.

"Chaney!" Katie Jo bounded out of the wagon.

Billy Jack vaulted over the side. "Hey, Chaney!"

"Hello, Sheriff." Even John Mark sounded as if he were truly pleased to see the sheriff.

Morrow Beth, caught in his unwavering black stare, felt her stomach dip and smiled weakly. "Hello."

* 11 *

IRRITATION COURSED THROUGH her. Drat Chaney White anyway! Morrow Beth had expected him to help her down from the wagon, then make a nuisance of himself. He'd said hello and followed John Mark without even looking back.

Piqued, she watched him walk away, her heart thumping harder at the sureness of his smooth saunter, the breadth of his shoulders. She could tell herself she didn't feel anything for Chaney, but it was a lie.

Her gaze slid down the straight proud back, then lingered on the dark trousers that hugged his muscular buttocks. Sensation fluttered deep in her belly. Caught up in admiring him, she didn't realize at first where he had stopped or who he was talking to.

She straightened, concern slicing through her haze of pleasure. Chaney was talking to John Mark and four men. They might have been strangers to Scrub, but Morrow Beth knew them. Rick Blansford, Frank Carter, Pete and Swish McSween—cowboys from Kansas.

Before she even thought, Morrow Beth hurried toward the men. What was John Mark thinking, to meet with them right in the street?

She neared and slowed to a stop just behind Chaney. John Mark had a hand on Frank's shoulder, introducing all the cowboys to Scrub's new sheriff.

Chaney nodded, his hands on his hips. "Nice to meet you, gentlemen. Hope you'll enjoy the celebration today, but be warned. I don't want any trouble."

"That's just what I was telling them." John Mark grinned like a possum and Morrow Beth wanted to smack him.

"We ain't here to cause trouble," Frank said. "Just want to have a little fun."

"As long as you do it without liquor, we'll have no problem." Chaney let his gaze settle on each one of them.

"Aw, well, sure, Sheriff." Frank smiled as if the thought of liquor had never crossed his mind.

Chaney nodded. "Good. I wanted to be sure we understood each other."

"Yessir." Frank looked meaningfully at the others.

"Yessir," they all echoed.

Chaney turned, his eyes widening as he saw Morrow Beth.

She smiled tentatively. Pleasure flared in his eyes, then disappeared. He tipped his hat and walked away.

John Mark disappeared with the other men and Morrow Beth stared after Chaney, irritation rising again. Drat it all!

She tightened her arms around the box holding her lunch and made her way over to the front of Henry's Mercantile. A table had been set up on the porch of the store. Bonnie and Polly Bell stood there, taking lunches and arranging them in preparation for later.

Morrow Beth suddenly hoped Chaney hadn't noticed her box, then wondered what difference it would make.

She had refused his invitation to the picnic. He wouldn't be interested in choosing her or her lunch.

Betsy Jones giggled shrilly and Morrow Beth glanced over to see Chaney smiling at the girl as if she were a prize filly.

Behind Morrow Beth, Bonnie snorted, "What's he want with that one?"

Morrow Beth smiled at the other woman. "There's no accounting for taste."

"Don't you fret, Morrow Beth. It'll work out just fine."

She blinked at Bonnie's soothing tone. "I'm not—I don't care who the sheriff spends time with, Bonnie."

"Of course not." Bonnie winked and walked off to arrange several baskets at the other end of the table.

Morrow Beth frowned and turned away, dismissing her friend's comments. A crowd gathered in front of the store.

Will Bell stepped up on the porch. "Looks like everybody's ready."

The crowd murmured in agreement as Morrow Beth searched for her family. John Mark and the twins stood on the edge and she threaded her way through several groups of people to reach them.

"Did you put your basket up there, Sister?" Katie Jo asked.

"Yes."

Katie Jo rose on her tiptoes, waving frantically.

Morrow Beth looked down in time to see her sister mouth something to Chaney. She pinched Katie's arm. "What are you doing?"

"Telling Chaney which box is yours."

"He doesn't care. Now leave him be." She glanced at the Jones sisters, tamping down her irritation. "He probably already knows who he wants to have lunch with."

"But—"

"It's all right, Katie," John Mark interrupted. "We'll have a good time eating Morrow Beth's pecan pie. You can give some to the sheriff later, if there's any left."

Katie Jo glared at Morrow Beth but nodded.

Morrow Beth spared one last glance toward Chaney before she turned away. Hah! She wouldn't give him another thought. She didn't care who he had lunch with.

"Ooooo!" Bonnie exclaimed, holding up a deep-bottomed basket festooned with blue-and-yellow curling ribbon. "This lunch is fried chicken with honey, biscuits with marmalade, and cherry pie."

"That's gotta belong to Betsy Jones," Hal Morland called out. "That girl's sweet tooth can't be beat!"

Laughter sifted through the crowd and Betsy giggled in that downright annoying way she had.

Hal stepped up to take the basket and made his way over to claim Betsy for lunch.

Morrow Beth refused to acknowledge her relief in knowing that Chaney wouldn't be eating lunch with Betsy.

"Here's the next one," Polly Bell's sugary voice piped up. "Yum yum. This one has chocolate cake, a fresh loaf of bread, venison steaks, liver and onions, and pickled okra. Who do you guess, gentlemen?"

Someone hollered out Morrow Beth's name, but she smiled and shook her head.

She could feel the weight of Chaney's stare, but kept her attention deliberately fixed on Bonnie and Polly.

After three tries, Bundy Rafferty correctly guessed that the lunch belonged to Miss Cholly Warner.

"It's about time," she called out as she walked forward to meet Bundy. "That bread was going stale."

The pair of them sauntered off, joking and laughing.

Morrow Beth smiled and as she looked away, her gaze crashed into Chaney's. His black eyes captured hers. Her heartbeat kicked up and she tore her gaze away.

She didn't want him to be nice to her. She needed to stay away from him. Far away from him. She wished someone would hurry up and guess her lunch so she could get away and try to ignore him. But it seemed impossible.

Though her attention was strictly focused on the light-hearted game around her, Morrow Beth was distinctly aware of Chaney as he milled through the crowd.

Bonnie and Polly's laughing voices carried over the crowd, but it was Chaney's baritone that Morrow Beth heard. The scent of fresh-baked cakes and pies and bread fluttered in the air, but it was the heady blend of male scent and bay rum that tickled Morrow Beth's nostrils.

All the while, his gaze lingered on her, stroking, silently urging her to look at him. Finally she could ignore him no more. She turned, her gaze lifting to his.

Hunger burned in the black depths and one corner of his beautiful mouth tugged up in a smile. Warmth flowed through her and before she knew it, she smiled back.

Someone jostled Chaney from behind. He stepped out of the way, breaking the moment. Morrow Beth's smile faded and she turned away. What was wrong with her? She had refused him and now stood here making eyes at him.

Only then did she realize how thin the crowd had become. Even her family had wandered off. John Mark had won Molly Jones and her lunch. The twins had been cajoled off with Miss Clara.

Morrow Beth's basket was still up there—*some-where*—and she tapped her foot, craning her neck to try and see it.

Several people mingled around her, but she was aware of only one man. Chaney stood well away from her, arms crossed over his broad chest as he talked and laughed with Sada and the mayor.

Morrow Beth couldn't see her basket anywhere. It didn't bother her much that no one had been given the opportunity to claim it, but she did wonder where it was.

"Everyone enjoy!" Will Bell urged.

Just as Morrow Beth started forward to find her basket, Polly said, "Oh, wait, here's one we forgot."

"Sheriff?" Bonnie smiled at him. "Why don't you take this one?"

Chaney shrugged. "I haven't been here long enough to be able to guess who it might belong to."

"Why don't you try?" Polly urged, looking as if she were trying to keep from smiling.

"It shouldn't be that hard," Sada said drily, looking from Chaney to Morrow Beth and back. "There's only one person left."

Chaney frowned, his gaze sliding to her.

She stiffened. Surely he didn't think she had anything to do with this? Why, she wouldn't eat lunch with him if he begged her, paid her, and made it himself!

"Come on, Sheriff," Bonnie coaxed prettily. "Why don't you give it a try?"

What was going on here? Morrow Beth had *never* heard Bonnie speak that way and she stared at the other woman as if Bonnie had come unhinged. Bonnie refused to look at her.

Suspicion inched up Morrow Beth's spine, matching that which she'd seen in Chaney's eyes.

"Well . . ." He glanced at Sada and shrugged. "What's it got?"

"There's ham and biscuits and eggs and, yum, pecan pie."

At the mention of the pie, Chaney suddenly looked at her, as if he knew about her pies. Yet she'd never told him. Apprehension formed a knot in her and she watched him carefully. *Pick Sada,* she urged. *Not me.*

"Sheriff?"

"Well, I don't know." He laughed, sounding a bit uncertain as he pulled his gaze from Morrow Beth.

"There's only one girl ain't been picked. That should make it easier for you," Will Bell boomed.

Morrow Beth's heart skipped into double time. He didn't want to pick her, not after yesterday. Why didn't they let her have the box and everyone could enjoy lunch? She started forward to claim her own lunch.

Chaney's gaze locked with hers and she could see the questions in his eyes as if he were as uncertain as she were. His voice was loud, seemingly too enthusiastic. "Well, it has to be Miss Huckabee's, doesn't it?"

He didn't want to do this any more than she did. How had this happened? Surely Bonnie and Polly hadn't done this on purpose.

A flush heated her neck, her cheeks. Her breath shuddered out and it was all she could do not to close her eyes against the longing she hoped didn't show on her face.

"Is it yours, Morrow Beth?" he asked quietly.

She nodded, her gaze moving from Polly's innocent features to Bonnie, who seemed to be biting back a smile, to Will Bell, who smiled smugly.

Morrow Beth frowned.

Polly stepped down from the porch and handed the box to Chaney. "Here's your lunch. Enjoy it, you two."

The three of them exchanged satisfied looks and walked off.

Holding her box, Chaney stared at Morrow Beth expectantly. "Well, it looks like we'll be eating together after all today."

"Yes." Her eyes narrowed as she watched Bonnie, Polly, and Will stride toward the creek.

Chaney stepped closer to her, drawing her attention. "You didn't bring chicken, did you?" he teased gently. "Fried rooster?"

She couldn't help a smile. "No chicken."

"Darn."

Bonnie and Polly glanced back, then bent their heads close together, whispering furiously. Something about the neat way she'd ended up with Chaney nagged at Morrow Beth. "I think *someone* went to an awful lot of trouble to make sure we had lunch together."

"This was definitely planned."

Startled that he'd echoed her thoughts, she nodded. "If you'd rather not—"

"I'd rather." He offered her his arm, his warmth circling around her. "I *did* ask, remember?"

She looked into his eyes, reading pleasure and hope. Placing her hand on his arm, she nodded. "I'd like that."

He smiled, setting off a burst of heat in her belly. As they walked up the hill toward the creek, warmth spread through her. Despite her efforts, it seemed she would spend the day with the sheriff after all.

"You looked as if I were about to clap you in wrist irons!"

"I did not!" Morrow Beth's protest was ruined by laughter.

An hour later, she sat with Chaney under the welcoming arms of an ancient oak tree close to the water.
She was stuffed full of ham and biscuits. "I simply
couldn't imagine that you would want to eat lunch with
me after—"

She broke off, looking away.

"After you refused to come with me?"

"Yes." Tension knotted her shoulders and she plucked
at a blade of grass beside her.

He was quiet for several seconds and Morrow Beth finally chanced a peek at him.

He watched her with a look of fond impishness. "I
might be tempted to believe you had those women set us
up."

"I never did!"

He chuckled, reaching for his napkin and blotting away
the small pie crumbs at the corner of his mouth. Morrow
Beth felt a flutter of sensation and she looked down.

The rustle of grass was crowned by laughter. All along
the creek, couples and families sat eating their lunch.
Morrow Beth hadn't expected to enjoy herself so much
or to relax as much as she had.

Only inches separated her from Chaney where they sat
on a checkered tablecloth that had mysteriously appeared
in her box.

Chaney leaned back on his elbows and cast a lazy
glance at her. "That was delicious."

"I'm glad you liked it." She knew the flutter in her
stomach was due to more than his comment about her
cooking. She plucked a loose thread from the cloth. "John
Mark told me you have no brothers or sisters."

"That's right. No kin at all now."

She hesitated, then ventured timidly, "You didn't see
your pa much?"

"No. I was raised by a lawman named Axel Dumont."

"That seems a hard life for a child." Her heart squeezed at the thought of Chaney as a lonely little boy.

He shrugged. "I never thought about it much. What about you? Things had to be hard after your father passed on. I mean, with you and John Mark having to take over the raising of the twins and providing for your family."

She was surprised at the depth of compassion in his eyes. "I guess we do what we have to."

"I guess so." He was quiet for a moment. "I had only to worry about myself. You've got the twins and I admire you a great deal for raising them. You have a nice family."

"Thank you." She smiled. "You didn't turn out too badly."

His lips tilted in a lazy grin that caused anticipation to curl through her. "You like working at the restaurant with Bonnie?"

"I don't mind it. I've learned how to cook from her."

"I can vouch for that." He rubbed his belly, his eyes sparkling mischievously.

"And we've become friends. Or we were until today," she joked, referring to Bonnie's part in throwing her and Chaney together for lunch.

"Your family is close. I guess that's due to you and John Mark?"

"He wants us to all stay together. That's why he works so hard." She wished she could explain to Chaney that John Mark had never intended to take over Pap's business.

Demand for the moonshine had necessitated that John Mark keep the still running. As much as she disliked it, she couldn't deny that it kept food on their table and shoes on the twins' feet.

"Your brother told me he can't read," Chaney observed casually, looking up at her.

She nodded. "He wasn't very good in school and Pap decided he needed John Mark at home more than they needed him at school. Because I was a girl, I was allowed to go."

"So, does he like working the farm or does he only do it because it's all he knows?"

Suspicion niggled at her. His questions had seemed innocent enough before, but now they seemed all about John Mark. "He likes the farm. He likes doing things with his hands."

He nodded, folding his arms behind his head and staring up at the sky. Around them, children screeched and hollered. Splashes sounded in the river and mockingbirds trilled from the tree above them.

Morrow Beth frowned. "Do you like being a sheriff? Or do you only do it because that's what Axel taught you?"

"I like it." Chaney's eyes narrowed as if he were surprised at her question. Then he chuckled disparagingly. "It beats stealing horses."

She smiled at the reference to his father, then sobered. "It's a shame we all have to live under the shadow of what our parents did."

Why couldn't he see that John Mark had been forced into making moonshine? He had never chosen that for himself. At least not until Pap died. She plucked at another piece of grass. "Why do you like your job? What do you like about being a lawman?"

Chaney eyed her thoughtfully and pushed up to his elbows, his arm brushing hers. "It gives me something.

It's steady, I guess. You always know where you stand. There's no gray.''

''But people aren't like that.'' Morrow Beth turned toward him, wishing suddenly she could explain about John Mark. ''People are never just right or wrong. There are always two sides to everything.''

''I agree.'' He shifted, placing one hand on the ground. The other rested on his knee as he turned toward her. ''But people need some rules. And everyone knows right from wrong.''

''What if it's not exactly wrong, but the law says it is?''

He stared at her for a long moment, causing her to shift uneasily. He knew she was talking about John Mark and moonshining.

Finally he said, ''I have to do what the law says.''

''Even if it hurts people?''

''More people could be hurt if I didn't do my job.''

She glanced down, trying to keep her voice steady. ''That's why you're so determined to catch all the moonshiners?''

''Partly.'' His voice rumbled low across her ears. ''It's also my job. I was given three months to shut down the moonshiners. If I don't do what I promised, I won't be hired. It's that simple.''

''No matter what happens to the people you catch?''

A frown furrowed between his dark brows and understanding glimmered in his eyes. ''Just because I do it, Morrow Beth, doesn't mean I like every part of it.''

She looked at him, trying to read if he were talking about John Mark, too. ''You mean, like what happened with the Warner sisters?''

''Yes.''

She knew he hadn't liked that. And he had handled it

very kindly. If he learned something about her brother, perhaps he would be just as kind.

Chaney cleared his throat and looked out over the river. "Where'd your family get off to?"

She pulled her gaze away from his strong jaw, the rugged profile, and glanced out toward the water. She spied the twins with Bonnie. "There go Billy Jack and Katie Jo."

"And John Mark?"

Perhaps because they had just talked about her brother, Morrow Beth grew immediately wary. "John Mark?"

"Yes." Chaney glanced around, eyeing the people scattered over the hillside. "Haven't seen him in a while."

Her eyes narrowed. His tone was casual, but tension laced his words. Chaney thought John Mark was up to something. And he was probably right. "He's probably still with Molly."

"Nope." Chaney stretched. "Saw her a little while ago, all by herself. Now, where do you suppose he got off to?"

Anger ripped through her. She'd been having a wonderful time talking to him, but she suddenly felt he'd been leading up to questions about her brother. Her voice shook. "Do you suspect him of something, *Sheriff*?"

Chaney's gaze snapped to hers, his eyes clear and determined. At first she thought he would laugh off her question, but then his jaw firmed. "You know I do."

He really was trying to find out about John Mark! She rose, shaking with the effort to keep her voice down as people sauntered past on their way back to town. "Did you have anything to do with what happened back there?"

"Back where?" He stood, too, glancing around at the

few people who'd stopped to stare when they heard Morrow Beth's angry voice. "What are you talking about?"

She fluttered her hand, anger boiling through her. "In town. Did you get Bonnie and Polly to help you—"

"No!" he roared, drawing even more stares. He stepped toward her. "I had nothing to do with that and you know it."

"But you still didn't mind eating with me, just so you could ask about my brother!"

"That's not why I ate with you!"

"Oh, really?" She stepped right up to him, angling her chin. "So you aren't trying to prove he's guilty of something?"

"Moonshining," he said stubbornly.

"What?"

"He's guilty of moonshining—"

"You don't know that!"

"Well, I'm trying to prove—No, I'm trying to find out—Oh, hell!" He planted his hands on his hips. "Listen to me, Morrow Beth. This lunch didn't have anything to do with—"

"And if you prove my brother is guilty, then what?"

Reluctance spread across his features and he arched his neck, sighing deeply. "You know I'll have to do something about it."

"Worse than what you did to the Warner sisters?"

His gaze leveled on her. "It depends."

Chaney had never stated outright his intention to catch her brother. Anger and fear and a sense of loss collided inside her. Snatching up her skirts, she marched past him.

"Hey, wait a minute!"

She wouldn't be used to incriminate her brother.

"Morrow Beth!"

She'd thought she and Chaney were getting along so well.

"What about your pie?"

"You eat it!" She turned and glared at him. "You'll need it to keep up your strength for all the moonshiners you're going to catch."

He winced, but she turned her back and kept walking.

She hoped desperately John Mark wasn't in town selling liquor, but if he was then he would be on his own. She didn't want Chaney to discover John Mark's operation, but neither was she going to tell her brother about Chaney's suspicions.

She didn't like what either of them was doing and she was washing her hands of them both.

Chaney watched her go, fighting the urge to follow her. He had nothing to apologize for. Except maybe being stupid enough to tell her that he was trying to catch her brother in some nefarious activity.

"Shoot."

He wanted to kick something, aimed for the empty basket, and got his foot caught in the cloth he'd spread for them on the ground. A curse twisted violently out of his lips.

"Tsk, tsk, Sheriff." Cholly Warner's voice was unmistakable behind him.

Chaney turned his head around to see her.

The older woman walked by, shaking her finger at him. "That's no way to treat a young woman."

Protests rose to his lips that he hadn't done anything wrong, but he *was* the one standing here alone. "Yes, ma'am."

He bent down and bunched up the cloth, tucking it under one arm.

"Forevermore, Sheriff, what was all that about with Morrow Beth?"

Royce Henry sounded genuinely concerned. Chaney grabbed up the box, which still held part of the pie. "Nothing to concern yourself with, Royce. Everything's just fine."

"Hmmmph! Don't seem fine to me." The older man trudged off down the hill.

Chaney glared after him. Why didn't people mind their own business? Morrow Beth would probably never speak to him again, but he had done nothing wrong.

Muttering under his breath, he started down the hill toward town. The afternoon stretched emptily before him. He had thought, *hoped,* that he might enjoy the Easter festivities with Morrow Beth. Obviously not.

"I don't see how you could run that girl off, Sheriff." Sada Pickins marched by him with her nose in the air.

Chaney frowned and wondered if *everyone* in town had seen his set-to with Morrow Beth.

"You'd best see about making things right with her." Will Bell passed on Chaney's other side. "That just ain't right, what happened. Just ain't right."

Chaney stopped, his jaw clenching as several more townspeople streamed around him on their way back to town, giving him advice or clucking their tongues in disapproval.

He sighed. Was nothing a secret in this town? One would think Chaney had compromised the woman in the worst way.

By the time he got to town, he was hard put to keep a rein on his temper. She was the one who'd asked his intentions regarding John Mark. She was the one who'd asked if he was suspicious of her brother.

Regret sawed through him. He'd hurt her, or frightened her. He wasn't sure which. He didn't want to discover that her brother was guilty of anything because then he'd have to do something. If worse came to worst, he would have to separate the family and he definitely didn't want to do that.

He walked through the back side of the livery and deposited the blanket and tablecloth in the Huckabees' wagon. She thought he'd been in on that blatant attempt to get them together for lunch, that he wanted to eat with her so he could ask questions about her brother.

He simmered with resentment. He hadn't known a blamed thing about that little plan Bonnie and Polly had cooked up. It was obvious Morrow Beth hadn't either. Furthermore, he *had* wanted to have lunch with her! Now besides this sinking sense of disappointment, he felt cursed by this inexplicable urge to apologize.

Why should he apologize? He was only doing his job. He had only been answering *her* questions.

Once outside the livery, he angled around the corner. Catcalls and whistles sounded from up the street and he saw the riders for the horse race were poised to begin in front of the bank. He stepped up onto the porch of the newspaper office and leaned against one of the pillars.

He set his jaw stubbornly. No, this time he wasn't apologizing.

The mayor fired the shot to begin the race and horses pounded toward Chaney. Screams and hollers carried on the March wind and he eyed the riders as they thundered past. He spied Hal Morland and Cholly and Davie Warner on the three lead horses.

The riders whooped as they flew past, the horses'

hooves spraying dirt across Chaney's boots. He smiled in anticipation as he watched Davie Warner's horse over-take the lead. She rode to the end of town and circled around the back side. Between the buildings on the other side of the street, Chaney caught sight of them, Davie still leading.

They disappeared for a moment, the sound of thudding hooves mixed with the calls and whistles from bystanders. Then the riders appeared at the other end of town, where they'd started. The crowd erupted in a roar of encourage-ment.

Davie Warner still held the lead and Chaney grinned. Hal Morland closed in on her, but Davie crossed the finish line first.

"Yippee!" Even among all the other cheers and yell-ing, Chaney recognized Billy Jack Huckabee's voice.

He grinned, starting toward Royce's store where the seed-spitting contest would be held. Squinting against the midday sun, he quickly spied the straw hats of the cow-boys from Kansas.

There had been no disturbance during lunch. Of course, if there had, would he have noticed? he wondered wryly. He'd been so wrapped up in Morrow Beth he doubted he would have noticed if a twister had touched down right in front of him.

Just her name stirred up a passel of longing and frus-tration and stubborn pride. He couldn't afford to get tan-gled up with her. No matter that his heart seemed lighter when she was around or that he somehow felt he belonged here in Scrub. No, he should definitely keep a distance from her. He should—

Who the hell was she with?

She was standing next to one of those Kansas cowboys. They stood at the back of a throng of people gathered to witness the seed-spitting contest. That cowboy, Rick something, was standing a little too close for Chaney's liking.

The man's chest brushed her shoulder and she stood there as if she didn't mind it one bit. Chaney clenched his teeth. She was none of his concern. She could do what she wanted, with whomever she wanted.

Even as he told himself that, he eased up behind them, his gaze boring into her back. She shifted from one foot to the other, then looked over her shoulder.

Her eyes frosted over and she turned away. His irritation notched up a level.

"Why don't you go get her?" Sada's voice sounded at his elbow and Chaney jerked, startled.

He edged back, asking nonchalantly, "Who?"

Sada smiled knowingly and pointed toward Morrow Beth. "Aren't you thinking about her, Chaney?"

"Only when I'm awake," he muttered in resigned frustration. "Or asleep."

"Then go get her," the older woman urged. She nodded, then walked away and took a place next to Rick Blansford.

Chaney's gaze moved to Morrow Beth just as the cowboy next to her leaned close and whispered something in her ear. She smiled up at him, nodding. An unfamiliar burn spread through Chaney's chest and he clenched his teeth so hard he nearly snapped his jaw clean in two.

Rick took Morrow Beth's arm and guided her down into the street. Chaney's eyes narrowed. The cowboy didn't seem too steady on his feet. Suspicion inched up Chaney's spine and his gaze scanned the crowd for John Mark. No sign of him.

Now that Chaney thought about it, John Mark hadn't

been seen since the beginning of the picnic. Exactly where was Morrow Beth's brother and what was he doing? Chaney quickly spied both of the Jones sisters, so he knew John Mark wasn't with them.

"Go, Billy Jack! Go!" Morrow Beth's voice was somehow distinguished over the cluster of other yells and encouragements.

Chaney's gaze honed in on her. Excitement flushed her face and she leaned forward, urging her brother on. She said something to Rick, who laughed, and Chaney once again felt that unidentified heat go through him.

He kept telling himself he should go look for John Mark, but he suddenly decided Morrow Beth needed looking after as much as her brother.

He wanted to march over there and kiss her until her knees buckled, but she had made her choice. And it hadn't been him. He eyed the cowboy, hoping the guy was drunk, hoping he would take liberties with Morrow Beth, anything so that Chaney could get his hands on him just once.

"So, what do you think of the festivities, Sheriff?" The elusive John Mark stepped up beside him, hooking his thumbs in his waistband.

Chaney shot a glance at him. John Mark didn't look inebriated. Nor did he smell it. Chaney smiled. "Everyone seems to be having a good time."

"Yep." John Mark rocked back on his heels, his gaze skimming over the crowd, then he frowned. "I thought you had lunch with Morrow Beth."

"I did."

"Then why is she with Blansford?"

"Her choice, I suppose." Chaney tried to keep his voice even. What had happened at lunch wasn't John

Mark's fault. "I don't have a claim on her, John Mark."

The other man grinned. "Maybe you oughta get one."

Chaney arched a brow and John Mark stepped off the porch, walking toward the crowd. "Somebody needs to keep up with her."

Chaney's gaze followed the other man and as he looked over the crowd, he stiffened. He searched through the crowd, seeing dark hair, gray hair, auburn hair, but there was no sign of a woman with hair the color of golden fire.

Panic flared through him and he stepped forward, skirting the crowd, searching again. She was gone. With the cowboy.

❖ 12 ❖

THE WHOLE IDEA that Chaney might only be interested in her because of John Mark chafed. She had feared it all along, but to have it thrown in her face . . .

She didn't care. The defiant words rang hollow, but Morrow Beth vowed to prove them to Chaney White. Rick Blansford, one of the cowboys from Kansas, had seemed the perfect way to do that.

Now she wasn't so sure. Her anger had cooled and Rick was getting more inebriated by the minute. Morrow Beth didn't know where he had gotten the bottle of liquor he kept pulling from his back pocket, although she suspected it had come from John Mark. Where was Chaney when there was a legitimate reason for him to be around?

At the moment, he was nowhere to be seen. Morrow Beth thought if Rick breathed the raw odor of liquor in her face one more time, she would retch. If he put his arm around her waist once more, she was going to break it. And if he mumbled another drunken suggestion in her ear, she was going to scream.

Between the horse races and the seed spitting, she had politely tried to excuse herself, but then she'd seen Chaney looking at her with that possessive, stubborn look and she'd pretended to enjoy Rick's company.

After the three-legged race, which Billy and Katie won, Morrow Beth saw her opportunity. As the crowd moved to the east end of Main Street to watch the egg toss, she slipped away from Rick and headed around the back of Henry's Mercantile.

She was still angry at Chaney's declaration of intending to prove his suspicions about John Mark, but she regretted accusing him of using her to get to John Mark. Still, he hadn't denied it.

She should remember *that,* instead of the hurt that had flared in his eyes.

She should remember that he had stated outright his intention to prove her brother's guilt. Maybe that would help dull the ache that speared through her like a broken blade and would cool the heat that seemed to flush her body whenever he was near.

Standing in a narrow strip of shade provided by the store's roof, she leaned against the back wall of Henry's store and fanned herself. Her carefully braided chignon drooped. She was hot and clammy. Wisps of hair tickled her nape, her ears, her cheeks.

She pushed away the stray strands and closed her eyes.

"You're not hiding from me, are you?"

Morrow Beth's eyes flew open.

Rick stood at the corner of the store, leaning against the side of the building. Which was probably the only way he was able to stand.

The sharp tang of liquor floated to her and she straightened, moving back a step. "Just needed a breath of air."

"There's air all around—" *Hiccup.* "Oh, 'scuse me."

He grinned and tilted forward, gripping the edge of the building to keep from falling.

Morrow Beth sighed. "You'd best get on back, Rick. I want to be alone for a minute."

"Can't be alone." He shook his head, his words slurred as he slunk toward her, his gait loose and liquid. He hiccupped again. "You're with me."

Her eyes narrowed. He was most assuredly drunk. She smiled, trying to decide the best way to handle him.

"We can stay back here if you want." He waved a finger at her, then grasped the wall for support as he felt his way toward her. "All kinds of privacy."

She did not want privacy with *him*. She retreated another step. "We should get back before we're missed."

She couldn't pick him up and carry him as she would Flower, but she could probably coax him back to the crowd. Moving away from the wall, she stayed well out of his reach as she inched around him. "Let's go back to town."

"Let's not." He swayed toward her and somehow managed to latch on to her wrist.

"Rick, let go."

"Wanna kiss."

She wrinkled her nose in distaste, trying to tug away from his surprisingly strong hold. "How about some lemonade?"

"No, not lem'nade." He tugged her toward him. "Kiss."

She planted her feet in the dry hard ground. "Let go of me, Rick," she said softly. "You're hurting me."

"Don't wanna hurt. Wanna kiss. C'mon, honey." He tugged harder. "Just one little kiss. C'mon."

"No." His slurred endearment made Morrow Beth's skin prickle with distaste. She sidestepped him, dodging hands that, though clumsy, were quick. "Maybe when we get back to town. Let's go, now."

"Justalittleone." His words ran together and he pulled her into him.

The odor of liquor hit her square in the face and she recoiled in distaste, trying to push him away. "No, Rick!"

"The lady said no."

Chaney! Morrow Beth looked over Rick's shoulder to see the sheriff scowling darkly.

Rick squinted, his head bobbing as he looked over his shoulder at Chaney. "Oh, Sheriff." He turned back to Morrow Beth, whispering loudly, "It's the sheriff. I'll take care of him."

She shook her head in exasperation, trying to pry Rick's strong fingers from her wrist.

Chaney walked up to them, his gaze raking over Morrow Beth. In a hard voice she'd never heard him use, he rapped, "Blansford, release the lady."

"But I—we—" The cowboy stuttered, frowning in confusion.

Morrow Beth took advantage of Rick's diverted attention to pull out of his grasp. "He wasn't hurting me," she said quietly. "He just wouldn't take no for an answer."

Chaney completely ignored her. He reached up and grasped Rick's shoulder. "Why don't you come with me, cowboy?"

"I think I can handle it now, Chaney." She didn't like the accusing light in his eyes, as if he thought she were getting what she deserved. "It *is* my business, after all."

"Actually, since your friend here is drunk, it's *my* business."

Chaney snarled the word "friend" as if she and the cowboy had been doing something illicit. Rick might have been doing something wrong, but he'd been doing it alone.

"Leave us alone, Sheriff." The other man straightened and stared down at Chaney, his eyes crossing. "Can't you see we want some privy—I mean—" He hiccupped again. "Privacy."

Before she knew what he was about, Rick grabbed for her. She hopped easily out of his reach.

He frowned and shuffled toward her. "C'mon, honey."

Chaney reached for Rick again. "Let's go, mister. You know I'm the law. Don't make me do something we'll both regret."

"Like what?" sneered Rick, swaying toward Chaney.

His lips flattened and impatience tightened his features. "I'm getting real tired of playing nice. Now, come on."

"Ain't goin' nowhere." Rick squinted at Chaney, trying to look fierce and looking only as if he were nearsighted.

Chaney sighed, eyeing Rick the way he would an obnoxious fly.

Morrow Beth stepped back, rubbing her wrist. It wasn't Rick's touch she could still feel on her skin, but Chaney's.

The drunken cowboy swayed toward Chaney, wagging his finger. "I haven't done nothing wrong. I don't have to come with you."

Chaney caught the man by the shoulders. "You're drunk. That's against the law."

"I ain't hurtin' nothin'."

"Where'd you get the liquor?"

Rick blinked slowly, then smiled adoringly at Morrow Beth.

She frowned. Why was he looking at her?

Chaney glanced at her, suspicion narrowing his eyes.

She drew herself up. Surely he didn't think Rick had gotten that liquor from her?

Rick hiccupped again and grinned. "Can't tell you."

"You're going to have to sleep it off in the jail, Rick."

"But I didn't do nothing!"

"You can hardly stand up. Come on, let's go."

Rick shook his head, his hand moving to the pistol at his hip.

Chaney groaned. "You don't want to do that."

"Me and the girl want some privacy. Now git!"

Chaney looked at Morrow Beth. "Do you want to be alone with him?"

Part of her wanted to say yes, but only out of wounded pride. "No."

Relief flared in Chaney's eyes and he looked back at Rick. "You heard the lady. Let's go. You can sleep it off in the jail."

"Do you have to do that, Chaney?"

A muscle flexed in his jaw and his eyes looked brittle. "Are you saying you do want to be alone with him after all, Morrow Beth?"

"No!" Her temper flared. "No, I wasn't asking because of that. I was hoping you wouldn't have to put him in jail."

"He's drunk. Since he can't behave, he can sleep it off in one of my cells. He'll be fine. It's to keep the peace."

Her gaze flickered to Rick and back to Chaney. Although she was unfamiliar with this hard-edged side of him, she didn't believe he would put Rick behind bars just to satisfy his anger at her. "All right."

Surprise flitted across Chaney's stern features as he turned to the other man. "Let's go."

"I ain't!" He fumbled for his gun, managing to look fierce despite his glazed eyes. "I told you—"

Chaney grabbed Rick's arm and at the same time pulled the flat bottle of liquor out of Rick's back pocket. "I got better things to do than play nursemaid to you."

Rick stiffened, yanking his arm out of Chaney's grasp and swinging at him.

Chaney ducked and rose fluidly. "C'mon."

She stepped back, frowning. Even though Rick was drunk, he outweighed Chaney by maybe twenty pounds and stood about three inches taller. If he hit Chaney—

Rick swung again, his fist connecting with only air. "Damn," he mumbled.

Chaney shook his head, looking more annoyed than angry. He unscrewed the lid on Rick's bottle, labeled Extract of Sarsaparilla, and poured out the contents. A stout odor bloomed between them and Morrow Beth knew as well as Chaney did that the contents weren't sarsaparilla at all, but corn liquor.

Rick saw his liquor watering the ground and cried out, "Sheriff! Sheriff, no!"

Chaney eyed the other man with a mixture of irritation and amusement.

Rick swung out again and Chaney sidestepped him. Before Rick's arm had dropped to his side, Chaney wrenched the cowboy's arm behind his back and pushed him forward. "Enough dillydallyin'."

Rick protested and struggled, but Chaney held him easily. He glanced over his shoulder at Morrow Beth. "You coming?"

"I don't think so—"

"You're coming."

Who did he think he was, ordering her around? She took in the fierceness in his eyes, the stubborn angle of his jaw, and opened her mouth to refuse.

"Please?"

His tone went from forceful to gentle and she blinked at the abrupt change. She found herself nodding.

Irritated, she told herself she was only going in order

to make certain that Rick didn't turn on John Mark. But as she followed Chaney and Rick around the store toward the jail, she knew it wasn't true. Not completely, anyway.

"You can't do this!" Rick protested. "Let me go. My friends will be looking for me. They'll be here any minute."

"Got plenty of room for them, too," Chaney said.

Morrow Beth bit back a smile. Did anything ever faze him? She looked over her shoulder, watching for Rick's friends or John Mark or anyone from town. The townspeople were gathered in front of the school for the egg toss. No one even noticed Morrow Beth or the two men in front of her.

She hoped no one noticed at all because she was pretty sure Rick had gotten that moonshine from John Mark.

The cowboy hadn't told where he'd gotten the liquor, not yet, but that wasn't to say he wouldn't. Morrow Beth hurried to catch up to Chaney, listening intently to the cowboy's mutterings. His words were incoherent except for the occasional curse at the sheriff.

Still holding his prisoner by the arm, Chaney pushed Rick up the steps and into his office. He guided the man into the first cell and loosed him. "Have a seat. You're gonna be here awhile."

Rick lunged at him, but Chaney stepped neatly aside, then out of the cell. Locking the door, he peered through the bars at Rick. "You're my first prisoner. Don't you feel honored?"

Rick stumbled forward, grabbing the bars. "Let me outta here! Morrow Beth, honey, go get Frank."

She looked away, watching as Chaney walked over and shut the door.

"Just have a seat on the cot there, Blansford. Take a little rest. When you wake up, you can probably leave."

"I can't stay in here. I ain't never been in jail." Rick flopped down on the cot, burying his head in his hands and bawling like a new calf.

Chaney shook his head, walked over and tossed the empty liquor bottle into his bottom drawer.

Morrow Beth watched with trepidations. She didn't want to talk to Chaney about her brother.

Sadness pulled at her and she turned to go. "Guess I'd better get back. My family will be looking for me."

"Stay."

She paused, feeling the tension circle the room around her. "I don't think it's a good idea."

"I think it's the best idea." He stood behind her, so close that his breath stirred the hair at her nape.

She turned her head slightly, catching his strong jaw and chin in her line of vision. "Chaney, we both know—"

"Something's going on, Morrow Beth. Something's . . . changed. I know it and so do you. Stay."

Her breath hitched in her chest. Did he mean *something* about her and him?

Over in the cell, Rick flopped back on the narrow cot, blubbering, "My friends ain't gonna like this. They're gonna be real mad."

Chaney leaned closer to her. "Stay. Talk. We can go out back."

She turned then, uncertainty winding through her. But there was also curiosity and anticipation. Something told her she shouldn't leave just yet. She should hear him out. She *wanted* to hear him out.

She sensed this wasn't about John Mark at all, but her. Chaney and her. She swallowed hard, hating the way her heart raced, the way her palms sweated. "All right."

* * *

Chaney wasn't sure what he was going to say, but he couldn't let Morrow Beth walk away. A sense of urgency unwound inside him. He cared for her, somehow amidst all this business with his job. He thought she might care for him, too. And he wanted to explore that.

Because of his investigation of John Mark, Chaney had told himself to stay away from her, but he couldn't do it any longer. He didn't want to do it. He didn't know how, but somehow he was going to keep his feelings for Morrow Beth separate from his investigation of her brother.

He thought, he hoped, that Morrow Beth didn't have anything to do with moonshining. Even if he'd suspected her in the beginning, Chaney wouldn't have believed it now. She was too honest, too responsible for those kids, and he just felt it in his gut.

She might not be making the stuff herself, but her brother very well could be. And when Chaney thought about her associating with people like Rick Blansford, his temper flared. He was glad he'd found her before Blansford had gotten out of hand.

The memory of that cowboy touching her sparked a core of anger. Chaney yanked off his hat and slapped it against his thigh. "What were you thinking to go off with him? You knew he was drunk—"

"I didn't go off with him." Her eyes widened. "He followed me."

Chaney was pleased to hear that Morrow Beth hadn't suggested Rick accompany her behind the store, but it still got under his skin that she'd left him standing high and dry at the picnic to be with Blansford. "If you hadn't been leading him on in the first place, he might not have followed you."

"I wasn't leading him on." Her features tightened and her eyes shot green fire.

"Oh, no?" Chaney slammed his hat back on his head. "You weren't laughing up at him as if he were the only man on earth?"

Her jaw dropped and she stared at Chaney. "Are you jealous?"

"No!" he roared. "Yes. And I'll tell you why. Because of this." Before he even thought about what he was doing, he grabbed her and hauled her to him.

She squirmed, pushing at his chest. "Let go of me."

"No." He anchored her to him, one hand to her head, the other arm locked tight around her waist. Before she could draw a breath, his mouth slammed against hers.

Anger and desire and regret swelled through her and she fought him, pushing and straining to pull away.

Then his lips turned coaxing, stealing the life from her anger. She felt him relax just slightly. Afraid he would pull away, she gripped his shirt front and held him to her.

But he didn't go anywhere. His hard thighs braced against hers. His gun belt dug into her belly. His chest was solid against her breasts. His lips ravaged hers and she gloried in it. She wanted him to kiss her forever.

Her chest tightened. Her head swam at the insistent pressure of his lips. He raised his head, his breathing ragged. She stared up at him, her own breath shallow in her chest, her heart thumping painfully against her ribs.

"Oh, my stars."

His eyes gleamed with male satisfaction. His gaze dropped to her lips. "We gotta talk."

He planted his hands on his hips and walked the length of the jail.

She was still searching for a full breath. So was he.

He paced back to her and stared for a long hard minute.

Her lips throbbed from his and she wanted to feel them again. Wonder coursed through her at the sensation, the pleasure, the sense of completion she felt. And in his eyes she saw the same wonder.

She wanted to fling herself against him, kiss him again, but she fought the urge. She trembled and clasped her hands, looking away, searching for composure.

He rubbed the back of his neck and heaved a deep sigh.

"If you apologize for that, I'll hit you," she said quietly.

He froze, his gaze locking on hers. "No, I'm not going to apologize."

Pleasure shot through her and she swallowed. "Good."

Blood raced through her veins and her skin felt on fire. Her heart thundered in her ears.

"You are something else, Morrow Beth."

The low timbre of his voice shot sensation up her spine and she clasped her hands tighter, searching for control, fighting the urge to lean into him again.

She didn't want to think about anything except Chaney, but she forced herself to ask why he'd brought her out here. She licked her lips, then froze as she noticed his heated gaze locked on her mouth. "Chaney."

His name was a plea, a question.

He cleared his throat, dragging his gaze away for a moment. He wanted to kiss her again, wanted to kiss that creamy patch of skin just below her ear, to bury his hands in the thick satin of her hair.

"What do we do now?" Her question mirrored the racing doubt, the same question he'd been tiptoeing around.

"I want to see you. I want to call on you," he blurted. "I want you to be my girl."

She started, her eyes growing wide.

He cursed under his breath. "I should've asked. I *am* asking."

"Why?"

"*Why?* How can you ask me that after what just happened?"

"I want to know." She stared at him with a mixture of uncertainty and defiance. "I have to know. You just told me that you suspect John Mark, that you're going to try and prove him guilty. I won't help you do that."

"I don't expect you to." He frowned, puzzled. "I haven't asked you to. Nor would I. One doesn't have to have anything to do with the other."

"How can you say that?" She pulled her hands from his and walked past him, her skirts brushing his leg. "That's why you started coming around in the first place."

"Well, it's not why I want to keep coming around." He snagged her elbow and turned her to him, staring straight into her eyes, urging her to believe him.

He cocked his head, wondering how she could question him after what had just erupted. Then he understood. She wanted to hear him say it.

"Because I can't think about anything but you. Because I want to see you every day. Because I dream about you." He stepped toward her, noting how she watched him warily, but didn't move away. "Because I want to kiss you again right now."

Pleasure flared in her eyes, but she remained where she was, arms folded tight against her body. "That's all?"

Want bored straight through his middle and he gave a hoarse laugh. "Isn't that enough?"

"I mean—" She licked her lips, looking straight at him. "Are you sure you're not interested in me because of my brother?"

"Morrow Beth, your brother has nothing to do with what I feel for you."

She arched her dark brows. "Nothing?"

"Nothing." He moved closer, his heat joining with hers, the soft scent of her driving him crazy. "This isn't about your brother at all. I don't want to talk about him when I'm with you. In fact—" His gaze dropped to her lips. "I don't want to talk at all."

She blushed and a small smile played about her lips.

"I want to see you. *You,*" he said authoritatively. "If you'll allow it."

"What about your job? What about John Mark?"

"What about those things? Ask me whatever you want."

She twisted her hands. "You told me at lunch that you suspect him of moonshining."

"Yes," he said softly, his gaze caressing her features.

"Are you—will you—" She drew a deep breath and faced him, her jaw firming stubbornly. "Are you planning to use me to try and trip him up? Because I won't be used. I won't allow that. I won't—"

"No." He gripped her shoulders, forcing her gaze to his. "No. I would never do that. I couldn't use you like that. I can keep my job separate from my feelings for you."

"Your feelings?" Her heartbeat stuttered.

He caressed her cheek, hoping she could see his heart in his eyes. He would have Morrow Beth and his job, too. "We can try, can't we?" He raised his right hand. "I swear I can keep the two things separate. I can. If you'll agree."

"I want to."

"But?"

"I can't risk my family, Chaney. I'm not saying they're doing anything wrong, but if *you* believe they are, I can't help you."

"Silly woman, haven't you heard anything I've said?"

She searched his eyes.

"I swear, Morrow Beth," he said fervently.

"I want to believe you."

"Then do."

Uncertainty flitted across her features.

He clasped her hands in his. "Say yes, Morrow Beth."

"I want to see you, too," she admitted, lacing her fingers with his.

"Tell me when. Where?"

"You promise you won't try to get information out of me?"

"As if I could!" He laughed.

"Promise."

"We don't even have to talk about your family if you don't want. Lord knows, when I'm with you, it's not your brother I'm thinking about."

She smiled and looked down, suddenly shy. "And what about when you're kissing me?"

"Haven't got a thought in my head," he teased gently, tipping her chin up and staring straight into her eyes. "Want me to prove it?"

She smiled into his eyes. "Yes, I think so."

He leaned in, touching his lips gently to hers.

This kiss was different, not desperate but gentle, exploring. He wanted to taste her, learn every sweet inch of her. Fueled by curiosity and pleasure, his mouth coaxed hers wider and she opened to him.

Looping her arms around his neck, she gave herself up to him. Fire lanced his gut and Chaney pulled her closer, sliding a hand down the trim length of her back to the flare of her hip.

He pulled her into him, throbbing, wanting her to see how she affected him. When she didn't stiffen or try to pull away, he pressed her against him. Her breasts flattened against his chest. He felt her nipples pearl through the fabric of her dress. Sweet desperation shot through him.

He forced himself to pull away, reluctant but aware of his responsibilities. Her face was flushed; her eyes dark with passion. "I think we'd better get back."

"Oh, of course." She pulled away and smoothed her hands over her skirts. "You probably need to keep an eye on things."

He lifted her hand, brushing a kiss across her knuckles. "I was actually thinking I might be tempted to lose my manners altogether if we stay back here much longer."

She blushed and laughed softly. "We'd surely better go then."

He tucked her hand into his arm and they walked out to the street.

• *13* •

CHANEY HADN'T EXACTLY made a promise to Morrow Beth, but he was going to act as if he had. There was no reason he couldn't keep his feeings for her separate from his investigation of her brother. There was no need to even discuss John Mark with her or to involve her in anything to do with moonshining, unless she chose to involve herself. And Chaney didn't think that would happen.

She'd only aligned herself with the Warner sisters because she'd thought to protect them. Now that she knew him a little better, she would know he wouldn't deliberately harm anyone. She would learn that, although he was determined to become the sheriff of Scrub, he was also determined to pursue this attraction he felt for her.

As they rounded the corner of Henry's store, the Warner sisters spied them.

"Oh, look," Cholly called. "It's the sheriff. And *Morrow Beth*."

It seemed to Chaney that her voice was unusually loud, but he didn't much care. All four of the Warner sisters hurried over, smiling and laughing, wanting to know if Chaney was enjoying the day.

"I am indeed, ladies." He smiled down at Morrow Beth. "But I'm really looking forward to the dance."

"Looks like you've already found a partner," Davie said with a quiet smile.

Morrow Beth blushed and smiled up at Chaney.

He patted her hand, still tucked in the crook of his arm. "I hope so, Miz Davie. I hope so."

The Warner sisters circled them, herding them back toward the crowd where the egg toss had just finished. Broken eggs littered the street and Chaney picked his way across, careful to guide Morrow Beth around the gooey mess.

"Look, everyone," Miss Clara called out. "It's the sheriff. And *Morrow Beth*."

Chaney bit back a smile, exchanging a look with Morrow Beth.

She grinned, saying in a low voice for him alone, "It's kind of charming, don't you think?"

He chuckled. "I've never been the object of a matchmaking scheme."

"Me, either."

Polly and Will Bell walked up. Will, looking extremely satisfied with himself, clapped Chaney on the back. "Glad to see you came to your senses, Sheriff. Miss Morrow Beth, I hope he apologized to you for that business at the creek."

A smile tugged at her lips. "Oh, yessir, Mr. Bell. He certainly did."

Chaney squeezed her hand, pleasure and arousal flowing through him.

Polly patted both their hands. "You make a lovely couple, dears."

"Thank you, ma'am." Morrow Beth searched through

the crowd, murmuring to Chaney. "Do you see my family? I haven't seen the twins in a while."

Scanning the crowd, his eyes narrowed thoughtfully at the group of cowboys standing at the back of the crowd. Those were the other men who had ridden in with Blansford. Chaney didn't want any trouble, but he had every intention of keeping an eye on the visitors.

Just behind them he spied John Mark and nodded in that direction. "There's your brother."

Morrow Beth followed the direction he was looking and John Mark waved at both of them. Chaney lifted a hand in greeting, wondering at the close-knit circle of men and what they were talking about.

He'd lay odds it was moonshine, but what would they dare to do right in front of him? He couldn't monitor every conversation of every citizen in this town.

It was difficult to be too concerned when Morrow Beth stood so close to him. Her breast slightly brushed his bicep, her sweet scent floated around him. She had agreed to let him call on her and Chaney's heart jumped in anticipation.

Bonnie strode by and stopped, speaking in a low aside to Morrow Beth, but eyeing Chaney with a satisfied smirk. He grinned at her.

"Morrow Beth! Morrow Beth!" Katie Jo ran up, her braids straggling into her face, her white pinafore stained with grass and dirt. "Hi, Marshal!"

Billy Jack was right on her heels. "Chaney, we won the three-legged race."

"I know." He smiled down at them. "I saw."

"And the egg toss. Did you see that?" Katie demanded.

"I missed that one."

"Well, we would've won if it hadn't been for Billy dropping that last egg."

"You didn't throw the dang thing far enough," her brother protested. "I could hardly reach it."

Morrow Beth wagged a finger at him. "Billy."

"Oh, shoot. I mean, oh, darn—" He stomped his foot. "Well, *what* can I say, Morrow Beth? Ain't no other words to use when you're mad."

Katie Jo stuck out her tongue, then smoothed her hair back, staring up at Chaney. "Are you gonna dance with me, Marshal?"

"I'd be honored." He bowed slightly and Morrow Beth smiled up at him. Chaney decided he would do just about anything to get her to smile at him like that all the time. "How about you, Billy Jack?"

The little boy's eyes rounded in horror. "I ain't dancin' with you, Chaney!"

He threw back his head and laughed. "That's not what I meant."

Morrow Beth and Katie laughed, too. Billy's face crumpled in relief. "Boy oh boy."

Katie sidled up to Chaney's other side and took his hand. He smiled down at her.

"I think they're about to put out supper."

"Shall we go, then?" He glanced at Morrow Beth and she smiled in agreement, holding out her other hand to Billy Jack. "Ready to eat, Billy?"

"Yes!"

Together they walked over to the front of Bonnie's restaurant where the owner had set up several of her tables piled high with breads and cakes and vegetables. One table was reserved specifically for meat, everything from ham and beef to quail, squirrel, and rabbit.

Chaney and Billy seated Morrow Beth and Katie at one

of the tables inside and went out to fill plates for the women. He saw John Mark again squiring two of the Jones sisters and raised his hand in greeting. John Mark smiled and walked to the far table, filling plates for the two women.

Chaney saw no sign of the cowboys from Kansas and he wondered if they'd figured out yet that Blansford was missing. He returned to Morrow Beth with her plate, then excused himself to fill his own.

After making a quick run over to the jail to assure himself that Rick was still asleep, Chaney returned to Bonnie's restaurant. He ate a pleasant dinner with Morrow Beth and the twins, then watched as Billy and Katie darted off with Bonnie's boys.

Chaney pulled out Morrow Beth's chair and held out his hand to her. As soon as everyone had finished eating, Bonnie would move the tables aside to make room for dancing.

Taking Morrow Beth's hand, Chaney pulled her to her feet. "Would you care for a walk before the dance begins?"

"Yes." She looked at him shyly, but he read eagerness and pleasure in her eyes.

So far things were going very smoothly and he intended to keep it that way. They stepped outside, speaking to the Bells and Sada and Mayor Bushman.

"It's going to turn out to be a nice evening," Sada remarked, glancing at the sky already streaked with vibrant red and orange and yellow.

"Yes, it is," Chaney murmured, looking at Morrow Beth. He couldn't stop thinking about that kiss they'd shared and figured they were about due for another one. He lifted his hat in farewell. "If y'all will excuse us, we're going to take a turn around town before the dance begins."

"Certainly," Will boomed, eyeing them like a proud papa.

Sada and the mayor watched them speculatively and Chaney could still feel them watching as he and Morrow Beth stepped into the street and walked toward the east end of town.

"They're staring," she whispered.

"I know," he said in a low voice.

She glanced up at him, her eyes dark in the encroaching dusk. "Do you mind?"

"Not at all."

"Me either," she said with a soft catch in her voice.

That little breathlessness made Chaney's gut tighten and he glanced over his shoulder. The Bells and Sada had turned away with the mayor. Chaney pulled Morrow Beth into the alley between the land office and the dressmaker's shop.

"Chaney—"

He kissed her full on the lips, pulling her hard against him. She melted into him, her arms going around his neck, her mouth opening under his. A thrill shot through him that only this woman seemed able to give him, a sense of possession, of building need.

He wanted to kiss her forever, hear that little sound she made deep in her throat, feel the sweet curve of her body fitted to the hard length of his, but he drew away. His hands moved to her face and he stroked her cheeks gently. "I probably shouldn't have done that, but I couldn't help myself."

"You don't hear me complaining." She snuggled closer to him and her belly nudged his, causing a kick of arousal. In the darkness, her eyes were deep and trusting.

She stared up at him, looking as dazed as he felt. He stroked a wayward strand of hair from her cheek, pressing a light kiss to her lips. She smiled up at him and his heart turned over.

He could easily fall in love with Morrow Beth Huckabee, moonshining brother or not. Down the street, they heard the pluck of the fiddle, the whine of a harmonica.

"Sounds like they're starting," Morrow Beth murmured, her breath misting his lips.

He wanted to drink her in, run his hands over the lush curves of her body, but he forced himself to keep his hands lightly at her waist.

She stared up at him, desire sharp in her eyes. He pressed another kiss to her lips, soft and slow and wet. After a long minute, he raised his head, breathing roughly. "We'd better get down there before I lose my manners again."

She laughed softly. "I don't think you would ever lose your manners, Chaney. No matter what."

He smiled, but didn't say that he was perilously close to the edge right now. He wanted to peel that dress from her body, run his hands over every inch of velvety peach skin.

He gathered her hands in his and kissed them. "We'd better go."

They stepped out of the alleyway, and, hand in hand, walked back to Bonnie's. Light streamed out of the restaurant. Voices gathered in a dim roar. The fiddle and harmonica and banjo strummed to the tune of "Jimmy Crack Corn" and Chaney's blood picked up the rhythm of the song.

They stepped inside, staying close to the door. Bonnie's restaurant was nearly full to bursting. The musicians were crammed into the corner closest to the door. The tables were pushed to the opposite side of the room. They held lemonade and crocks of buttermilk and pitchers of water.

Couples skipped and glided around the room, swinging partners from one person to the next. Chaney's gaze searched through the crowd, but he saw no sign of the cowboys from Kansas. Maybe they'd already gone. And left Blansford to fend for himself. There was no sign of John Mark either.

Chaney determined to enjoy himself with Morrow Beth. With Blansford in jail, there wasn't likely to be further chaos. Chaney hadn't spied anyone else who looked to be intoxicated.

Just then the mayor whirled by with Clara Sue. She wriggled her fingers at Chaney, and trilled, "Hello, Sheriff!"

He smiled, the music's rhythm thumping around him. He turned to Morrow Beth. "Shall we dance?"

"Yes." She put her hand in his and they joined the group on the floor, becoming part of the weaving circle.

The band started "Pop Goes the Weasel" and Chaney twirled Morrow Beth around the room. She smiled up at him and his heart tightened. His hand flexed at her waist and he stared down at her, wishing he could kiss her right here.

She colored and glanced down. "Chaney," she said so low he could barely hear her. "You shouldn't look at me like that."

He squeezed her waist. "I can't help it. You're beautiful."

A smile bloomed on her face, lighting her eyes in a way that took his breath away. The music trailed off and they slowed, then stopped, clapping with the rest of the dancers. The crowd milled around them, several people inching past and going toward the drink tables.

Chaney turned to Morrow Beth. "Can I get you something to drink?"

"Lemonade would be nice," she said. Color flushed her cheeks, her eyes shining like polished emeralds.

He smiled down at her. "Don't run off anywhere."

"I won't."

Chaney turned to get their drinks, but paused when he heard a commotion at the door. Loud irate voices carried into the room and Chaney frowned.

John Mark stood in the doorway, his eyes zeroing in on Chaney.

Frank Carter pushed in behind John Mark, his voice loud enough to be heard over the din of voices and shuffling feet. "I wanna talk to him. Let me by."

He pushed past John Mark and stalked toward Chaney. The other two cowboys, Pete and Swish, followed. Their faces were red, their eyes bright with anger.

Chaney moved toward them. "What seems to be the problem, gentleman?"

"You do." Swish sneered over the heads of people standing between him and Chaney. Swish flanked Frank's right shoulder.

Pete moved up to Frank's left, glaring at Chaney.

"Shut up, boys." Frank threw his friends an irritated look and moved his attention back to Chaney, straining to be heard over the people between them. "Rick's gone. Something's happened to him and we want you to find him."

"Yeah," Pete put in. "We want to report him missing."

Trying to close the distance between him and the cowboys, Chaney elbowed his way between Will Bell and the mayor, who watched avidly. "He's not—"

"We were supposed to meet him in the livery," Frank said loudly. "But we been waiting over an hour and he's

not shown up. Since this is your town, we want some help
finding him.''

Chaney tensed. He wasn't close enough to smell liquor
on the three men, but he was almost positive they'd been
drinking. He knew they had to have gotten it here, because he'd checked all of their saddlebags when he'd gone
through the livery after lunch. ''I know where he is.''

Frank's eyes narrowed. ''You do?''

Chaney nodded. ''He's in my jail.''

Abrupt silence sliced through the room and Chaney
thought he heard a collective gasp.

Frank shook his head as if he hadn't heard Chaney
correctly. ''He's *where*?''

''In my jail.'' Chaney's voice sifted over the now-silent
crowd like dust over the prairie.

Rage gathered on Frank's blunt features. ''Well, let him
out.''

''Afraid I can't do that.'' People were tittering now,
eyeing Chaney with apprehension and foreboding. He was
well aware of John Mark making his way through the
crush of people toward him.

Morrow Beth stood behind him, quiet, but tense. The
crowd was heavily silent. He flexed his fingers, reassured
by the weight of his Colt at his hip. ''Your friend was
drunk. You know the rules in this town and so does he.
He's sleeping it off in jail.''

''You can't do that,'' Pete exploded, lunging for Chaney.

He drew his gun at the same moment that Frank
slammed a restraining arm into Pete's chest. ''Watch it,
Pete. He's got a gun.''

The crowd gasped, but Chaney didn't take his eyes off
the men in front of him. ''Now, unless you gentlemen

want to join Blansford, I suggest you step back and leave the party.''

"What the hell—'' Swish bellowed, moving toward Chaney.

"Hold on, hold on.'' John Mark finally managed to push his way through the crowd and placed himself between the three cowboys and Chaney. "Now, don't come any closer, fellas.''

He gazed at the three men in front of him, casually crossing his arms over his chest. "You boys heard the sheriff. We don't want no problems, not today on Easter. Why don't you just go on? You can wait on your friend or I'm sure he can find his way home.''

Chaney wondered when John Mark had become his ally, but he didn't take his gaze from the men in front of him. Chaney waggled his gun. "Blansford is free to go tomorrow. But I warn you, if I catch any of you with liquor on your breath, I'll have to do the same to you.''

Swish opened his mouth to say something and John Mark stepped in.

"Now, Swish, you were just saying you hoped Rick didn't show so you could dance with one of these pretty women.''

Swish flushed and glanced around.

"Looks like this is your chance.''

Chaney eyed them all. "You can stay, but only if you stay peaceably. I've got room in my jail for all of you.''

"There won't be no call for that, will there, Frank?'' John Mark's voice hardened.

Frank's gaze sliced to John Mark, measuring.

"Will there?'' Morrow Beth's brother asked again.

Frank looked down at Chaney's gun. Reluctantly, hesitantly, he nodded. "No.''

"Good.''

Though relieved, Chaney couldn't stem a flare of curiosity. When had John Mark become his deputy?

"Let's just go on outside, get a breath of air," John Mark urged cordially.

The three men eyed Chaney, clearly fighting anger, but at last they nodded and turned away.

"Why're you taking his side, Huckabee?" Frank muttered.

John Mark winked at Chaney then followed Frank. "Cool down, Frank. The sheriff's just doing his job."

Frank muttered something, glaring over his shoulder at Chaney.

He held the cowboy's gaze, slowly holstering his gun. The four men walked outside and disappeared into the darkness.

A sigh of relief eased out of Chaney and the crowd suddenly came alive again. Excited voices tittered and laughed nervously. Tension seeped slowly out of Chaney's shoulders. He turned to see Morrow Beth watching him with a combination of pride and worry.

"It's all right," he said quietly, taking her hand.

She smiled brightly. "At least John Mark helped you."

"Yes, he did." Chaney glanced thoughtfully at the open doorway, wondering again *why* John Mark had done such a thing.

Chaney hadn't smelled liquor on their breath, but then again he hadn't been close enough. John Mark had seemed awfully careful to stay between Chaney and the cowboys.

The crush of bodies in the restaurant, combined with the faint hint of sweat and perfumes, made it difficult to detect liquor on their breath. But he would bet his badge they'd been drinking, just like Blansford.

And they had probably gotten the stuff from John Mark.

Morrow Beth touched his shoulder. "Are you all right?"

"Sure." He wondered where John Mark and those guys had gotten off to, what they were doing. He should probably follow them.

"Do you need to leave?" Her gaze dropped uneasily to his gun and worry clouded her eyes.

He gave her a reassuring smile. "I should probably check on Rick."

She glanced at the door, then wistfully at the couple moving back to the middle of the floor. "One more dance?"

One dance wouldn't ruin his chances of catching those cowboys if they were doing something that needed catching.

Disappointment darkened her eyes and she glanced around. She looked over at the corner of the room. "Billy and Katie are already asleep. I guess we should probably go."

"One more dance won't hurt." He held out his hand as the fiddle player tuned up for "Silver Threads among the Gold."

"All right." She smiled up at him and as they twirled around the room, Chaney forced the incident with Frank Carter to the back of his mind.

But as he helped Morrow Beth carry the twins to the livery, he found himself scanning the streets for the cowboys. They were nowhere to be found. John Mark, however, was in the livery, hitching up the wagon.

He smiled at Chaney and took Billy from him, laying his brother gently in the back of the buckboard. He did the same with Katie Jo.

John Mark glanced at Morrow Beth, then Chaney, his eyes twinkling. Silently the big man walked around and climbed into the wagon.

Stepping a few feet away from the wagon, Morrow Beth's eyes shone at Chaney. "I had a wonderful time tonight."

"So did I." He wanted to kiss her, but not in front of John Mark. He also still needed to ask John Mark's permission to call on her. He took her hand, squeezing it warmly. "I hope to see you tomorrow?"

"Yes, I'd like that."

"How about a picnic?"

"Yes!" She squeezed his hand in return.

He walked her over to the wagon and helped her up. She was warm and light in his hands and he wanted to pull her against him. Instead he released her and gave her a little wink. She smiled and smoothed her skirts.

Moving around the head of the team, he came up on John Mark's side. "Thanks for your help tonight."

"Just being neighborly. You obviously had it handled."

Chaney nodded, his gaze shooting to Morrow Beth. She watched him with pleasure simmering in her eyes and he cleared his throat. "I was wondering . . . I'd like to call, er, I mean I'd like to get your permission to call on your sister."

John Mark's eyebrows shot up and he glanced in surprise at Morrow Beth. "Well, well."

She hit her brother on the thigh. "Just tell him yes."

He grinned, resting one hand on his thigh, frowning. "Let me see . . ."

Morrow Beth smacked him again and John Mark laughed. "That'd be right fine, Sheriff. Right fine, indeed."

Chaney grinned at Morrow Beth, but he couldn't stifle the feeling that John Mark seemed too pleased. As if he'd been hoping for just such a thing. But why would John Mark care?

Did he think Chaney's relationship with Morrow Beth would take precedence over his investigation into John Mark's activities? He would be sorely disappointed if he did.

Chaney grinned up at the other man, silently acknowledging a new challenge in the man's eyes. John Mark clucked to the team and they drove out of the barn.

Morrow Beth turned and waved. Chaney lifted a hand in farewell, pleasure sifting through him. He'd done it. Despite the interruption that could have turned ugly at the party, Chaney had handled Frank and his friends. And he'd also spent a delightful evening with Morrow Beth.

He walked back to the jail, whistling tunelessly. Yessir, he could certainly keep his feelings for her separate from his job. It wasn't nearly as hard as he'd expected.

Stopping at the jail to check on Blansford one last time, Chaney stepped inside and lit the lantern. He turned and walked over to the cell. Lantern light slanted between the bars, making deeper shadows, throwing into relief the ticked mattress.

He froze, staring from the cot to the floor and beneath the bed. What in the Sam Hill!

He toed open the cell door and walked inside, turning in a slow circle. Not one thing was disturbed, but Rick Blansford was gone.

From the corner of his eye, Chaney caught a glimmer in the strip of lantern light. He turned his head and his gaze fell on a bottle full of liquid. It lay on the cot, glaringly conspicuous. He hastily set the lantern on the floor and picked up the bottle.

Even before he opened it, he knew what it was. Anger started a slow build inside him. He unscrewed the lid on a flat bottle similar to the one he'd taken earlier from Blansford and the pungent odor of corn liquor hit him in the face.

Obviously Rick's friends had broken him out of jail while Chaney danced with Morrow Beth. They'd left this bottle as an affront to his authority.

Rage boiled through him and he stalked to his desk, coldly calculating a new plan. With deliberate movements, Chaney placed the liquor in his bottom drawer, well in the back. He would use their own joke to learn who'd made this liquor. And who'd sold it to them.

With a cold knot of dread forming in his gut, Chaney hoped it wasn't John Mark.

❖ 14 ❖

THIS HAD BEEN the best day of her life. She had fought her feelings for Chaney White, tried to deny them, but tonight they burst free like a bud springing from the ground. And he seemed to feel the same way about her.

He was taking her on a picnic tomorrow, just the two of them, with no talk of John Mark or moonshining or sheriffing. Morrow Beth could still feel the burn of Chaney's lips against hers, his strong hands gently stroking her face.

Anticipation wound into a tight knot in her belly. She had had plenty of beaux before, but none had ever made her feel this breathless eagerness, this tightness in her chest.

Night air wrapped around her and a full orange moon hung heavy in the sky. The wagon wheels grated on hard packed earth, creating a squeaking rhythm that lulled Morrow Beth, drawing her back into the memory of the dance she'd shared with Chaney.

She'd felt locked in a moment with him, uncaring of anything except the intense hunger in his eyes, that cocky grin. Music had flowed around them, webbing them in a place spun from light and sensation and their mingled scents.

Beside her, John Mark shifted, reminding her that she wasn't alone.

He slid a sideways glance at her. "Looks like you enjoyed yourself today."

"Yes, I did." She smiled at him, still wrapped in the warmth of Chaney.

Except for that one instance during the dance with the cowboys from Kansas, today had been almost perfect. "I appreciate you helping Chaney at the dance. I know he could've handled it on his own, but I'm glad he didn't have to. That was nice of you."

He shrugged. "Didn't do it to be nice. I didn't want no trouble."

She smiled. "Neither did he."

John Mark shot her a funny look. "I'd just sold those guys a fresh batch of moonshine. The last thing I needed was for them to get close enough to the sheriff for him to figure it out."

Morrow Beth's eyes widened. "Oh, John Mark, you didn't!"

"Of course I did. Do it every year. 'Course I was lucky that Rick didn't let on."

Morrow Beth shook her head, a sick feeling unraveling inside her.

"I don't know how you did it, Sister, but you did better than I ever hoped."

She frowned, trying to figure out exactly what John Mark intended. Because it was obvious that he intended something.

At her puzzled look, her brother said, "Chaney. How'd you get him to ask after you, ask to call on you?"

"I didn't!" Her brother's assumption that she could

have *convinced* Chaney to do something like that shattered the fragile memories she'd been reliving. "How could you even think it?"

"I know you said you didn't think it was a good idea, but even I never thought of this." Her brother gazed at her admiringly. "I never thought you had it in you."

"I don't!" she protested, casting a quick glance over her shoulder to make sure the twins still slept. They hadn't moved, but Morrow Beth lowered her voice anyway. "I can't believe you think I would do such a thing."

"Hey, I think it's good."

"I don't. And furthermore, that's not why I did it."

"Sister—"

"And another thing—" She leaned close, her voice harsh and low. "We agreed not to talk about you at all, so you don't talk about him either."

She crossed her arms, irritation spiraling through her.

"Well, I thank you anyway. He'll be so preoccupied with you he won't have time to bother about me."

She frowned at him, feeling suddenly uneasy with this new shift in her relationship with Chaney. "Don't think for a minute, John Mark, that I'm doing this to benefit you. My seeing Chaney has nothing to do with you."

"Of course not, Sister."

She sometimes hated that smooth confidence in his voice. "It doesn't! It has to do with me. And Chaney. I think I might love—"

"You think you what?"

"Never mind." She wasn't sure of her feelings for Chaney and she certainly wasn't going to share them with her brother who would probably try to use those to his advantage, too. "You know he's going to call for me. Don't use that to your advantage."

"I'm not taking advantage, Sister. It's family helping family."

She folded her hands in her lap, taking a deep breath, telling herself that John Mark wouldn't use her relationship with Chaney to protect himself. It didn't matter that he'd been urging her to do just that for him. He'd only been trying to goad her. She would explain to John Mark how important this was to her. He would understand.

Quietly, she said, "I like him. And he likes me. That's all it has to do with. We're not going to talk about you at all."

"Suits me fine. You don't have to talk about me. Just let me know if he plans to come after me."

She turned disbelieving eyes on him, whispering loudly, "Did you hear what I said? We're not going to talk about you! At all. He won't tell me anything. We both agreed and I'm not going to be the one to break the agreement."

John Mark studied her for a long minute, speculation narrowing his eyes. "You wouldn't even tell me if you knew he was coming after me?"

Unease curled through her. After tonight she didn't believe Chaney would worry too much about her family. Not after the things he'd said to her, *about* her, but if he did discover something about John Mark, he wouldn't tell *her*.

"You can't turn your back on family, Morrow Beth. You don't have it in you."

When had this become a choice between Chaney and her family? Even Chaney had promised to keep his job separate from his suspicions about her brother. Misery pinched at her. "There's no way I'll know that, John Mark."

"Even if he tells you? Or you ask him?"

"He *won't* tell me and I won't ask him."

"Not even to save your old brother?" John Mark turned suddenly serious and a chill skittered up her spine.

Morrow Beth shivered. "I can't ask anything about you, John Mark. Chaney and I agreed. In fact, it was my idea."

"I see." Hurt flared in his eyes and he turned away, quiet and stoic.

Morrow Beth ached inside. She laid her hand on her brother's arm. "Can't you see he's different from all the other beaux I've had? I think there could be something there. Please don't ask me to use him that way. I can't do it."

He sat there for a long moment, then straightened, his features once again relaxed. "It's okay, Morrow Beth. I'll do just fine."

His abrupt change caused her to frown. "What are you thinking of doing?"

"Nothing for you to worry about."

"John Mark—"

"I don't want to compromise you, Morrow Beth. It's best if you don't know."

She gritted her teeth, fuming as they pulled up to their barn. "Sometimes you make me so mad."

He leveled a long look on her. "I know the feeling, Sister. I know the feeling."

He jumped down and led the team into the barn.

"Don't you be getting any ideas," she whispered roughly. But he ignored her.

Chaney couldn't get the thought out of his mind. Ever since last night, when he'd discovered Rick gone, Chaney couldn't help wondering if Morrow Beth had been involved in some way.

Oh, Chaney knew she hadn't actually busted Rick out of jail, but had she been a distraction while her brother had done so?

Chaney didn't tell a soul about Blansford being sprung from jail, didn't tell a soul about the liquor bottle left as a taunt. But he made a thorough sweep of the town that morning.

He chatted with Bonnie while scanning her dining room. There were no jars to match the one he'd found, no odor of liquor. When she went into the kitchen, he searched the sideboard and found only china and silverware and glassware.

Following her into the kitchen on the pretense of getting a piece of pie, he tasted or smelled everything in sight, from pickles and pecans to mincemeat and cheese. He found nothing suspicious.

Just as thoroughly, he searched Royce's general store, Sada's newspaper office, the bank, the mayor's office, the dressmaker, the blacksmith, all while making pleasant conversation about the Easter festivities.

At every establishment except Royce's store, Chaney found tiny little brown bottles. They were all empty, all lettered with crooked handwriting that read Tonic.

With a sigh of resignation, Chaney realized where the "tonic" had come from. Half an hour later he stood in the doorway of the Warner place.

Clara Sue opened the door and smiled broadly. "Good day, Sheriff."

He removed his hat, wishing he didn't have to do this again. "Good day, Clara Sue. I hope your sisters are home."

"Why, yes!" She invited him inside, her blue eyes warm. "What can we do for you?"

"I've come about this." He pulled his hand from behind his back, revealing a fistful of tonic bottles.

Her gaze froze on the bottles then moved slowly to his. "Oh, dear."

"Yes, I'm afraid so."

Chaney had broken down the Warner sisters' still again. Despite their arguments that Congress was sure to declare their land as Oklahoma Territory and legalize liquor, Chaney wouldn't be swayed. He couldn't be.

"Please don't make me come back, ladies."

The four of them stood quietly at the doorway, watching with wide, sad eyes as if he'd just arrested their best friend. He hated doing this to them *again*, but what choice did he have?

He walked away, hoping this wouldn't set the tone of his day. The prospect of spending the afternoon with Morrow Beth was marred by the suspicion that wouldn't leave him be. The suspicion that had taunted him since Blansford's disappearance.

Had Morrow Beth been used to distract him while Blansford was sprung? And during the celebration yesterday while John Mark sold his liquor in town?

Chaney's visit to the Warner sisters left him feeling unsettled and he wanted to talk to Morrow Beth, let the gentle warmth of her laughter wash away the heaviness of his day. He wanted to look into her green eyes and forget, for just a minute, that he'd once again hurt those four ladies.

He picked up the picnic basket that Bonnie had packed for him and rented a buggy from the livery. Reaching the Huckabee place, he reined up in front of the house and set the brake.

Hopping down, he strode to the front door and knocked. After several seconds, he knocked again, but there was still no answer. Perhaps she was out back or in the barn.

He moved down the steps, went through the gate, and walked into the barn. But there was no sign of her. "Morrow Beth!" he called.

There was no answer. Chaney turned, walking out the door and toward the house. As he reached the corner, he opened his mouth to call out again, but heard a noise.

John Mark's deep voice carried around the corner. "You don't have to do anything other than what you've been doing. It's working out just fine."

"I keep telling you—"

Chaney strained to hear. He recognized Morrow Beth's voice, but couldn't understand what she said. He started down the side of the house to announce himself, but halted when he heard a reference to himself.

"You're not hurting the sheriff and he's not hurting me. I think that's a pretty good situation."

Chaney froze. What was John Mark talking about?

Morrow Beth said something, obviously perturbed.

John Mark chuckled. "He enjoys your company. He'll never suspect a thing."

Realization sliced through Chaney like a razor. It sounded as if John Mark wanted Morrow Beth to distract him from his job. Is that what had happened last night?

All the suspicion he'd tried to deny came pouring back. No, Morrow Beth would never do such a thing. Would she? He wanted to ask her, but that would tip his hand. He strained to hear more, but Morrow Beth and her brother were silent. He wanted to hear her deny it, but she didn't.

He called in a loud voice, "Morrow Beth!"

She hurried around the house, her eyes glowing, her

face flushed. Even after hearing what he had, her smile still caused his body to harden.

He forced himself to smile, his gaze searching hers.

She paused, smiled questioningly at him, and he moved forward, taking her hand.

"You look pretty." He circled around her, admiring her creamy yellow dress and her thick hair caught in a low chignon.

"Thank you." She smiled, which caused a kick to his gut. "Let me get my hat. I'll be right back."

She hurried up the front steps and into the house.

"Hello, Sheriff." John Mark leaned indolently against the corner of the house, a blade of grass poking out one side of his mouth.

"Hey, John Mark." Chaney kept his voice easy, but his muscles tensed as he studied the other man.

Morrow Beth returned, tying a floppy straw bonnet on her head.

"Where y'all off to?" John Mark's question was innocent enough, but the interest in his eyes was avid and real.

Chaney smiled. "That's a surprise for Morrow Beth." He met her at the bottom of the steps. "Ready?"

"Yes." She waved to her brother and walked with Chaney to the buggy.

He helped her inside, then climbed in himself. Gathering the reins, he turned the gray mare he'd rented and waved to John Mark. One way or another Chaney would discover if Morrow Beth was feigning interest in him to help her brother. He didn't see how she could fake her response to his kisses, but he couldn't dismiss the possibility.

He could discern no deceit in her eyes or her open smile. She pointed out a blue jay sweeping down from a tree and a chattering squirrel on a branch overhead. Pleasure warmed her features as she spied a cluster of pink and yellow flowers beside the road.

She didn't refer to last night or even ask about Rick Blansford. Chaney had learned of this spot from Sada and when he could see the creek through the trees, he guided the mare toward the water.

Thick tree branches crisscrossed overhead, providing a canopy of shade. Chaney stopped the horse, throwing the brake before helping Morrow Beth down.

"It's beautiful." She turned in a circle, surveying the small clearing and the sparkling water. "I didn't know you knew about this spot."

"Sada told me." He picked up the basket Bonnie had packed for him and a worn checkered tablecloth she'd given him. An old pecan tree guarded the creek bank and Chaney chose a spot beneath the tree.

Morrow Beth removed her hat and placed it in the buggy. "It's so shady here I don't need it."

He smiled, wondering if her innocent chatter was designed to keep his mind on her and off of her brother. He didn't like thinking it, but he couldn't dismiss what he'd heard.

He spread out their lunch and they ate. Occasionally she would ask him a question or point out something at the creek. He watched her, hoping to hell he had misheard her brother, that she wasn't involved in any way in trying to keep him from learning something about John Mark.

They had agreed to keep away from topics of her family or his job. Chaney was curious to see if she would abide by their agreement. After lunch, he packed everything away.

"What would you like to do now?"

She sat on the tablecloth with her feet tucked under her. "Do you need to get back?"

"Not particularly."

"Then why are you standing all the way over there?" She smiled up at him and he walked over, his muscles drawing tight.

He didn't want to believe she would help her brother. Now she would probably ask him something about his investigation. Or say she wanted to stay here all afternoon.

She held up her hand to him. "Maybe we could wade in the water."

He blinked. "What?"

"Well, if you think the water's too cold—"

"No. No, that would be fine." Relief coursed through him though he told himself he was being ridiculous. Just because she hadn't brought up John Mark yet didn't mean she wouldn't.

She unlaced her tiny white boots and he toed off his own. Then he helped her up and they walked to the edge of the creek.

She lifted her skirts just above her ankles and he could see the lace of her petticoats. Dipping one toe into the water, she sighed and closed her eyes. "Oh, that feels heavenly."

The words rolled out of her in a throaty sigh and Chaney's body hummed. She looked at him from beneath her lashes. "Aren't you going to try it?"

He grinned and rolled up his pants legs. Plowing into the water, he splashed both of them. She laughed and he found himself smiling back. They waded in the water for a while.

"Have you traveled a lot in your job? I've never been anywhere but here."

"Went to Kansas City once." He stared at the pale

skin of her ankle, the dainty fingers holding up her skirts.

"What was it like?"

"Big and loud. Had a train." If she was leading up to John Mark, she was damn good at it. Chaney's nerves were strung tauter than fence wire and if he was being distracted he wanted to know it right now.

"If Congress passes the Organic Act, we'll be our own territory." She picked her way across a broad rock.

"Yes." He pulled his gaze from her ankles. Here it came, something about her brother.

"If it passes, what will you do?"

Taken aback at her unexpected question, he blinked. "Sheriffs do things besides close down moonshiners."

She tilted her head, a smile lighting her eyes. "So, you would stay?"

"I'd like to." Drawn by the invitation in her husky voice, he stepped carefully toward her, his feet finding purchase on the rocky creek bottom.

She laughed up at him. "I love it here, don't you?"

His eyes traced her lips, her breasts.

"Chaney—"

"Do you want to ask me anything else, Morrow Beth?" He eased up next to her, hating the steel in his voice, but tired of playing games. If indeed she was playing a game, he wanted it in the open. "Is there anything else you want to know?"

She looked up at his lips. "Like what?" she asked huskily.

He very nearly kissed her right then, but he stayed focused on what he was doing. "Like if I've learned anything about your brother? Or how my investigation's going?"

Her face was blank for a moment, then confusion

clouded her eyes. "I thought we weren't going to talk about my family."

He hated himself for destroying the light in her eyes, but he couldn't halt a rush of euphoria. This would have been the perfect opportunity for her to learn something to pass along to her brother.

Her smile faded. "Chaney?"

He stared into her eyes, searching hard for deceit, but he found only genuine puzzlement and uncertainty as she stared back at him.

"Chaney—Oh!"

He scooped her up, one arm at her back, the other under her knees.

She grabbed him around the neck for balance. "What are you doing?"

"Getting you to dry land." He set her down, sliding her body against his, her skirts bunching at his knees. "So I can kiss you proper."

He framed her face in his hands and pulled her to him. She gripped his arms, holding him close, returning his hot openmouthed kiss with the same abandon. Want and triumphant satisfaction sang through his veins.

She couldn't be deliberately helping John Mark. She couldn't. Her tongue touched his shyly and his hands moved to her shoulders, then her back, pulling her into him.

His arousal throbbed against her belly and he thought she might stiffen or pull away but she melted into him, completely trusting, in complete surrender. Her fingers skimmed his face, slid through his hair to hold him tight.

He pulled his lips from hers, wanting to taste her all over. His lips trailed across her cheek to her ear and then down her neck. She arched back, sighing in pleasure.

Want lanced him, urging him on, and he was barely

aware of where they were. He breathed her in, the sweet scent of her mingled with budding flowers and loamy earth and trees. Driven by the desire pounding through him, he cupped her breast.

She gasped and went taut in his arms. Only then did reason trickle back. Chaney realized where they were, what he was doing. He slowly dropped his hand, aching to touch her everywhere, knowing he couldn't take the liberty.

She stared up at him, her lips swollen from his, her eyes cloudy with the same desire ripping through him. She caught his hand and laced her fingers with his.

He nearly groaned. "Did I hurt you?"

"No! I liked it," she whispered, flushing furiously, but not moving her gaze from his. "But we shouldn't. Not yet. I mean—" She colored deeper.

He understood. He wanted more than one afternoon with her. He was starting to wonder if a lifetime would be enough. "You're right. I apologize."

"Don't. We'll just be more careful from now on."

He nodded, feeling as if he'd been trampled. His chest hurt, he couldn't get a full breath, and he had never wanted to have a woman as badly as he wanted Morrow Beth. But he wanted more than the physical with her. He wanted to keep that trust in her eyes. He wanted—

"I love you, Morrow Beth." He froze in astonishment. Now it all made sense—why he couldn't concentrate, why he couldn't forget her.

Her eyes widened and her mouth formed a perfect O. "Wh-What?"

Shock hit him, washed away by a sense of rightness, of belonging.

"Chaney?"

He shook himself, seeing the disbelief, the hope in her

eyes. "It's true, Morrow Beth. I didn't realize it until now and I don't dare hope that you return my feelings. But maybe in time—"

"I do." Her hands flattened on his chest and she gazed earnestly up at him. "I love you, too."

"You . . . do?" His breath caught in his chest as realization spread through him.

For a long moment, they stared at each other caught in the throes of surprise and comprehension. Then Morrow Beth threw her arms around his neck, hugging him tight.

"Oh, is this real?"

"I think so." He drew back, cupping her jaw in his hand. "It better be."

She rose up on tiptoe, her mouth brushing his. He pulled her close, his lips closing over hers, soft and pliant and warm.

Moments later, he lifted his head, breathing hard. Her face was flushed, her lips swollen from his. Pleasure turned her eyes to the deep green of polished emeralds. Chaney thought she'd never looked more beautiful.

Gripped by desire, he clenched his fists against the urge to peel the clothes from her body, explore her.

Her fingers touched his lips, her eyes cloudy with need.

His control slipped a notch and he knew they should go now, before he was no longer able to walk away. He squeezed her hand. "We'd better get back before I forget myself again."

She smiled up at him. "I like knowing I can make you forget yourself."

"I'm not so sure I like you knowing that," he teased, gathering up the basket and the cloth.

She wrinkled her nose at him and walked beside him back to the buggy. They talked quietly on the way back, about her mother and Axel, of plans for the future.

They pulled into the yard and he helped her down.

"I had a wonderful time."

"Me, too." The yard and barn were quiet so Chaney pulled her close for a brief kiss.

Pulling away from her, he opened the gate and guided her through, walking her up to the door.

"I love you," she whispered, her eyes shining.

"I love you, too."

Still staring raptly at him, she fumbled behind her for the door and opened it. "Maybe you could come to supper tomorrow night?"

He leaned against the doorjamb, nuzzling her cheek, his chest nudging hers. "Maybe I could."

"I'd like that." Her breath feathered his lips, inviting him.

He kissed her, lightly, slowly so he wouldn't get carried away again. Pulling away, he straightened. "I'll see you tomorrow."

"All right." She backed into the house, wriggling her fingers at him.

He smiled, his gaze on her as she backed into the house. He was peripherally aware of the cleanly swept floor and orderly kitchen, the burst of colorful flowers on the table. Something about those flowers—

He pulled his gaze from hers, staring over her shoulder.

She gave a small smile and turned, following the direction of his gaze. "Would you like to come in?"

The flowers were in a jar. The jar—Realization hit him, and then disbelief.

"Chaney, what is it?"

He heard her voice as if from far away. Dread filled him, then a sharp denial. No, it couldn't be the same jar. Rage ripped through him, so powerful it blocked his vision for an instant. "That jar. That damn jar." He grabbed her arm. "Where'd you get it?"

She blinked up at him, looking genuinely confused. "Wh-What?"

He pushed past her, grabbing up the jar of flowers and staring at the glass. It was exactly like the one he'd found in the tunnel. *Exactly.*

"Chaney, what is wrong with you?" She glanced from him to the jar and back again. "What is it?"

"Where'd you get this?" His voice cracked like a whip on stone and he gripped her wrist with his free hand. "Tell me, Morrow Beth."

"What are you doing?" Confusion sharpened her voice and she tried to pull free of him. "What's wrong with you?"

He thrust the jar into her face. "I found a jar just like this."

Tears glittered in her eyes. "I don't understand—"

"In the tunnel."

❖ *15* ❖

BETRAYAL, SHARP AND overwhelming, pumped beneath the seething rage. He couldn't believe he was holding a matching jar in his hand. He looked at Morrow Beth, absently noting her pale color, the questions in her eyes.

"Where's the still?"

"What!"

Rage settled into a hard knot in his chest. "Where is it, Morrow Beth? I know what John Mark uses these jars for."

"That jar doesn't prove anything!" Desperation darkened her eyes and she clenched her hands into fists at her sides.

Frustration rolled through him. In the back of his mind, he knew she was right. The jar didn't prove a connection between Huckabee and moonshine at all. But in his gut, Chaney knew, he *knew*, the connection. "I found a jar in the tunnel, smelling of moonshine, and I know it belongs to your brother. I'm going to prove it."

Worry etched her features and she took a step toward him. "What do you mean?"

"What do you think I mean?" he snapped. "I know

good and well your brother is operating a still. I'm going to prove it and when I do—''

"It's just a stupid jar, Chaney!" she yelled. "A jar! There are dozens of them, hundreds!"

"I would tend to agree," he said coldly. "Except I've been looking for jars just like this and there aren't any in the town of Scrub, except here at your place."

Fear dilated her eyes and a wild pulse tapped in the hollow of her throat. "Well, you can ask John Mark. I'm sure there's an explanation."

"I'm sure there is. There *always* is. Of course, your brother isn't around, is he?" Disgusted, he turned for the door.

"What are you doing?" She hurried behind him. "No!"

He halted on the porch and up-ended the jar. Flowers and water gushed out. The bright buds lay limp on the ground, small pieces of color against the wet red earth.

Agony pumped through Chaney with every heartbeat, a numbing pulse of pain with every breath. He couldn't believe she had agreed to use him the way her brother wanted. He couldn't believe the love in her eyes had been a lie.

You'd better believe it, White, or you're not only a fool, but an unemployed one.

She stared down at the flowers, sadness pulling at her delicate features. She looked at him then, her eyes bleak and dark. "Don't do this, Chaney. Please—"

"Don't you want to try and convince me, Morrow Beth?" He hated the silkiness of his voice, hated the way he slid his gaze over her. But she was the one who'd lied to him.

She looked confused and shook her head.

He eased up to her and ran a light finger down the

buttons in the middle of her bodice. "Maybe you can think of a way to make me forget what I've found."

She drew in a breath and went as pale as moonlight. "Don't talk to me that way."

"Why not? Aren't you supposed to make me forget?"

"What?"

"Weren't you supposed to distract me so John Mark could carry on as usual?"

Realization bloomed, then horror spread across her features. "You heard that? But why—"

"Yes, I heard it." His voice was clipped, unforgiving. "What I can't believe is that you'd agree to it."

"If you heard, why did you still take me to the creek? How could you—"

"I wanted to prove to myself that you wouldn't do it, that I hadn't heard what I thought I did." His gaze raked over her and he sneered. "I was wrong, wasn't I?"

Hurt flashed across her features. "I would never do such a thing. I didn't agree. I didn't!"

"I heard you, Morrow Beth. I heard you talking to John Mark about me."

"That was John Mark talking. I told him I wouldn't do it. I told him not to take advantage."

"I just bet you did."

She grabbed his arm, desperation in her eyes. "Chaney, you've got to believe me. I wouldn't do that. I couldn't. I love you."

"How unfortunate for you," he said coldly. "Too bad it didn't work out the way y'all had it planned."

Her eyes were frantic and her grip tightened on him. "Were you using me, too?"

"No, I wasn't."

"But you can see how it looks?" she questioned urgently. "You can see that it might look as if you were?"

He hesitated, uncertainty welling up inside him. But he couldn't let himself soften.

"Chaney, please! Listen to me. I had no part in John Mark's scheme." Her gaze searched his, pleading. "From the beginning, I told him no."

His nostrils flared. "From the beginning?"

She flushed, hesitating.

He gripped her arm. "All of it, Morrow Beth. Tell me."

Misery pinched her features, but she acquiesced. "John Mark wanted me to be friendly with you from the first, but I said no. I liked you even then and I didn't want to do that. At least not for the reason my brother wanted."

He stared at her, wanting to believe that her brother had done all this on his own. But he simply wasn't sure. He shook his head, turning away.

Her fingers tightened on his arm. "You've got to believe me. I didn't—I wouldn't . . ."

He let his gaze deliberately rake over her. "You should've tried a little harder to distract me. I would've been willing."

She stilled, her voice coarse with hurt. "You're just angry."

He was more than angry. He'd never felt so betrayed in all his life, not even by his father, and his voice vibrated with rage. "You should've let me have you, Morrow Beth. It would've been a welcome distraction. A worthy price for me to turn my head."

She gasped, his words sinking in. The color drained from her face, then two spots of vivid color flagged her cheeks. She drew back her hand and slapped him.

The sharp *crack* sliced through the rasp of their breathing, the still air.

Chaney's cheek burned, but it didn't compare to the raw growing ache inside him.

"Get off my land." Her voice trembled and the pain in her eyes cut right through him. "Now."

An apology rose inside him, but he squelched it. He was the one who'd been used. He was the one who'd been led around by the nose. He stalked down the steps and shoved through the gate.

"Don't come back."

At the buggy, he turned, his fingers clenching the reins so tightly his knuckles ached. "I *will* be back, and when I am, you can bet it'll be to get your brother. If you're smart, you'll keep your distance from him."

She angled her chin at him, angry tears glittering in her eyes. "I should've kept my distance from you."

Regret and anger sawed between them like a blade, severing the trust he thought they'd had only an hour ago, the trust he'd given her, the trust she'd destroyed.

She watched him go, pain drilling into her. She loved him. He'd said he loved her. How could he believe she would use him that way? Why wouldn't he believe her?

She gripped the rough wood of the porch rail, uncaring that a splinter burrowed deep into her palm. He was driving away and his threat to come after John Mark paled in comparison to the fear that what had blossomed between them was now dust.

Pain, anger, frustration churned inside her. What about John Mark? Chaney had made his intentions clear and Morrow Beth was sorely tempted to warn her brother. But she had made a promise to Chaney.

Was it null, now that he'd accused her of such duplicity? Upon learning that he'd overheard her brother's plans, she had been stunned. But she hadn't been able to convince Chaney that she refused to play along with John Mark.

She *hadn't* asked Chaney one thing about his plans for John Mark or his investigation into moonshining. No, he'd been the one to bring it up.

Why, oh why, hadn't she thought to throw that in his face? How could he say he loved her, then believe her capable of this? Didn't he trust her at all? Didn't he know that she would never force him to choose between her family and his job?

That was exactly what had happened. He felt his hand had been forced, but she hadn't been the one to force it. She had kept her word and though she was sorely tempted to break it now and warn John Mark about what Chaney had said, she wouldn't.

The time had come for the entire thing to end. She wasn't going to help Chaney. And she wasn't going to warn John Mark. If she never saw either of them again, it would be fine with her!

The next day, Morrow Beth was still smarting from Chaney's accusations, but a deep sadness had taken the place of her anger. As she took orders and carried food and cleared tables from the lunch crowd at Bonnie's, she worked hard to keep Chaney from her thoughts.

She tried to focus on the cold unforgiving words he'd thrown at her, the harsh accusations he'd made. But layered with those hurtful memories were the sweeter ones of the fun they'd had at the picnic, the confidences he'd shared about his father and his growing up, the heated desire in his eyes when he looked at her.

She wanted to find him, wanted to make him believe her, but she'd told the truth. If he didn't realize that, then he wasn't the man for her.

It took all her willpower not to go after him, all her willpower not to ask Bonnie casually if she knew what the sheriff was doing today or where he was.

Just after the restaurant emptied for lunch, Bonnie pushed her way into the kitchen, carrying an armful of dirty plates. She glanced over where Morrow Beth stood washing dishes.

"Looked like you and the sheriff had a mighty good time at the dance, Morrow Beth."

"We did." She couldn't disguise the grimness in her tone.

Bonnie looked closely at her and laughed. "That didn't sound very convincing."

Morrow Beth glanced at her friend, then sighed. "We were getting along so well . . ."

"And?"

She shook her head, drying her hands on a towel. "He thinks I was trying to interfere in his investigation of John Mark."

"Were you?"

"No. I told John Mark that I refused to do that. I like Chaney. I love—" She turned away, gathering up a stack of clean plates and going to the cupboard.

Bonnie stepped in front of her, her round face curious but kind. "You love him? That's wonderful!"

"He doesn't really think so," she said drily, stepping around her friend. "And I'm not so sure either."

"It is wonderful!" Bonnie took the plates from her and passed her two teacups. "If you're with him, then he won't worry about closing down John Mark. Your brother has a job. Chaney has a job. And you have Chaney."

Her jaw dropped as she faced Bonnie. "You're just like John Mark. That was his plan all along, but I won't do that. I won't force Chaney to choose between my family and his job. I could never take advantage of any feelings he might have for me by asking him to look the other way if he thought someone was breaking the law.''

"But—"

"No, Bonnie. It's not right.''

Bonnie fell silent for a moment, drying her skillet. "Then where is your sheriff now?"

"He's not *my* sheriff." Pain stabbed through her. "He believes that I was helping John Mark, that I was lying about my feelings for him.''

"Then go find him! Tell him again.''

She wanted to. Oh, she did! But she shook her head. "I've told him the truth. If he can't see that, then there's nothing for us anyway.''

"Morrow Beth, you can't just let him walk away.''

She shook her head. "You don't know Chaney. He has to do his job. Whether he likes it or not, that's just who he is. I can't ask him to turn away from that.''

"Then my solution is perfect! If he's with you, he surely won't mess with John Mark.''

"He won't go back on his word, Bonnie. I would think less of him if he did. And I won't beg him to believe me. He has to realize on his own that I told the truth.''

"Or not at all?"

"Or not at all,'' Morrow Beth echoed sadly, not sure she could bear it if he never saw the truth. "He has to do his job. He's a fair man. He won't throw John Mark in jail, at least not the first time. The rest is up to John Mark.''

Bonnie's eyes widened. "You're not going to ask for any leniency?''

Morrow Beth shook her head. "I'm not going to interfere at all.''

She wondered if Chaney would ever know. Or even care.

All the next day, Chaney wavered between anger and guilt. He shouldn't have been so hard on Morrow Beth. He shouldn't have accused her of being in cahoots with John Mark. And how could he have said such awful things to her?

But how could he ignore what he'd heard? He wanted to believe her when she'd denied it, but doubt burrowed deep inside him. He loved her, he wanted to believe she loved him. Would she really use him to protect her brother?

Right now he couldn't afford to believe otherwise. His job was on the line and he was fed up with dancing around with John Mark Huckabee.

Chaney had suspicions and today he was going to prove them. He was going to find John Mark's still. Or he was going to abandon the investigation altogether.

He felt a twinge of guilt at his ruthless determination. Part of him hoped he found nothing to prove John Mark's guilt. After coming to know the family, Chaney believed they were getting by the only way they knew.

But he was trying to do the same himself. He had an obligation to this town and he had to do his job.

He had no answers about Morrow Beth, but he had to admit she was right about one thing. That jar didn't prove anything, but he was bound to finish this. If he couldn't pull in another moonshiner by the end of his time here, then so be it.

He could leave this town behind, but he wasn't so sure he could do the same with Morrow Beth. He loved her, though he didn't know if it would matter in the end. He'd said some horrible things to her, things she might not be able to forgive.

Walking quickly from his house, he strode through the field behind town, then around to his office.

"Ah, there you are." Royce Henry rose from the chair in front of Chaney's desk as Chaney walked in the door.

He gritted his teeth. "What do you need, Royce?"

The store owner's eyebrows lifted at his sharp tone. "Just came by to remind you that you've only got about a month left."

"I'm well aware of that." Chaney crossed behind his desk and yanked open his middle drawer.

Royce eyed him curiously. "Hmmm. You know you have to have a unanimous vote. Sada and the mayor don't have a problem with what you've done so far, but I'd like to see more."

"I'm aware of that, too, Royce." Chaney groped in the back of the drawer for the bottle of liquor he sought.

"Do you have anything new to report?"

Chaney started to tell him about the Warner sisters again, then decided against it. His fingers closed around the liquor bottle and he pulled it out, eyeing it balefully.

"What's that?" Royce leaned close to the desk, his eyes gleaming. "Sheriff, is that—"

"Yes, Royce." Chaney's head snapped up and he thrust the bottle at Royce. "Do you know what it is? Have you seen it before? Have you ever had any of it?"

"That's moonshine!" Anger clouded Royce's thin features. "Of course I ain't never had any. Devil's brew, I tell ya!"

Chaney gripped the bottle and started around his desk. "Well, I plan on asking everybody in this town before the day is through."

"Why don't you just ask Huckabee?"

"I plan to, Royce," Chaney bit out.

A satisfied light came into Royce's eyes. "I could vote for you in good conscience if you pulled in Huckabee."

"Good day." He slammed the door, leaving the merchant inside his office.

Chaney went from business to business and house to house. Everywhere he got the same response he'd gotten from Royce. No one knew anything about the liquor. No one knew who had made it, who had sold it, who it belonged to. Chaney didn't even care if they were lying.

It was after lunch by the time he got to Bonnie's. He had waited until last to go to the restaurant because he knew Morrow Beth was working today.

Bracing himself not to soften at the sight of her, Chaney pushed through the doors of the restaurant. The little bell above his head chimed, announcing his arrival.

Morrow Beth walked out of the kitchen with a bright smile on her face. At the sight of him, she turned straight around and went back into the kitchen.

He wanted to call out to her, but he bit his tongue. Instead, he hollered, "Bonnie!"

"I'm right here." The older woman ambled through the kitchen doors, glancing over her shoulder at a disappearing Morrow Beth. "What do you want?"

So much for cooperation. Morrow Beth must have told the woman what had happened between them. He walked over to her, showing her the bottle of liquor. "I need to know if you've ever seen this before."

Bonnie peered at it and shook her head, her sausage curls bouncing. "No."

"Are you sure?"

"I'm not that old, Sheriff. I'd remember a bottle of liquor."

He nodded, forcing himself to say the words even though he hated them. "And what about your employees? Can you ask them to come out here, please?"

Bonnie's thick jaw dropped. "Are you joshin'?"

Pressure squeezed tight across Chaney's chest and his throat closed up. "No," he said between clenched teeth. "I'm not."

She eyed him in frustrated disbelief but called over her shoulder. "Morrow Beth, you gotta come out."

Chaney hated it as much as she did. If he hadn't thoroughly turned her away yesterday, this was sure to do the trick. Seconds scraped by, pricking his nerves like hooks. His patience strained, he finally snapped, "Morrow Beth, get out—"

"I'm right here." She pushed through the door, looking cool and regal in a pale blue shirtwaist with her sleeves rolled up to her elbows. "What do you want?"

He wanted to erase everything he'd said to her, wanted to smash this bottle of liquor and forget he'd ever found it, wanted to spark some warmth in those green eyes. He cleared his throat and thrust the bottle at her. "Ever seen this?"

She barely glanced at it. "No."

"You have to look, Morrow Beth."

Sighing deeply, she looked at it for a long time before she stared at him pointedly. "No. Like I said."

He wanted to turn her over his knee. He wanted to push her up against that wall and kiss her until they both forgot why they were angry. "Do you know what it is?"

She gave him a flat stare, then tapped one finger against her lips. "Oh, my, whatever can it be?"

He clenched his jaw on the sharp words that threatened to roar out of him.

Seemingly tired of taunting him, she planted her hands

on her hips, staring straight into his eyes. "Of course I
know what it is, *Sheriff*. But I don't know where it came
from. Or *who* it came from."

Despite her anger, despite the hurt that circled around
them both, he believed her. Maybe it was because he
wanted to. Maybe it was because he was just damn tired
of knowing he couldn't have her *and* his job, too.

Quietly he said, "I have to do my job, Morrow Beth."

Tears welled in her eyes. "I know," she relented. "But
I can't side with you against my family."

"I know." He looked at her for a long moment, tracing
her dark brows, the delicate upturned nose, the dark green
of her eyes, the rose-petal lips. "And I know you were
telling the truth about John Mark."

Hope flared in her eyes, but quickly disappeared. She
regarded him warily.

He wanted nothing more than to settle things with her,
but he had to see John Mark, put this moonshining business behind him once and for all. "I apologize for saying
those awful things. I—I didn't mean them and I hope you
can someday find it in your heart to forgive me."

She nodded, tears glittering in her eyes, and he cursed
himself for hurting her the way he had. How could she
ever forgive him? He didn't know if he would ever forgive himself.

He tugged sharply on the brim of his hat and turned
away.

"Where are you going now?"

He heard the fear in her voice, the apprehension, and
he looked at her sadly. "To talk to your brother."

Agony ravaged her eyes, but she only nodded, saying
fiercely, "I hope you don't find anything."

"So do I." Chaney saw the surprise in her eyes and
she started forward. He walked out the door before he

changed his mind about going altogether. "Thank you, ladies."

Behind him, he heard a smothered "Hmmmph!" But when he looked back, both Bonnie and Morrow Beth had disappeared into the kitchen.

Chaney closed the door and stared down at the bottle in his hand and the liquor inside. He knew what he had to do. He'd only been putting it off, hoping to gain some other clue, evidence that pointed elsewhere. But now he knew. He was going to have to confront John Mark, face-to-face.

As he rode reluctantly toward the Huckabee homestead, Chaney found himself hoping he would find nothing to prove that John Mark was moonshining.

Besides having fallen in love with his sister, Chaney liked John Mark. He honestly didn't think the man meant any harm by making and selling moonshine, but neither could Chaney overlook it.

He'd brought the jar, too. It nestled in the saddlebag alongside the bottle of liquor.

He reined up in front of the Huckabee homestead. He could tell by the quiet stillness of the place that no one was home. There was only the occasional rush of wind, the soft sporadic cluck of the chickens and the clatter of the cow's bell.

Pauuuck!

Chaney smiled at the rooster's familiar croak coming from the back of the house. He strode into the barn, making certain John Mark was nowhere to be found.

In front of the house, Chaney stood for a long time looking at the little house, the porch, the neatly laid out garden, wondering if he should go inside.

It didn't stand to reason that John Mark would brew

his liquor indoors. Moving to the side of the house, Chaney carefully searched the base of the house, looking for a point of entry that would lead beneath it, but he found none.

He meticulously waded through the high grass around the house, but found nothing.

Flower shot out from behind a tree, startling him.

"Whoa, there!" Chaney stepped back, eyeing the rooster warily. He didn't want a repeat of the last time they'd met when Flower had tried to peck his toes off.

Paaauck! Flower strutted out of a cluster of honeysuckle bushes and stared unblinkingly at Chaney. Then, as if he recognized him, he fluttered his wings and zigzagged through the grass toward him.

Chaney frowned, hoping the rooster wasn't about to have another of his spells. Morrow Beth seemed able to handle the animal fine, but Chaney had no experience with sick roosters.

Flower screeched and lunged toward Chaney, angling past him to weave through the grass, flapping his wings and crowing hoarsely.

Chaney shook his head and started toward the clump of cottonwood trees.

Paaauck! Paaauck! Flower raced around Chaney, then between his legs before staggering to a stop in front of him.

Chaney froze. What in the Sam Hill was wrong with that rooster? And what was that smell?

His gaze narrowed on the bird. Flower gazed back unblinkingly and gave a low squawk that ended with a hiccup.

It wasn't possible! *Was it?*

He stepped closer to the rooster, trying to deny the

smell emanating from the bird. Sharp, raw, tangy. Chaney shook his head in disbelief.

This couldn't be. No.

He inched up to the rooster, who peered up with unfocused eyes. Suddenly the rooster's head drooped and he teetered over to the ground.

Chaney knelt, inches from the bird, confident the animal wasn't capable of attacking him at the moment. He leaned closer and that unmistakable odor wrapped around him, nearly suffocating.

Corn liquor! There was no doubt about it.

Chaney stared down at the bird, stunned. For a long moment, he simply knelt there, staring in puzzlement. Then realization slammed into him.

The rooster was drunk as a skunk, damn it! He'd been drunk the first time Chaney had come out here, when Morrow Beth had explained about Flower's "spells." *Spells!*

Chaney rose, his gaze probing the cottonwoods, the honeysuckle bushes, the woods beyond. The rooster had already imbibed today, which meant there had to be a still nearby.

Leaving the unconscious bird, Chaney moved purposefully toward the honeysuckle bushes. They were thick and lush, tangled together with bois d'arc thorn bushes. Chaney picked his way carefully through the bushes, careful to keep his gloves on.

He inched his way through the thick hedge of bushes, thorns scratching against the denim of his pants, the crunch of twigs and grass beneath his boots. Just when he reached the inside of the thicket, he saw it. Buried under a screen camouflaged with vines and leaves, he spied a curl of copper tubing.

Lifting the vegetation out of the way, Chaney saw a

large covered kettle sitting in the middle of a furnace. He'd been so close to finding it the other night, but his sense of triumph was dimmed by deep regret.

The still was set up similarly to the Warner sisters'. The tubing led out of the pot and spiraled up to droop over onto the ground. Two feet away, behind another screen of vines, was a barrel full of corn mash. Fermenting corn mash, Chaney amended at the ripe odor.

Altogether, he found two full barrels and one empty one. He also found an old cracked jug and next to that, several bottles. They looked exactly like the one Chaney had in his saddlebags. And beneath the bottom of a bush, Chaney saw the glitter of more glass.

Rolling the object out with his foot, he moved it into view. He didn't have to hunker down to know this jar would match the ones he'd found in town and on the Huckabee table.

Damn, he'd been right all along. John Mark was making moonshine. A lot of moonshine. This would certainly assure Chaney's job as sheriff of Scrub.

So why did he suddenly wish he'd never found it?

"Hello, Sheriff."

Chaney turned at the sound of John Mark's voice. His gaze met John Mark's, the other man's face more somber than Chaney had ever seen it.

John Mark indicated the still with a nod of his head. "Looks like you found what you were looking for."

With great regret, Chaney nodded and exhaled a deep breath. "I'm afraid so."

❖ 16 ❖

*I KNOW YOU were telling the truth about John Mark.
I apologize.*

She wanted to forgive him, wanted him to stay so she
could tell him that, but he'd left. To go after her brother.

Morrow Beth fought back the urge to follow Chaney.
She had promised herself that she wouldn't interfere. It
was time to let John Mark and Chaney work it out.

Grabbing the broom, she attacked the restaurant floor,
replaying over and over the genuine regret in Chaney's
eyes. Moving the broom briskly, she covered the width
of the room.

Bonnie stepped out of the kitchen, drying her hands on
the damp, wrinkled apron she wore. "I'd like you to leave
me some part of the floor, Morrow Beth."

She stilled and glanced up. Realizing she'd been sweeping with a vengeance, she smiled and loosened her hold
on the broom. "Sorry."

"It's all right." Bonnie moved to the nearest table, rolling up the soiled tablecloth for laundering. "That sheriff
really set you off, didn't he?"

"Of course not!" She swiped at the floor with the
broom, telling herself again not to go after Chaney.

Bonnie clucked her tongue, tucking the wadded cloth under her arm and moving to the next table. "It was pretty nice, what he said."

"Yes." Morrow Beth stopped sweeping and leaned against the broom. She remembered every word and she had wanted to say she forgave him, but the words stuck in her throat.

Bonnie yanked off another cloth. "Maybe you should go after him."

"I don't think so." Despite her quick refusal, Morrow Beth couldn't stanch the ache in her heart. They were both doing what they had to. Neither wanted to ask the other to choose.

Bonnie walked over to her and took the broom. "Look, dumpling, it's obvious you want to go after him."

Morrow Beth chewed on her lip. "Yes."

"Then go!"

"He thought I was using him to help John Mark."

"Sounded to me like Chaney apologized for that. Or was I hearing things?" Bonnie arched an eyebrow, though compassion glowed in her eyes.

Morrow Beth looked at her friend. "No, you weren't hearing things. He did."

"Well, then?"

"I said I wouldn't interfere. You heard him say he's going to talk to John Mark."

"Maybe you can stop him," the other woman urged, her dark eyes concerned.

Morrow Beth shook her head. Bonnie didn't understand that she wouldn't, *couldn't,* ask that kind of favor from Chaney. But neither could she bear to lose her brother.

Yanking at her apron in dread and apprehension, she tossed it on the table. "Can you find the twins after school, tell them I've gone home?"

"Good girl!"

She didn't have the heart to tell Bonnie that she wasn't chasing after Chaney for the reason her friend thought. Hurrying toward the door, Morrow Beth yanked it open, hoping she reached Chaney before he reached John Mark.

She ran smack into Sada. The two women literally bumped into each other and Sada stumbled back.

"Oh!" Morrow Beth grabbed the other woman's arm, preventing her fall.

Sada laughed, gaining her balance and readjusting her poke bonnet, which had slid to the side of her head. "Whoa, I guess we're both in a hurry."

"Are you all right?" Morrow Beth ran a critical eye over her friend.

Sada patted her arm. "I'm just fine. Where are you off to in such a hurry?"

"I've got to catch Chaney." She stepped around the other woman. "Please excuse me."

"Wait." Sada smiled triumphantly and thrust a piece of paper at Morrow Beth. "Tell him this, too."

She started to tell the other woman she didn't have time to read it.

"Go on, read it," Sada urged.

Morrow Beth's gaze scanned the telegram and her breath caught in her throat. Surprise and pleasure wound through her and she looked up at Sada. "Oh, my stars," she breathed. "Do you know what this means?"

"I certainly do." Sada nodded vehemently. "Get busy and find that sheriff."

"I will." Morrow Beth hurried down the steps then raced back up, hugging Sada tightly. "Thank you so much."

Sada laughed, patting her on the back. "My pleasure. I hope this means Chaney will stay anyway?"

"So do I." Morrow Beth hugged the other woman again, then hurried down the steps.

"Good luck," Sada called.

"Thank you." Morrow Beth hurried to the livery, hoping to reach Chaney before he reached John Mark.

Chaney faced John Mark, uncertain of how the other man would respond. He wanted no trouble, especially with Morrow Beth's brother, but he had come prepared. His palm covered the butt end of his Colt.

John Mark's expression went from surprise to guarded speculation. "Well, this is bad, isn't it?"

"I'm afraid so."

The big man walked over, staring at his stillpot and the barrel half full of corn mash. "Pretty clever of you to find them."

"Pretty clever of you to hide them in plain sight."

John Mark grinned. "How *did* you find it?"

"Well . . ." Chaney's gaze slid around the other man to the bird still laying motionless in the grass. "Flower led me to it."

"That stupid rooster." John Mark's voice was calm, but Chaney sensed the tension beneath the words. "Was he over here having a little?"

Chaney couldn't stop a grin. "I think he'd already helped himself. I noticed he was acting strange and when I got close enough to him, smelled liquor on his breath."

"Guess I'll have to make chicken and dumplings out of him after all."

Chaney grinned. "Be a shame to get rid of him. He's right entertainin'."

"I guess so." John Mark's grin faded and he turned, eyeing his stills with a resigned expression. "So what happens now?"

"I'm going to have to tear them down."

The other man nodded, exhaling wearily. "I figured. Don't think I can help you do that, though."

"Wouldn't expect you to." Chaney walked around him and paused. "Look, I'm sorry about this. I know it's been hard, getting money from the farm and all."

John Mark stared at him for a long moment, admiration erasing the resentment in his eyes. "We'll make do somehow. Morrow Beth's pretty smart."

"Yes, she is." Chaney turned away, his heart aching at the sound of her name.

She would throw a fit if she knew what he'd found and what he was doing. Despite his apology, she'd probably never speak to him again.

Walking over to the nearest barrel, which contained water and the "worm," Chaney plucked out the tubing.

"Don't see how we'll get along without her."

At John Mark's casual observation, Chaney straightened. "Is she going somewhere?"

Her brother grinned, his eyes sparkling impishly. "Thought she might be gettin' married."

"*Married!* To who?" Alarm kicked through him and Chaney's voice cracked like a whip. "Who's she been seeing?"

John Mark eyed him for a long moment, then a grin split his face. "You."

"Me?" Chaney turned and faced the man, his jaw dropping. "What are you playing at?"

"I know what's between you two—"

"Then you know she's too angry to even talk to me right now."

"She was pretty mad when you accused her of using you." John Mark rubbed his chin thoughtfully. "But you know she wouldn't do it. Don't you?"

Chaney sighed. "I do know."

"It was my idea." John Mark looked chagrined. "But she wouldn't have any part of it."

"I see that now. I apologized, but I think it may be too late. I hurt her pretty badly."

"Yep, you did."

Chaney couldn't help a rueful smile. That was one thing he did like about John Mark. The man never white-washed the true state of things.

"So you apologized?"

"Yes."

"And?"

Chaney just looked at the other man. "And nothing. I think it's going to take more than an apology to mend things between us."

"You're probably right," John Mark agreed easily, leaning against one of the cottonwoods. "Females are funny about things like that. You'll probably have to propose."

"Propose?" Chaney's heart kicked in a painful rhythm. "Now, see here, John Mark, there are some things you shouldn't stick your nose in."

"Don't you want to marry my sister?"

Struck dumb, Chaney considered him for a long moment. It wouldn't be right to confess to her brother what he hadn't confessed to Morrow Beth. "Even if I did, it wouldn't change what I have to do here."

"I know that." John Mark waved his hand dismissively. "I guess my days as a moonshiner are numbered, but that doesn't mean you have to quit courting my sister."

"I'm betting your sister doesn't agree," Chaney muttered drily, thinking that right now would be a nice time to have a drink of the very stuff he was supposed to destroy. He turned back to his task. "I've been thinking—maybe I can help you out, John Mark."

"How's that?"

"If I get the sheriff job, I could use some help."

"You mean, like a deputy?" John Mark asked incredulously.

"Yes." Chaney looked over his shoulder, gauging the response on the other man's features.

Disbelief clouded John Mark's eyes, then he threw back his head and laughed. "Me, a deputy? Who would believe that?"

Chaney shrugged. "It's an idea. You're good with people. You could learn the law."

"I can't read or write."

"You could learn or not, as you chose. I can tell you most things you need to know."

"Me, a deputy?" John Mark's grin faded. "You'd trust me to do that?"

Chaney's gaze met his, measuring, probing. "Yes, I would."

"You're no fool, Sheriff." John Mark's admiration was colored with disbelief.

"I like to think I'm not," said Chaney.

"Then why would you ask me?"

"I think you'd be good at it. And I'd like to help."

"So I wouldn't go back to making moonshine?"

"Partly, yes."

Chaney weighed his words, gesturing toward the still. "I think you do it mainly to help your family and because you don't know much else to do."

John Mark stared at him and Chaney found himself hoping urgently that the other man would accept his proposal.

"Are you doing this to win back my sister?"

Chaney snorted. "You and I both know it would take more than that."

John Mark nodded. "That's right."

"You can think about it."

"I don't have to start now, do I? I couldn't tear down my own still."

Chaney chuckled, turning back to the task at hand. "You can think about it as long as you want. Or you can turn me down flat." He piled the tubing in the kettle and set the pot on the ground before moving to look into the next barrel.

Behind them, Flower crowed hoarsely and struggled to his feet. The ground vibrated and the thunder of horses' hooves pounded toward them. Morrow Beth's voice came from the front of the house.

"John Mark! Are you here? Chaney!"

The two men looked at each other and Chaney braced himself to face her anger. Though he knew she didn't approve of her brother's operation, she was very loyal to her family. That loyalty was just one of the things he loved about her.

"Chaney, don't—" She raced around the side of the house and toward the cover of trees where they stood, skidding to a stop in front of the two men. "What's happened?" She panted, looking from Chaney to John Mark. "Is everything all right?"

"Chaney found me out, Sister," her brother said easily.

"You can't do this." Morrow Beth stepped toward Chaney, her chest rising and falling rapidly, her face flushed, her eyes bright. "You can't."

Flower squawked in agreement.

"Morrow Beth, I don't like it any better than you, and having you here doesn't make it easier for me."

"Oh, I said that wrong." She took a deep breath, her

eyes searching his, pleading. "I mean, you don't have to."

He stared at her for a moment, then shook his head. "You know I do. Flower was drunk and I found the still—"

"It's against the law. I mean—" She took a deep breath, closing her eyes and frowning in concentration. She said carefully, "The Organic Act passed this morning. We're now Oklahoma Territory."

"So we're not under the laws of Indian Territory any more?" John Mark eased forward, his words tentative. Tension corded his body.

Morrow Beth nodded. "That's right."

Chaney frowned, doubt and hope mingling. She wouldn't lie to him, would she? Even if she thought it might help her brother? "Morrow Beth, it's all right. I'm not putting John in jail. I'm only tearing down the still."

"I'm not lying, Chaney." She was still breathless, her eyes earnest. "I'm not. It's true. The act was signed this morning. Sada got a telegram."

"A telegram?" Dazed, Chaney stared at her.

Flower strutted between them, clucking quietly.

John Mark frowned, eyeing his sister as if trying to decipher a riddle. "Morrow Beth?"

"It's true, John Mark. It is." She squeezed his arm. "I swear."

Chaney looked into her eyes, wanting to believe her. If he did and it wasn't true, it would cost his job. But he had doubted her once and deeply regretted it.

More than his job was riding on whether or not he believed her. His future with her, if indeed there was one, could be at stake.

Flower pecked at Chaney's boots, but he ignored the bird. He knew then that she told the truth. She and her brother stared at him, eyes wide with apprehension and urgency.

Her face fell, her eyes bleak with hurt. "You don't believe me."

"I do." He stepped up to her, reaching for her hand. "I do believe you, Morrow Beth."

"You do?" she said softly.

"You do?" John Mark echoed. "Yee haw!"

Flower let out a cheery *pauuck*.

"I promise it's true." Morrow Beth gazed earnestly into his eyes. "I wouldn't make it up. Because I—I know you wouldn't hurt John Mark." She slid a glance at her brother, her eyes twinkling again. "Unless he forced you to, of course."

John Mark laughed, moving behind Chaney to the still. "I'll just hook this back up. Hey, Sheriff, that deputy job still stand?"

"If you want it," Chaney said absently, gazing at Morrow Beth, unable to believe she was talking to him, touching him. "I love you, Morrow Beth. I'm sorry for ever doubting you."

"Oh, Chaney." She walked into his arms and pressed a soft kiss to his lips.

Flower crowed hoarsely.

Chaney's arms tightened around Morrow Beth and he wanted to sweep her into the trees, hidden from sight where he could kiss her properly. A sudden burst of noise from the front of the house drew their attention. He pulled away from her and they looked toward the house.

John Mark moved up beside them. "What's all the racket?"

"Best go see." Chaney pulled Morrow Beth along with him and John Mark followed.

The Bells, Sada, Royce, the mayor, Bonnie, and the

twins walked around the corner of the house and toward Chaney.

"It looks like the whole town," John Mark muttered. "What's this about?"

Sada, heading the procession, stopped in front of him. "Sheriff, did Morrow Beth tell you?"

"Hi, Marshal!" Katie singsonged.

"Hi, Chaney!" Billy Jack chimed.

Both of them threaded their way around the Bells and toward their older sister.

"About the Organic Act?" Chaney asked. "And the fact that we're now officially Oklahoma Territory? Yes, she did."

"Good," said Will Bell. "So now you can leave off torturing these people."

"I wasn't torturing—"

"He wasn't torturing—"

Chaney and Morrow Beth spoke at the same time, then laughed.

"Marshal White would never torture anyone," Katie said loftily.

"The point is liquor isn't prohibited anymore." A smile lit Sada's eyes.

Chaney eyed the group in disappointment as he realized why they'd all come to the Huckabee homestead. "So, you've all come to tell me you don't need a sheriff."

"That's right," said a disgruntled Royce.

Flower tilted his head at Royce and squawked in loud protest.

"It certainly isn't right." Sada took a piece of paper from her reticule and handed it to Chaney. "We came to show you the telegram."

He scanned it, smiling at Morrow Beth as he finished. She squeezed his arm.

Sada smiled at him. "We've also come to ask you to stay and be our sheriff."

"Oh, yes, please stay!" chorused the twins.

Mayor Bushman stepped forward. "That's right, Chaney. We're very pleased with the way you handled things."

"But I only discovered the Warner still." He felt more than saw John Mark's questioning gaze, but Chaney saw no reason to mention the still hidden in the trees directly behind them.

"That doesn't matter. You did a fine job and we'd like you to stay on."

"Now, see here—" Royce began.

"Oh, hush, Royce," Sada exclaimed. "We want Chaney to stay and we're overrulin' you."

"Here, here," the crowd echoed.

"Thank you." A warmth spread across Chaney's chest, but there was still one thing to be done. "I'd like to stay, but I'm not sure I can."

"What?" Sada's question was echoed through the crowd.

"You have to stay!" Katie wailed.

Flower fluttered his wings and let out a string of hoarse squawks.

Morrow Beth looked at him, alarm darkening her green eyes. "What do you mean?"

He wished they were alone, but he had to say this, regardless. "I love you, Morrow Beth. I want to marry you, but if you say no—and I could understand why you would—"

"She ain't gonna say no, are you, girl?" Bonnie put in.

"Say yes, Morrow Beth," Polly urged.

"Go on, girl," came Will Bell's voice.

"Oh, yes. Do, Sister," sighed Katie Jo.

Chaney focused on Morrow Beth, on the pure love shining from her green eyes, the soft sigh of his name coming from her lips.

She covered his hand with hers. "Yes, Chaney White. I will marry you."

He smiled, his eyes promising for later what he couldn't do now. He turned to the crowd, "Well, folks, looks like your new sheriff is about to take a wife."

"Here, here!" This time the cheer resounded through the crowd.

"Heck fire!" Billy Jack yelled, then slapped a hand over his mouth, his eyes wide with misgiving.

"Billy Jack," Morrow Beth warned.

The boy groaned and Chaney chuckled.

John Mark clapped him on the back. "Well done, Chaney. How about a drink with your new brother-in-law?"

Chaney laughed as loud as everyone else, hugging Morrow Beth close.

Her brother grinned. "Now, about that job—"

"Later, John Mark." Chaney anchored an arm around Morrow Beth's waist and pulled her to him. "Later."

Amidst the congratulations and good wishes, Chaney took Morrow Beth around to the back of the house and kissed her long and properly.

Flower followed, squawking hoarsely and strutting around Chaney's legs.

"Dang rooster," Chaney murmured against Morrow Beth's lips. "Gonna make chicken and dumplings out of him yet."

Morrow Beth pressed her lips to his and drove all thoughts out of his head. Instead there was only a warmth, a sense of belonging. A sense . . . of home.

Our Town

...where love is always right around the corner!

■■■■■■■■■■■■■■■■■■■■■■■■■■

__*Harbor Lights* by Linda Kreisel	0-515-11899-0/$5.99
__*Humble Pie* by Deborah Lawrence	0-515-11900-8/$5.99
__*Candy Kiss* by Ginny Aiken	0-515-11941-5/$5.99
__*Cedar Creek* by Willa Hix	0-515-11958-X/$5.99
__*Sugar and Spice* by DeWanna Pace	0-515-11970-9/$5.99
__*Cross Roads* by Carol Card Otten	0-515-11985-7/$5.99
__*Blue Ribbon* by Jessie Gray	0-515-12003-0/$5.99
__*The Lighthouse* by Linda Eberhardt	0-515-12020-0/$5.99
_*The Hat Box* by Deborah Lawrence	0-515-12033-2/$5.99
__*Country Comforts* by Virginia Lee	0-515-12064-2/$5.99
__*Grand River* by Kathryn Kent	0-515-12067-7/$5.99
__*Beckoning Shore* by DeWanna Pace	0-515-12101-0/$5.99
__*Whistle Stop* by Lisa Higdon	0-515-12085-5/$5.99
__*Still Sweet* by Debra Marshall	0-515-12130-4/$5.99
__*Dream Weaver* by Carol Card Otten (9/97)	0-515-12141-X/$5.99

Payable in U.S. funds. No cash accepted. Postage & handling: $1.75 for one book, 75¢ for each additional. Maximum postage $5.50. Prices, postage and handling charges may change without notice. Visa, Amex, MasterCard call 1-800-788-6262, ext. 1, or fax 1-201-933-2316; refer to ad # 637b

Or, check above books   **Bill my:** ☐ Visa ☐ MasterCard ☐ Amex _____ (expires)
and send this order form to:
The Berkley Publishing Group   Card#_____
P.O. Box 12289, Dept. B   Daytime Phone #_____   ($10 minimum)
Newark, NJ 07101-5289   Signature_____
Please allow 4-6 weeks for delivery.   **Or enclosed is my:** ☐ check ☐ money order
Foreign and Canadian delivery 8-12 weeks.

Ship to:

Name_____	Book Total	$_____
Address_____	Applicable Sales Tax (NY, NJ, PA, CA, GST Can.)	$_____
City_____	Postage & Handling	$_____
State/ZIP_____	Total Amount Due	$_____

Bill to: Name_____

Address_____City_____
State/ZIP_____

FREE
Romance
(a $4.50 value)

Send in the Coupon Below

To get your FREE historical romance and start saving, fill out the coupon below and mail it today. As soon as we receive it we'll send you your FREE Book along with your first month's selections.

- -

Mail To: **True Value Home Subscription Services, Inc. P.O. Box 5235**
120 Brighton Road, Clifton, New Jersey 07015-5235

YES! I want to start previewing the very best historical romances being published today. Send me my FREE book along with the first month's selections. I understand that I may look them over FREE for 10 days. If I'm not absolutely delighted I may return them and owe nothing. Otherwise I will pay the low price of just $4.00 each: a total $16.00 (at *least* an $18.00 value) and save at least $2.00. Then each month I will receive four brand new novels to preview as soon as they are published for the same low price. I can always return a shipment and I may cancel this subscription at any time with no obligation to buy even a single book. In any event the FREE book is mine to keep regardless.

Name _____

Street Address _____ Apt. No. _____

City _____ State _____ Zip Code _____

Telephone _____

Signature _____
(if under 18 parent or guardian must sign)

Terms and prices subject to change. Orders subject
to acceptance by True Value Home Subscription
Services. Inc.

12130-4